Tangled Webs

Book of Short Stories

Theresa Lennon Blunt

Trafford Publishing
Victoria B.C.

Other books by Theresa Lennon Blunt

Judas in Kilkenny

The Boodyman

On Broken Wings

This book is a work of fiction based on fact

Certain character's names have been changed to protect their anonymity.

Order this book online at www.trafford.com
or email orders@trafford.com

Most Trafford titles are also available at major online book retailers.

Printed in Victoria, BC, Canada.

ISBN: 978-1-4269-1891-9 (sc)

Our mission is to efficiently provide the world's finest, most comprehensive book publishing service, enabling every author to experience success. To find out how to publish your book, your way, and have it available worldwide, visit us online at www.trafford.com

Trafford rev. 1/14/2009

 www.trafford.com

North America & international
toll-free: 1 888 232 4444 (USA & Canada)
phone: 250 383 6864 ♦ fax: 812 355 4082

CONTENTS

* * * * * * * * * * * * * * *

PROLOGUE

In the storehouse of my mind I have a trillion memories, some happy, some sad and some just in between, but all of them an integral part of me. I've heard people say you can forget the past, but I don't think you can. You may push it aside temporarily, but it springs back to mind every chance it gets, and though all of us tend to suppress certain ugly realities, memories once unleashed are difficult to rein in. Even now as I put my pen to paper, an avalanche of memories come tumbling through my head bringing clear, precise images of people and events.

Some of the incidents in the following stories I have personally experienced and remember clearly, though many of the words and conversations are my own. In others I recount events that were either related to me, or whose history I happened on by chance. A few of the names you may recognize; the Old Man, Malachi Dempsey, for example whom I wrote about in my first book, and to whose memory I devote three stories here. However, to make his stories easier to read, I have dispensed with his unique vernacular.

Other stories may have found expression through the influence of characters in my earlier books, and though not all of them played a direct role in the day-to-day vagaries of my own life, their existence clearly enriched it. Of one thing I am certain, without their colorful attributes these stories could never have been written.

THE GIRL IN THE VELVET DRESS

I am three years old or thereabout, sitting on the doorstep of our house. My uncle's dog Shep is by my side, licking the ice cream from my cone. Behind me my mother is busy in the kitchen, washing, ironing and cleaning house. She is singing as she goes about. An open coal fire burns brightly in the grate with the folding metal guard in front of it, and on which she has placed wet articles to dry. She sticks her head around the door to check that I'm still there, then pulls it back in again. Behind her the big clock in the corner begins to strike the hour and I hear my mother mutter to herself as she hurries past it to the scullery. Incidents before, or immediately following, elude me.

I know I am one of seven children, yet except for my brother Mikey, I have no awareness of my siblings. For some strange reason only his existence holds dominion in my mind. He is the eldest child in the family and often takes me with him on his excursions around the town, buying me sweets and lollipops.

The two things I remember most about him are his smell, a mixture of soap and cigarettes and the feel of his powerful arms around my legs while being borne aloft on his stout shoulders. At night I am lulled to sleep in the comfort of his arms and the soft, sweet tones of his tenor voice.

Once when he left me standing alone on a gravelly path I had fallen and cut my hand on a discarded light bulb. The cut wasn't deep but the blood frightened me, until Mikey kissed it better and wiped it clean with his handkerchief. I was too young, of course, to be taken to the cinema but had slight acquaintance with his idol Flash Gordon and his daring acts of chivalry when we leaped together off the roof, me straddling Mikey's back, my

9

arms around his neck, and he with one arm braced beneath my bottom, the other holding an enormous black umbrella.

Outside of parental awareness, his is the only distinct memory to occupy my mind around that time. According to my mother I worshipped him and followed him about like a faithful dog. It almost broke my heart when he left home for good. I was nine years old before we met again and still loyal in my affection. The family had increased to ten and though not *the baby* any longer, I was confident of Mikey's sole attention. I was so excited when I heard he was coming home, had lain awake the night before imagining how it would be when he saw me, the fuss he would surely make of me.

But it wasn't like that at all. Mikey hardly noticed me as he mingled excitedly with the others in the kitchen. Except for the few scant words 'look at you, a big girl now', he totally ignored me. Didn't even say my name, or ask anything about me. The hurt went deep, but I kept it to myself. I have often wondered, though, whether Mikey ever knew or was even marginally aware of the depth of the love I had for him. I never got a chance to ask, because a few years later he died in England of pneumonia.

Strange, that I should have no clear memory of other family members, or events inside the house around that time. Except for the bedtime stories on my father's knee and the scent of polish on my mother's hands, I remember nothing.

My first clear memory outside the house is of the day I started school, or kindergarten as it is known today. The rain was falling from the sky in buckets and I had hoped that the two-mile walk would deter my mother. Not yet four years old and no taller than a tailor's thimble, I trudged along beside her wondering what terrible fate awaited me. And if it be true that the voices of childhood memory remain longer in the mind than the faces, which are forever changing, it was not so with me, for the voices of that day remain forever lost to my memory. Events of the opening and closing hours, which I ought to remember, remain in every way a blur. Only the sounds and images of the intervening hours have remained vigilant in my mind, presenting an impression which comes back to me now as it did then, but with less lucidity.

We are walking across a stone bridge under which a river is flowing noisily. I can hear the water rushing and splashing against the pillars below trying to squeeze beneath the arch. I want to stop and look but my mother hurries me along. Ahead, and lashed by the slanting rain, I see a steep hill. On one side there is a solitary house, followed by some deserted sheds. Later I would learn the occupant's name, old Mrs. Clooney, for whom the hill was named. Opposite her house there's a high stone wall with an iron railing, and behind that the tops of tall trees stand like silent sentinels around a grey church.

From somewhere in a street ahead comes the sound of horse's hooves clomping along the hard ground, and the sound of a man's voice swearing. A faint tingle of bells announce their arrival at the bottom of the hill and I listen to the jingle of the harness changing rhythm with the movement of the cart. It stops. Then starts up again and the dull thud of hooves is coming closer. Together we reach the bottom of the hill and start up the steep slope. Water running in a swift current down pours over my shoes and socks, and I feel the chill of cool water against my ankles. My mother, letting go of my hand in a hurried jerk, picks me up in the crook of her arm and I am drenched with the drip of her umbrella.

The cart rumbles past and the driver, wrapped in a black oilskin cape and a dripping wide-brimmed hat, speaks to my mother in a kindly tone. He climbs down from the seat and approaches. Now I am taken from my mother's arms and lifted to the shelter of a heavy canvas, covering the upright churns in the cart. I crouch down quietly in the warm straw, wary of the horse's tail, flicking roughly against the cart. The sound of my mother's voice below brings small comfort to my ears.

The cart moves slowly up the hill, the metal wheel rims grinding into the ridged cement. It creaks and groans as the horse slips and falters, and I am sure that he is going to fall. Suddenly the driver disappears to the back of the cart and my mother walks along in silence, her body hidden beneath the black umbrella. Fat beads of water plop around the tip of the umbrella and I watch them break apart and wriggle down the center to the edge, where they disappear along the rim. The driver reappears with a heavy rope coiled around his shoulder, and now I see we have reached the crest and a whole new world of wide streets and houses.

Turning the corner at the very top, we move along for a little while longer, the horse quieter now. Then the man stops the horse and makes him stand beside the path, fastening the reins to a nearby pole. He spends a long time rubbing the horse's head and fixing up the leather straps. But finally he lifts me down beside my mother and I cling to her hand. Around us the streets are empty and bare, but in a nearby school I hear the sound of boys singing.

Heavy black shawls, covering bent shoulders emerge now and then from behind closed doors, only to disappear again into a neighboring house or behind some hidden corner. Once a bareheaded man hobbled past on a stump, followed by a rain-soaked dog with round sorrowful eyes. At last we reach the little school and Mother opens the iron gate, shuffling me inside.

There's no sign of my sister Jane, who had started school the year before, and I wonder where she is. All I see is an empty yard with small clusters of pebbles scattered in every corner. Sensing my uneasiness, my mother whispers in my ear as we pass through the wide, wooden door into the hall. The air is heavy with the smell of damp wool, and I look above me to the rows and rows of hangers, laden with coats, scarves and caps. A small stout woman comes along the hall, snatching up fallen items from the floor. I cling to my mother's hand as the woman reaches for mine, but my mother tells me she cannot stay and will be back to get me later.

Taking charge of my wet clothes the woman opens the door to an inner room and ushers me inside. She disappears, and I stand alone in the large room feeling awed and frightened. Small groups of children are seated playing on the floor in front of a blazing fire. They look up when I enter but go right on playing. Across the room a small grave girl in a red velvet dress and white lace collar watches me from her place beside the chimney. She seems so solitary and alone and her image provokes my imagination. I note the paleness of her skin against her black shiny hair, and the hint of pain in the deep brown eyes.

A vague transient discomfort passes over me and I look in vain for my mother's face against the glass-paneled door. Now a slight pressure on my arm, and a strange but smiling woman leads me toward the fire. From her pocket she takes a small shell brush and ties a yellow ribbon in my hair. Then she sits me down beside the others on the floor. And now, for the first time, I see the doll's house with real glass windows and a slated roof. Each little window has a white lace curtain and I cannot see inside, so I crouch down to peer through the open door but am distracted by a movement barely perceptible from the corner of my eye.

It is a tiny mouse, with a small metal key jutting from its side. I watch it race along the floor between the sprawling bodies, until with a bump it comes to rest against someone's shoe. Hands pick it up and start it on its way again. But I am no longer interested in the mouse, my attention directed to the pursuit of more intellectual channels in the task of intricate construction. My brick house is beautiful with red windowpanes and green and yellow portals. I feel so proud to have accomplished it and all I want is to sit and look at it. But somewhere a bell is ringing and everyone has fallen silent. The children have stopped talking and some are standing, stiff and motionless. A tall, thin woman with white hair has entered and is beginning to speak in a mellow voice. The room is filled with the perfume of wild flowers, and all at once I remember Jane. Where is she? Why isn't she here, and why hasn't my mother come back for me? I begin to feel afraid again as I watch for her face in the glass panels of the door.

Here the scene fades and I remember nothing further. It comes to me again at a point later in time in a yard swarming with children. I'm no longer frightened or unsure as I race wildly with my friends. The teacher's names I know now are, Lawlor, Davin, and Brennan and the cleaning lady is Mrs. McDonald, who lives in a house across the road. We run to the gate to look out at where she lives. Then we hurry to the bottom of the yard to watch her scrub the blue china flowers on the lavatory bowls and to look over the wall into Meany's garden.

Phyllis Hogan, who lives nearby and knows a lot of things, says that if we stand on top of the wall we can see all the way past Blunden's Wood to the fairy glen where Jack the Lantern is living. So, we all climb up on the wall to look, but can see nothing but the irate form of Mr. Meany, waving his spade and yelling for us to 'get down out of there this minute'.

Undaunted, we head back along the yard, skipping and jumping till our bodies hurt, our shouts echoing through the galvanized shed. And when we reach the gate again, breathless but content, I am saddened by the sight of the timid little girl in the red velvet dress standing alone in her corner by the door. Day after day I have seen her there and I wonder about her shyness, and the cold that is causing her to shiver even when the sun is shining.

I have no conscious memory of any moment of decision, but I recall with clarity her instantaneous reaction to my outstretched hand, and the grave expression on her face dissolve into a grateful smile. I remember also the pinch of my fingers in a vice-like grip that belied all my notions of her fragile frame. So unexpected is the spontaneity of her response and so intense her pleasure as we dash about in a flurry of excitement, flinging open our coats in total dissolution.

Her name is Peggy Donnelly and she lives only streets from the school. And during the weeks that follow, in our attempts to copy the mild conventions we have picked up from our mothers, we share a mutual satisfaction as we wander together through the school grounds, sharing every secret and finding new adventure under every stone. Those days I believe to have been among the happiest of my life and I can see myself now, strutting about like a little fat hen, discovering the strength of my own will in puffed up airs of ownership.

But soon the long days of summer came and the school year ended, as hand in hand Peggy and I strolled together for the last time, exchanging vows of friendship. I watched her cross the road to her house and listened to her last farewell as she wheeled out of sight around the corner. For a moment I stood and listened, expecting to hear her call again, but she didn't. Seconds later, I am speeding down the hill to home, to my mother, freedom, and a world of great adventure.

I never saw Peggy again. When the summer holidays ended and the first day of school came around, I waited by the gate of the new school as I had promised, but she didn't come. Each morning I waited hopefully, but she never came. I found out later that she had died that summer of tuberculosis.

BIDDY'S BURDEN

It was a routine day for Biddy Bolger until four o'clock that Thursday in July when a frantic scream from inside the house ripped apart her quiet afternoon. Biddy, who had been idling on the swing in their back garden, had been left to mind the house. She had been passing time looking at the latest edition of the Dandy while waiting for her little sister to wake up. Maddy, the baby of the family was two and Biddy was almost eight. She leaped off the swing and ran indoors, to find her baby sister standing barefoot by the fire, her nightshirt in flames. Not knowing what else to do, Biddy dragged her to the scullery where she filled a pot with water and doused it over her.

"Mammy! Mammy!" the little girl kept screaming as the flames crept up around her ears and her beautiful hair began to burn. Frantically, Biddy screamed for help and tried to calm the child, to get her to hold still so she could drown the flames with water. But the little girl was terrified, screaming for her mother, and in her frenzy, dashed into the garden. Biddy followed, and in a moment of enlightenment pulled a blanket from the clothesline and threw it over her. The screams turned to stifled sobs and then to an eerie silence as the little bundle crumbled to the ground.

A neighbor who had heard the screams came running over and carried the traumatized child in his arms the whole way to the hospital. Maddy survived the terrible ordeal, and grew to be a lovely girl, though she never laughed and seldom spoke. Miraculously her face had not been burned, but her arms, legs and torso told the story. Biddy's mother never forgave Biddy for her carelessness, and reminded her of the pain she caused every chance she got.

Biddy had few memories of life in those last years before her father died. She was five when he passed away and all she remembered about that day was standing rigid in a strange white room that hadn't any furniture. She had been left to stand inside the door and could see her father lying in an iron bed with people standing around the bed in front of her. Everyone was silent. Instinctively, she felt that something terrible had happened to her father. His eyes were closed, his face pale. Her mother was sitting by the bed, her hand resting on his shoulder. *Why doesn't he open his eyes and look at her?* Only then did she become aware that people in the room were crying, and her mother too had begun to sob. Terrified, Biddy ran to her and her mother picked her up and hugged her.

"Poor little lamb," she heard someone say, "what a time for this to happen."

"Well, there's nothing more we can do for him," an old woman sighed. The next thing she remembered was standing in a bedroom crying, with the same old woman standing over her. Biddy didn't like her, she was old and smelly, and Biddy didn't want to wear the ugly black dress she handed her. It was rough and scratched her skin.

"Stop whinging and put it on. Be thankful that you've got it." She laid it on the bed beside her. Biddy made no move to put it on and after a few minutes another woman came and sat on the bed beside her. She draped her arms around her shoulders.

"There now pet, no more tears. You don't have to wear that old dress if you don't want to." She picked it up and tossed it carelessly across the bed. Then she whispered in Biddy's ear. "I'll tell you a secret, shall I?" Biddy nodded, and the woman hugged her closer and whispered in her ear. "I wouldn't want to wear that old thing either. It's a granny dress. Thing is, your nanny is from another world. She doesn't live in our time. The only thing she knows is practicality."

Biddy didn't understand what she was talking about, but she liked how the words sounded and the soft way the woman spoke to her. Later that evening, her mother told her that her father was never coming back.

"But why? Why doesn't he want to come back to us?"

"He can't love. God wants him in heaven with him." Biddy began to cry. Memory of her father's love and kisses came flooding back.

"I don't care about any old God. I want my daddy back." Her mother tried to console her.

"Listen pet, your daddy was a sick man, too sick to stay in this old world. He didn't want to go, but he had to. The doctors couldn't help him, couldn't make him better. At least up there he's in no pain." Biddy refused to be consoled.

"Why couldn't God make him better? Why did he have to take him?" Biddy's mother knew the time had come to tell her about the baby. Biddy looked at her with big round eyes.

"A baby! We're going to get a baby! When?"

"Any day now," her mother laughed, and Biddy couldn't wait for the day to come. The moment she laid eyes on the baby, Biddy knew she loved her more than anything else in the whole wide world. She had reached down to touch her hand and the baby clung to her, her fat little fingers curled around her thumb.

"We can call her Maddy, can't we Ma?" she asked, excitedly. It was the name she had given her very first doll, the one her father had given her on her fourth birthday. It had been stolen from the flat the day he went to the hospital and Biddy, inconsolable, had cried for days.

To some extent, Maddy had made up for the loss of her father. Biddy adored her little sister and after the accident, the two girls were inseparable. They went on living in the tenement, as they had before her father died. Only now she slept in her mother's bed, behind the heavy curtain. It had been a year since her father died and Biddy knew that her mother worried if she couldn't pay the rent. Though she never said as much, Biddy had heard her tell Bill Cunningham, the gasman, when he came to empty the meter.

"I don't know what is to become of us, or how we're going to manage. I simply don't make enough money washing, and can't seem to make ends meet."

The gasman listened patiently, sipping the tea she had made for him. He had been her husband's friend in the early days and often called in at the flat of an evening. Over the years he had become her mother's friend too. Then one day Biddy heard him ask her mother to marry him. She held her breath behind the curtain, hoping her mother would refuse. She didn't want him taking her father's place.

"Well it's nice of you to ask," she heard her mother say, "but I'd have to think about it Bill. There are the children to consider."

"Don't you think I know that? You said yourself it's hard to manage and surely a man's wages coming in can make things a lot easier." Biddy peeped out from behind the curtain in time to see her mother grimace, and then shake her head. She wasn't sure, she said. She'd need more time to think, she couldn't make her mind up just like that. They had talked about it for a little while, and then Bill rose to leave.

"Well, promise me you'll think about it," Biddy heard him say, before putting on his hat and going to the door. As soon as he left, Biddy flung herself down on the bed and cried, a wave of misery washing over her. She had hoped her mother would say no, now she felt certain she'd say yes.

Though in his prime, Bill was still a handsome man with broad shoulders, deep-set eyes and thick eyebrows that had grown together in the middle. His sleek black hair had a touch of grey, was brushed back from his forehead and slicked down at the sides. He had a way of holding his head erect, and swinging his long arms as he walked. A flashing smile revealed a set of neat, white teeth. People considered him a *good catch*, a widower with no children. Yet, he was a taciturn man, silent about his own life, and opening up only when people pressed him. In a way, Biddy's mother felt sorry for him, for at times he seemed more burdened than she. As the days went by, he began to call more often at the flat and soon, with his persuasion, her mother's fear gave way to practical thoughts. In the end, it was money that decided her. Not his looks or his appearance, but the fact that he already had a house, and a steady job at the Gas Works. She didn't love him and knew he liked a drink at the weekends, but what man didn't? Her maternal instincts told her she was doing the right thing. Marriage to him would not only help the children, but help him as well.

Within weeks of her decision they were married and moved into his house. At first Biddy was unhappy and didn't know what to make of him. She didn't exactly dislike him, but resented him taking her father's place, and taking her mother away from her. But as time went on she became convinced that it was he who didn't like her, or her sister Maddy. She decided to mention it to her mother.

"Now don't be daft, Bid," her mother chided. "What do you mean he doesn't like you? Of course he likes you. He told me so himself."

"Well, he doesn't like our Maddy, I know that. I've seen the way he looks at her, like she was a monster or something."

"That's only because he has a hard time coping with her scars, you know that."

"No I don't," Biddy screamed. "Maddy can't help the way her skin is, and I hate him for reminding her."

"It's a bit late to worry about that now, isn't it? Whose fault is it she got them in the first place?" The tears welled up in Biddy's eyes and her mother, swallowing for once the hard nub of retaliation, reached out and drew her close.

"Now listen Bid. I know he must seem a bit strange to you now, but you'll get used to him. He just can't show his feeling like the rest of us. Remember, he's doing the best he can for us. What chance would we have had to live in a nice house? And don't forget, he made that nice swing for you."

Biddy was twelve when he took her on his lap. It was an ordinary weekday in July and she was in the house alone. Her mother had taken Maddy to the doctor. She had not been well for ages and had been coughing and whimpering all night. That afternoon, her stepfather had come home unexpectedly and seemed in a jolly mood. Biddy could tell he had been drinking. He asked her where her mother was and she told him.

Then he pulled a chair out from the table and sat down. She could feel his eyes examining her and was about to leave the kitchen when he spoke.

"You don't seem happy to see me Bid. Why is that I wonder?" Biddy shrugged. "Come here and sit a while on my lap." Biddy frowned and twisted the hem of her dress around her finger. The last thing she wanted was to sit on his lap.

"Come on now, don't be shy. Come and let me see how much you weigh?" He adjusted his position and drew her to him.

"There we are now, that's better." He began to talk about her mother, saying what a wonderful woman she was and how he had always admired her. Then he talked about her dad, the best friend he ever had, and finally about Maddy and herself. All the time he talked she felt him press against her, shifting her bottom urgently from one side to the other. Though Biddy didn't know exactly what was happening, her common sense told her it was something bad. *He doesn't care about my weight,* she thought, and tried to wriggle free. But his fingers gripped her tighter, digging deep into her groin. Finally, with all the strength in her own wee fingers, she pried his open and darted off his lap.

What was she to do now? She couldn't tell her mother. Given the circumstances, she wasn't sure she should. Her mother would probably not believe her in any case, and would think she was making things up. Biddy was in a quandary not knowing what to do. She was spared the agony of decision, however, because by the time her mother got home, her stepfather had apologized. He didn't know what had come over him, he told her, genuinely sorry and begged her to forgive him.

"It won't happen again, I promise." Then he gave her sixpence and told her to buy some sweets. Biddy never told her mother and life went on as it had before.

Maddy's health improved, but the visit to the doctor had revealed a frightful truth. There was something wrong with Maddy. Two years earlier when she was four, a sudden transformation had come over her. She had begun to spend more time alone, sitting on the floor for hours swaying back and forth. Try as she might, her mother couldn't get her to stop. Maddy would just look at her with a vacant face, as if trying to understand what she was saying. Then she would utter some unintelligible remark and repeat the prior performance. Her mother decided to consult a doctor.

"Is it possible she could still be suffering from shock?" she had inquired, her face a mask of anxiety. The doctor, evidently unsure, yet feeling it incumbent on him to try to ease the tension had graciously replied. Yes, it was entirely possible, and she was not to worry.

"Just give her time, and with the proper care and God's help she will eventually pull out of it." Then he had given her a prescription and sent her on her way.

Now Maddy was six, with no sign of things getting better. If anything they had worsened. She had failed miserably at school, unable to socialize or communicate with other children. Time and time again the teachers had sent her home. Then this morning, the doctor at the clinic had confirmed her mother's worst fears.

"She is not going to pull out of it and needs to be in a special school where she will receive the proper care and tutoring." With no money for a specialized tutor and not wanting her child institutionalized, her mother decided to keep her home, to show a cheerful face and say nothing of the diagnosis. Yet Biddy suspected she had something on her mind as day-by-day she grew paler, and seemed in a constant state of anxiety. She had taken to watching and waiting for the girl's return every time they went outside. Biddy pretended not to notice when more and more she talked about their dead father, with big wet tears pooling in her eyes.

She didn't know what to make of it. All she knew was that once upon a time her mother had been happy, now she was always sad. What could have happened to bring about such change? She found out sooner than expected when on awaking early one morning she had heard her mother crying softly in her room. Biddy rose and hurried to her. She found her mother sitting by the bed, her hand resting on her husband's shoulder. A flash of memory came back to her and once again she saw herself in that cold, white room with her mother sitting by her father's bed, her hand resting on his shoulder.

"What's the matter Ma? Why are you crying?" Yet, even as she asked the question, she knew the answer, and it occurred to her then that her mother had been expecting it. As it turned out, she was right. Her mother had known for months that Bill had a heart condition, yet she had kept the information to herself. Biddy couldn't bear to look at him. Though she had never grown to love him as a father, she had in an odd way grown fond of him.

"Would you go next door please, and ask Mrs. Boyle to come over?" her mother asked, and without a word Biddy left the room. Later that day, the men came and took the body away. Her mother, a non-drinker, refused to have a wake and didn't want to go through all that fuss again. In the days following, he was buried. The girls accompanied their mother to the funeral, but neither one shed a tear. Biddy had wrongly suspected that Maddy had simply never taken to the man, had sensed his discomfort in her presence, but had never mentioned it.

They were back where they started at any rate, only this time they had a house. However, in the weeks following her husband's death, her mother's health began to fail. She became hostile and withdrawn and was hospitalized for several weeks. The girls were sent to live with their maternal grandmother, whom neither of them had ever met and who lived alone in another town. Biddy hoped it wasn't that smelly, bossy woman, whom she had met at her father's funeral. As it turned out it was, and she made no secret of the fact that she had little time for children. From the moment they stepped inside her door she had let them know they were not welcome. Her house was like a showplace of fine carpets, fancy furniture and fine china.

Biddy tried her best to make her like them, offering to do small jobs around the house and running to the shop for messages. But none of it made any difference. Her grandmother criticized everything she did. Nothing suited her. From her, Biddy learned the truth about her sister. Maddy had cried every day they were there, and one day in a moment of extreme distress she had broken a china cup. In a rage her grandmother flew at her.

"You imbecile! Look what you've done!" Biddy apologized for Maddy and bent to pick the pieces up, but her grandmother struck her on the arm with her cane and pushed her out of the kitchen. Later she told Biddy that her sister was *touched,* and was never going to get well. There was madness in the father's family, she said, and Biddy's mother never should have married him. Distressed and filled with anger, Biddy never spoke to her grandmother again. In days they were back home with their mother. However, with little money in the house and no other means of acquiring it, Biddy decided to quit school and look for a job. She had reached her fourteenth birthday.

Her neighbor, Mrs. Boyle, came to her assistance by suggesting that she apply at Whitefriar Hall, a once opulent estate, three miles outside of town. The home belonged to Mrs. Magda Morgan, a plump little lady with a lame leg, who was known for her generosity. Unlike many of her kind, she was well liked and was always ready to do a kind deed for the needy. Though her family had once been considered wealthy, with a large estate and many racehorses, poor financial management and ever mounting debts had necessitated the selling off of most of the estate. Whitefriar Hall was all that was left of it.

The house itself, large and solidly built, with a few architectural pretensions, was located at the end of a long narrow lane and opened onto a cobbled courtyard flanked by a hedge of clipped yew on one side, and a brown brick archway leading to the stables, on the other. There were no green spaces at the front, but the back of the house opened on to spacious grounds, with flower gardens and a huge ornate fountain. Yet, despite the many functions and activities on the premises, the household staff was limited, consisting only of a cook and house maid. Two full-time men and one young lad saw to the horses and the stables. It was Mrs. Morgan's habit, whenever the occasion called for it, to hire extra women from the town to help out with domestic chores.

In her married life she had been unlucky, losing her husband to a hunting accident, and the use of her own leg to a stray bullet. Her only daughter had died at birth, but she had two remaining sons. The youngest boy Johnny, the apple of her eye, had always loved horses and liked to ride. He had never married and eventually became a professional jockey. Markus, the oldest boy, was a married man living in London with his wife and two growing children. For a while he was engaged in politics, but later had entered the bar and became a successful barrister with a reliable practice in certain spheres of continental jurisprudence.

Biddy did as Mrs. Boyle suggested and applied for a job as a domestic. At first Mrs. Morgan had been hesitant, but on learning that Biddy was the daughter of Mick Bolger the blacksmith who had once worked on her father's estate and shoed all his horses, she invited her into the drawing room. Biddy's father had been an honest man, whom she had liked and trusted. Then she asked about Biddy's mother and Biddy told her of her failing health and the worry they both shared over Maddy. Mrs. Morgan nodded understandingly.

"Well, I couldn't pay you much to start, you understand. Half a crown with room and board! As it happens my present girl is leaving in three weeks to get married, and I will be in need of a replacement then. In the meantime, Chrissie will show you your duties and as soon as she leaves you'll have five shillings, if that will suit you?"

"Oh! Yes madam, yes," Biddy blurted, already planning in her head what she could do with it. Mrs. Morgan rose abruptly.

"Very well then, you can start on Monday, you'll meet Chrissie then. Biddy thanked her and hurried out, sprouting wings the whole way home to tell her mother and Mrs. Boyle the good news. As predicted, she loved her job and worked hard every day but Sunday, scrubbing, cleaning and polishing. The only drawback was the necessity to share living space in the servant's quarters with Mrs. Bell the cook, an older woman with strict ideas about one's respectability.

Now, Biddy had always been a pretty girl, with porcelain skin, large liquid eyes and jet-black hair, and by age eighteen had grown to be a desirable woman; a fact that did not go unnoticed among the male inhabitants. Although she was a virtuous and religious girl she was not above flirting with the boys. A harmless occupation, one might say, but one which one day would cause her grief.

It was a common practice of Mrs. Morgan's to hire odd-job men around the stables and Biddy had a smile for all of them, as she had for Johnny, her employer's son who, over time, had taken a shine to her, and had formed the habit of dropping into the kitchen when he thought she might be there. Biddy liked his company and sometimes strolled the lanes with him, sharing secrets and cigarettes and engaged in conversation, which she would never have expected a man of his position to share with a person of her denomination. Yet, never once had he looked down on her and once or twice, on a rainy day, had actually driven her to Mass.

So it was only natural then that Biddy in her naïve ignorance imagined him in love with her. When later he took to concealing himself on the narrow, backstairs landing and leaping out as she came by, she had not objected. Often they would kiss and cuddle there in the dark, Biddy unwisely allowing certain liberties. But apart from those minor indiscretions, he had always treated her with respect.

Then one warm Sunday in May, she was returning alone to the house after spending an evening with a friend. The sun had already left the sky and the stars beginning to appear. She had reached the lane leading to the house and turned into it, humming softly to herself. She had almost reached the end of the lane when she heard the footsteps. Biddy turned around and in a flash Johnny was beside her.

"Oh! 'Tis you Johnny. You gave me a fright. What are you doing here?"

"Waiting for you, of course. What else?" His voice had an excited and extra carefree note in it. Biddy giggled, noting the lock of blond hair fall across his forehead. She had always thought of him as handsome, and liked the way he looked, with his high cheekbones and laughing eyes. "I needed to talk to you alone", he whispered, "something I want to ask you." Biddy's heart began to quicken. She had anticipated something of this nature, for only days before he had given her a friendship ring to wear on her middle finger. His attention had excited her and drawn her into an atmosphere to which she was a stranger, filling her head with fantasies of marriage and life in a grand house.

Taking a firm grip on her arm, Johnny walked along beside her. At the entrance to the courtyard there stood a little shed, built to be a depository for utensils and pieces of discarded furniture. It was very small, very dark and incommodious, yet into this Johnny guided her. Biddy began at once to object but Johnny, as always, talked her round.

"Come on now Bid. Don't be difficult. You know that I adore you. You have no need to be afraid of me, and why should you be, I'm not going to hurt you." With those words Biddy foolishly relaxed.

"What is it you want to ask me?" she asked, her heart beating faster, and she barely able to contain herself with expectation. Johnny didn't answer, just wrapped his arms around her and drew her close, all the while whispering sweet nothings in her ear, while groping frantically for her breast. It was a maneuver he had carried out before, but never with such force or passion. Biddy tried to pull away from him.

"Wait Johnny, I ....," she began, wanting to tell him to leave her alone, that she didn't like the way he was behaving, but was unable to get the words out, so hard were his lips pressed against her mouth. Before she knew it, he had edged her over to an old settee and pulled her onto it. In a flash, he was all over her, tearing at the buttons of her skirt and yanking her underwear down around her legs.

"Please Johnny. Don't do this. It isn't right," Biddy pleaded, and tried to pry his hands away. But her pleading fell on deaf ears as Johnny threw himself on top of her. She tried to wriggle free but couldn't. Too polite to scream, she eventually gave up the struggle and lay still. Considering his small size, he was as heavy as an ox on top of her, panting and groaning and pounding into her.

Through it all, Biddy had remained silent, but when it was over she had cried and refused to look at him. She felt cold, dirty and ashamed. "You won't get away with this Johnny," was all she could think to say.

"And why won't I? Isn't it my word against yours?" Johnny laughed, but then in an instant of regret. "I'm sorry Biddy. Truly I am. I had not intended it to happen, but I lost control and couldn't help myself." He helped her up and draped his jacket over her, begging her not to say a word to anyone. "If the necessity arises I'll look after you, I promise. I won't let you down." Biddy nodded, but couldn't bring herself to look at him. She no longer trusted him and was bitterly angry at what he'd done. Yet in her heart she knew she should have fought harder and maybe have prevented it. She agreed to keep her mouth shut and not tell anyone.

As the weeks passed and she felt no ill affects she assumed that all was fine. Johnny didn't come to the kitchen again and after a while Biddy decided to put the whole ordeal behind her. Then one morning she began to vomit. As it happened, she and cook had become good friends and the older woman had, over time, become Biddy's confidante. So it was she who put into words what Biddy couldn't bring herself to say, that she was carrying Johnny's child.

"I thought as much," was all she said, when Biddy began to snivel and reveal what happened.

"Silly girl. Silly, silly girl," she scolded. "Surely you can't believe he will marry you?" Biddy hung her head.

"He said that he'd look after me. He promised." Cook sighed and shook her head tut-tutting.

"Listen to me child. Did nobody ever tell you that men are rotten? They'll say anything to get what they want. All they ever think about is that one thing, never of the consequences." Biddy began to sob as she continued. "You might as well make up your mind to that. That lad has no intention of marrying you, and never had. To his way of thinking, you're a servant girl and all servant girls are *easy,* and happy to oblige."

Not one to point the finger, yet wondering whether Biddy might have brought it on herself, she got up from the table and walked around the kitchen. She couldn't say she was shocked, because in an undefined way she had expected something like this to happen. She had seen the way Biddy behaved whenever Johnny was around, and once or twice had voiced her concern. "It's no use," she said finally, "I can see no way around it. His mother will have to be informed." She took hold of Biddy's arm.

"But I promised I wouldn't say anything," Biddy wailed, as cook pushed her up the stairs.

"My goodness me! What ails you girl?" Mrs. Morgan cried perplexed as Biddy stood in front of her, tears streaming down her face. She couldn't find the proper words to answer and looked to cook for help.

"Well madam it was like this...." Cook began to relate the sordid details. Mrs. Morgan groped behind her for a chair. She was in shock, but declined to let it show. *No, there must be some mistake. My son wouldn't do a thing like that. It's unthinkable, Johnny entering into a liaison with a servant girl. Hopefully, he has made no foolish promises.*

30

"But when? When did this happen?" she asked, her pallor pale. *Of course he would have to take responsibility for the baby.* Her mind already in turmoil had now gone into overdrive as another thought took root inside her head. Illegitimate children of mixed class did not fit well into the social fabric of the wealthy. This situation called for clearer thinking, yet her mind was in a whirlpool of perplexity. How could she think? How could she even render a decision? In a moment of complete confusion she had wrung her hands despairingly, and asked them both to leave.

Next morning she confronted Johnny, who for the first time in his life saw his mother in a rage. He admitted he had seduced Biddy, but his account of what had happened differed entirely from what cook had said. In the first place, he denied using physical force and went so far as to intimate that the whole incident had been Biddy's fault. "We'll that's beside the point now, isn't it? The girl is pregnant, and says you are the one responsible. There is no other way around it you will have to speak to her. Come to some arrangement if you must, but I want no scandal." Conscious of her mounting emotion and reluctant to put himself in opposition to her wishes, Johnny agreed.

In the meantime Biddy, ever trusting, eagerly awaited his decision. But, of course, nothing ever came of it, because a few days later Johnny disappeared. It was rumored he had fled to his brother's house in London. Yet, every day Biddy watched and waited, expecting his return. It had been her intention when in the fifth month of pregnancy to hand in her notice, which is why she was surprised when one Friday afternoon, in the middle of the fourth month, Mrs. Morgan summoned her to the drawing room and handed her an envelope containing twenty pounds. Not a fortune by any means, but to one earning less than two pounds per month!

"I'm truly sorry Biddy," she began distressfully, "but you must realize, that given the present circumstances, I can't possibly keep you on the premises any longer. A replacement has already been arranged, and it might be best for everyone concerned were you to leave today." She took hold of Biddy's hand. "I've arranged for the St. Vincent de Paul to look in on you. They will help you cope with any problems that may arise." *Well, thanks for nothing,* Biddy thought, thanking her and quietly leaving. She was beyond consoling as she packed her few belongings and left the house without saying goodbye to anyone.

With a heavy heart she returned to her mother's house only to find her mother lying on the couch, a damp towel wrapped around her forehead. *One of her migraines no doubt,* Biddy thought, unaware that her mother had not been eating and had been ill for weeks. In the bedroom she found Maddy, sitting on the floor playing with her doll. She wrapped her arms around her and began to cry. "What's the problem Biddy? Why are you home? You haven't been fired, have you?" Her mother had followed her to the door. She looked old and shrunken.

Biddy sighed and headed to the kitchen, her mother at her heels. "Sit down Ma," she said, "there's something you should know." She told her everything, leaving nothing out.

"Oh! The cad. I thought there must be something wrong when I hadn't seen you for so long. How far gone are you?" Biddy told her. "You should have made the bugger marry you." Biddy didn't know how she could have done that, but to keep her mother from getting more upset, she handed her the money. "So, this is what she gave you as compensation?" She shook her head disgusted.

"I had a good mind not to take it," Biddy said, "but I knew you could use it." Her mother nodded.

"At least she didn't send you home empty handed."

As the weeks went by her mother's health worsened and each day Biddy watched her grow weaker. But what? What was it that was eating her away? *Consumption. That's the only thing it can be.* "You ought to see a doctor Ma," she kept telling her, and always her mother shook her head.

"I know what's wrong with me, so what's the use? They'll just put me in the Sanatorium and what will happen to Maddy then. Who is going to look after her?"

"I'm home now. I'll look after of her." Her mother laughed.

"You have enough to do to look after yourself. Look at you, barely skin and bone and with a baby on the way."

"Don't worry about me, I'll be all right."

And so the weeks passed and at scarcely nineteen, on a cold wet day in December, Biddy gave birth to a healthy boy, with blond hair and laughing eyes. Anyone could see he was Johnny's son. Surprisingly, she felt a tenderness toward the baby that she had not felt since Maddy was born. The feeling was so strong as to make her bow to her mother's suggestion that she not give him up for adoption as she had intended, but try to bring him up herself. They decided to name him Michael after her father.

No sooner had the news got out about the baby when malicious tongues began to wag and snide remarks to circulate, until pretty soon Biddy found herself outcast, the talk of the neighbourhood. *Well, let them talk,* she told herself, *I don't owe them anything.* What upset her most was the fact that her mother refused to see a doctor, yet went on from day to day coughing and spitting blood. Her mother was dying and Biddy knew it. What made it even more difficult for her that winter was learning to be a mother, not only to her newborn baby but also to Maddy, who could do little for herself. Many nights she couldn't sleep and would lay awake thinking about Johnny. She couldn't believe he had deserted her, and clung like a vine to the glimmer of hope that one day he would return and marry her. Until then she decided, she would wear his ring.

In January her mother's health worsened and by the end of the following month she was deceased. Biddy was beside herself with grief. Not only did she have to deal with her mother's funeral but with those well meaning, but interfering social workers, intent on putting Maddy in a home. She had begged them to leave her be, determined to look after her herself, but the nurse was adamant.

"The child is being deprived," she said, "deprived of friends and special care. If she is ever to enjoy a normal life, then you'll have to let her go." Biddy was broken hearted, torn between her need to protect and cherish Maddy, and the desire to see her well. She agreed that Maddy needed special care, the kind of cerebral nurturing she could never provide, and in the end had allowed them to take her.

Alone now and miserable, she began to withdraw into herself and it was then that Paddy Purcell came into the picture. A little fellow with a ruddy face, the image of Mickey Rooney, who lived with his mother on a farm some distance from Whitefriar Hall. A shy sort of man, in his thirties maybe, Biddy wasn't sure for she didn't know him all that well, though she had visited his mother many times, mostly to pick up eggs for Mrs. Morgan. But once or twice she had passed him in the yard and had stopped to say hello. Shortly after her mother died, however, Paddy took to calling at her house, bringing eggs and rashers from the farm.

An observant man, he hadn't failed to notice how miserable she was. The way she worried over Maddy and the baby, and he couldn't help but notice the shabbiness surrounding her. Though he had never said so, he had always liked her and wanted desperately to help. There was no way he could offer money without insulting her. But he could ask her to marry him. At least she would have good food to eat and a decent place to live.

His offer was not entirely unselfish, mind, for he knew his mother was getting on and might not be around much longer. If something were to happen to her, he would need someone to replace her. Someone he could depend upon to clean house and cook for himself and the hired hands. The more he thought about it the more the idea grew on him, yet he refrained from asking, afraid that she might laugh at him.

As the months wore on, however, and their friendship deepened, so did Paddy's courage. In a casual but lighthearted way he contrived to win her over. "I know I'm not much to look at, not in comparison to Johnny boy, but if you'll have me I promise to make you a good husband." Biddy didn't know what to say. She liked Paddy, and knew he was a kind and generous man, but she didn't want to marry him.

Paddy persisted and on the third rejection, said with a trace of irony. "If you're waiting for him to marry you, you'll have a long wait. He's back home now and brought a wife with him." Biddy didn't believe him and thought he was just saying it so she would agree to marry him. She was about to tell him so when he spoke again, dragging his hand across his mouth like a little boy.

"I wouldn't pressure you where the other thing is concerned, if that's what's worrying you. I've seen enough poor animals in distress to want to do that." Biddy was astonished at his remark, until suddenly it all came back to her. The first time she had seen him, almost five years before. She had gone to the farm to collect the eggs, and Paddy's mother had sent her to the barn where a cow was giving birth to her first calf. She had stood inside the door watching.

The cow was standing in the corner groaning. Her contractions had already started and Biddy thought she looked terrified, her big eyes moiling in her head. Paddy was standing close by, stroking her, a length of rope draped across his shoulder. He hadn't seen her enter and Biddy liked the way he kept talking to the cow. Soft like. The way a mother might talk to a baby. "There now my pet, don't be frightened. Just relax, you're doing fine." As if in response to his ministrations, the cow's back legs buckled and she dropped down onto the straw.

Biddy saw Paddy examine her, and could tell by the grave expression on his face that he was worried. He kept coaxing and encouraging. But after some minutes he stood up and ran his hand across his forehead. It was then he saw her standing by the door. He shook his head dejectedly.

"It's no use. She can't do it by herself. The calf is the wrong way around." By now Biddy could see the two small hooves protruding, and signs of the infant struggling to get free.

"Can I help at all?" she had asked without thinking, and walked across to him. Paddy smiled and handed her the towel.

"There's nothing for it but the rope now," he said, and began to wind a length of it securely around the little hooves, while all the time reassuring the mother. "We're almost there now girl. Just you lay still and I'll take over." With one foot braced against the mother's back, he began to pull, gently at first and then with increasing strength until all at once the hindquarters were free, and a grey jelly-like mass slipped out onto the straw. A little brown calf, with a white star on its forehead was wrapped up in it.

"Yeuch!" Biddy had turned her head away in revulsion. "If that's the way a baby gets born, I want no part of it." Paddy laughed.

"Can't say that I blame you. I'd want no part of it myself. No woman should have to suffer that." He turned a questioning glance at her. "First time you've seen it then?" Biddy nodded shyly. She remembered thinking what a good man he was to treat animals so lovingly. But never in the world could she have imagined marrying him. Not wanting to hurt his feelings now, she thanked him again for his offer and said she would consider

it. Consider it was all she might have done, had it not been for
that Sunday morning walking home alone from Mass.

She had seen two people coming toward her on the path,
one short, the other tall, and one a woman, the other a man.
There was something familiar about the man, and as he drew
close she saw that it was Johnny, with a pretty blonde girl on his
arm. There was no time to turn around and no place to hide
and so she had kept walking toward them. As she passed, the
lady smiled and nodded, and Johnny looked at her, his lips
parting as though about to speak. But then his eyes slid past her
and he turned his head away. Biddy couldn't believe it. She
knew he had recognized her. She was utterly shattered, yet
somehow managed to walk past. She then stood motionless on
the path, looking after him, twisting the friendship ring round
and round her finger.

Fool! Fool! Blind, stupid fool! The words roared inside her
head as she pressed her fist against her mouth to stop herself
crying out. *So, Paddy had not been lying after all.* The tears
gushed unbidden from her eyes, as the ring slipped from her
finger and she flung it with all her might to the other side of the
road. There was nothing left for her now, she had lost
everything. She thought it best not to mention it to Paddy.

By the time Michael was three, she knew she would have to
do something. The last of the money had long ago run out and
like her mother before her, she had begun to take in washing to
help pay the rent. The work was tiring and the pay less than
minimal, but it helped. Then came a day she was so sick she
could barely stand and couldn't stay on her feet long enough to
do the necessary work. The weakness had hit her once or twice
before but each time she had managed to get the washing done.
This time the dizziness wouldn't go away and she was forced to
let it ride. A few days went by before a smart young girl came
knocking on her door. Biddy opened it.

"You have my mother's laundry and I want it," was all she said. Biddy tried to explain about her illness, but the girl simply repeated what her mother had said. That she had engaged another washerwoman and Biddy was not to call at the house again. After that, things went from bad to worse until one night she began thinking about her mother and the warning she had given her before she died. 'Don't make the same mistake I did and wait too long. Find a good man and marry him, for your own sake as well as the baby's'. Biddy made her decision. She found a nice priest willing to marry her and when Paddy came around again she told him what she had done. Slightly taken aback, he stared at her.

"Well, you do want to marry me don't you?"

"Of course I do. Only I'd like you to be sure you are doing the right thing."

"I'm doing the right thing. You know I don't love you Paddy, I've never lied about that. But I do like you a lot, and I know you'd make a good husband. Besides, what would Michael do without you now? Sure, he thinks you're his dad already." Those were the words that Paddy longed to hear. For months he had been remodeling the house, adding rooms and planting gardens. Only now that she had accepted him did he give her the good news. He was soon to inherit his uncle's farm, a plot of prime, fertile land over fifty acres, and adjacent to his own. "We'll be on the pig's back then my girl. We'll call it Oakridge Acres, and you can thumb your nose at the lot of them."

"I can. Can't I?" Biddy wept, calling up visions of a grand house surrounded by all those acres. At least her dream had come partly true, and though her new home may never share the same prestige as Whitefriar Hall it would, nonetheless, be hers.

THE COALMAN

"One hundred weight of coal for the Lennons," the voice calls out on the garden path and I hurry to the yard to watch Jimmy Murray empty the bulging sack, his back bent beneath its weight. From my place beside the apple tree I can watch the coal tumble to the ground, filling the air with that black silk dust that settles in a film over everything. I like watching this, I don't know why. Maybe it's the tiny motes settling so neatly over everything. But also I like Jimmy, a handsome man of about thirty years with deep brown eyes and jet black hair, who always has a kind word for everyone.

He folds up the empty bag while I go inside to get the money, then he roots in his pocket for a peppermint for me. Aware of the dirt so heavy on his hands, his fingers thick and calloused, I at first refuse but then I take it and hold it in my hand. "Go on eat it," he says, "'tis only dirt, it won't poison you." And so not to hurt his feelings, I place the peppermint behind my teeth waiting for a chance to spit it out. After a while I forget about the dirt and begin to suck on it. This pleases him and he pats my head approvingly, and then moves across the yard to the window ledge to count his money.

I wait as he unwinds the piece of crumpled paper wrapped around the notes and crosses off names with a stub of pencil. Then he puts the notes away and empties the change from his pocket onto the ledge for counting. This action usually embarrasses me for it seems rude somehow, though I know he means no slight by it. Yet, I find myself gazing up into the apple tree, pretending not to notice.

How things have changed, is what I'm really thinking. For when we knew him first he had no money, and no coal to sell. All he had was a rickety old cart that he used to gather wood from around the country roads. Then a friend and he began collecting scraps from lumberyards, chopping them into bundles and selling them around the neighbourhood. More often than not, both men could be seen any evening of the week, hail rain or shine, busy at their task. Their hard work paid off and in no time at all they were getting more orders than they could handle, and tired of using the empty space behind their house they rented their own yard and started up in business. With the passage of months and a new power saw, came the full-sized logs and the notion of expansion. After that, there was no stopping them as they moved full swing into turf and coal. Soon they were supplying a large portion of the city, with only one other coal merchant to compete with.

I know today will be Jimmy's last delivery and from now on the coal will be delivered by a recently hired hand. He has told me about this arrangement on his last delivery and I know he's looking forward to the change. I sense that he has finished counting and look in his direction. He is smiling now and gives me one of his appraising looks, admiring my hair and telling me I've grown much taller in the last few weeks.

This, for certain, I know to be an exaggeration for I haven't grown an inch. I shrug and smile at any rate, letting him believe he has said the right thing, but I can feel the blush coming into my cheeks and hope he doesn't notice. He is silent for a moment after, as he wipes the sweat from his blackened face, and then holds a match to his cigarette. He takes a deep drag.

"You're a quiet one, all the same. How old are you now?" he asks, blowing out the smoke. I'm not quite sure what to say about the *quiet* part for I really don't have an answer, except to say that adults sometimes have that affect on me. I tell him, however, that I'm twelve years old and soon to be thirteen.

"Ah," he expels his breath in a noisy burst as though I have told him something magical. "Do you like school?" he asks, and I say no that I can't wait to leave. He nods his head in understanding. "I know what you mean all right," he says, giving me a wink, "book learning has its place, but it's not everything." Why people can't use the brains that God has given them instead of relying on books for everything is something he can't understand.

"Look at me now!" he says, using his success as an example. Ordinarily, he does not engage in lengthy conversation, so I am surprised when he continues, telling me about his work and how it is that he succeeded. It is a lesson not included in the school curriculum. Taking the bull by the horns, he explains, is all very well, but one had to be able to see both ends of the situation. For the man who begins a task without foreseeing its end is doomed to failure. And did I know that the world is full of educated fools whose schooling never took them farther than the Labour Exchange?

No, I didn't know that I tell him, and wish he hadn't told me. For all at once I'm thinking about my father and the books he is always reading. Names like Dickens, Shakespeare and Dean Swift spring rapidly to mind, and I remember what my father said about these men. How their understanding of the habits and motivations of humanity has helped to shape the world. Good books help to make people smart, he said, and are beneficial to all ages; their lessons often leading men to greatness, or helping the less fortunate to promote themselves in life.

Surely then he has been using the brains that God has given him! At least that has been my understanding. His failure to climb the corporate ladder of success cannot be due to an inability to think, nor to any lack of labour, but to the *"slings and arrows of outrageous fortune"* or misfortune, whichever way you cared to look at it. If his achievements have fallen short of his goals, is he to blame? I want to say all this to Jimmy, to make things clear to him, and contradict to some extent his proclamation. Though I hear no actual criticism in his words, his thoughts make me uneasy, for I don't want him thinking my father a fool. I miss the opportunity to speak, however, when all at once he shifts his gaze and looks behind me to Mrs. Carroll's garden, where Paddy Commerford the hunchback has begun to hack at the long untended grass, the nettles and incipient weeds, with mighty sweeps of his scythe. His fine baritone voice begins to rise to the strains of *The Colleen Bawn.* Jimmy watches him a moment before calling out.

"Have you lost your wits entirely Pat. Aren't you too old now to be doing work like that?" Paddy stops what he is doing and waves to him.

"Deed and I can do all this and more," he makes a wide sweep of the area with his arm, then spits on his hands before gripping the scythe again. The action sends a tremor through my senses as I catch the gleam of the sharpened blade rushing toward the grass. It triggers a memory in my brain and I look about me worriedly. Jimmy, who has pulled out his dirty handkerchief and blown his nose in it, shoves it back into his pocket before asking.

"Does that man frighten you or what, because you look as though you're afraid of him?" *Afraid! Of course I'm not afraid. Why should I be, Paddy wouldn't hurt a fly.* The fact is, of course, I know little about the man. Outside of the fact that he rents a room with old Mrs. Carroll, tends the grounds at the Abbey Chapel and sings in the church choir with my father. Yet, I feel no reason to fear him.

The thing that has me worried is the story I once heard him tell my father about the time he was cutting hay in Morgan's meadow and sliced the legs clear off a nesting pheasant with one great sweep of that same blade. The poor bird had not even made a sound, he said, but flew some inches in the air before dropping back to earth. I have visions of that happening to one of our hens now. Especially to Hanna, my mother's pet, who usually wanders freely in our garden, and likes to sneak into Carroll's patch to nestle in the grass. If I reveal this fact to Jimmy I fear he will think me foolish, worrying about a hen.

By now Paddy is singing at the top of his voice and won't hear me even if I do shout a warning. So, I move away from Jimmy and take a peep around the side of the house to the chicken coop in the corner, where I catch sight of Hanna safe outside the wire fence, her head stuck under the wooden post pecking at the gravel. With an easier mind, I turn back to Jimmy who is silent now, his eyes staring into space like he doesn't want to speak, and as I can't think of anything special to say I wait respectfully for him to break the silence. Finally he does, looking anxiously once more at Paddy and shaking his head sympathetically.

"Poor auld devil. You'd wonder what he has to sing about, condemned to a life of misery." With alacrity, he tosses the butt of his cigarette clear across the garden and bends a little closer to speak to me. "Let me tell you something now," he says almost in a whisper. "'Tis a sad thing to say, but there's little hope in this world for a man born with a deformity." He nods his head knowingly and looks about him warily, before picking his sack up from the ground and flinging it across his shoulder.

"Mind you don't forget what I told you now. Healthy, wealthy and wise, that's my motto," and giving me another wink he goes hurrying off along the path, his lean, lively body moving in rhythm to the dictates of his club-foot.

THE CANDIDATE

Mickey Mulligan and his good wife lived together on a small farm, at the top of a steep hill some miles outside of town. It was a warm friendly place where town folk, out for a walk on a summer day, were free to drink from the cool *spring-water* well just inside the gate, or rest awhile on the wooden bench beside it. The house, which had been built in the nineteenth century, had a fine thatched roof and mullioned windows and stood firmly on its roots. On most days of the year a log fire burned brightly in the grate with a cast iron pot simmering quietly beside it. It was there Mickey could usually be found sitting with his good friend Mr. Dempsey, or the Old Man as he had become known to us.

Mickey, a jolly man in his middle fifties, was apt to adopt a comic role and liked nothing better than to raise issues with which to tease his friend. Whereas the Old Man, steeped in the wisdom of his seventy-five years, preferred to adopt a more serious note. Observing him now begin to fill his pipe, Mickey laid aside the newspaper he had been reading. Though he liked the smell of pipe tobacco he had never used it. If he smoked at all it was a cigarette, a Woodbine or Sweet Afton, and then only at Christmas time or Easter. He shuffled his chair back from the fire.

"I've said it before and I'll say it again, there's no surer way of helping a man to his eternal rest than a lung full of that stuff every day." The Old Man ignored the comment as he usually did, and after a while Mickey continued with the conversation.

There was nothing new about the things he said, just the usual complaints about the times, and the trials of farming in inclement weather.

"It's hard work for a man of my years, especially when you're doing it every day."

Unwilling to be drawn into an argument, the Old Man offered no response. He had heard Mickey's arguments before and had little time for them. For the truth was that Mickey was inclined to be indolent. The whole farm was in a state of disrepair and everything needed mending. Pieces falling off buildings in the wintertime were never nailed back, left to rot until the spring and then forgotten. But there was little use in trying to talk to Mickey, because no matter what anyone said to him, he never seemed get things done.

"I don't believe in hired hands," he was fond of telling people, but neither did he believe in doing it himself. The result, of course, was visible to everyone but him. Yet, he was a pleasant man and liked by all who knew him. A rare page in the annals of success he might never be, but for warmth of heart and public affability, he had no equal.

In spite of the difference in their ages and Mickey's persistent friendship with the Old Man's nemesis Barney Callahan, the two men shared a solid friendship. Mickey knew he had to tread lightly when he mentioned Barney, but he couldn't always resist the temptation to include him in their conversation. The feud between Barney and the Old Man had begun years before and was based solely on political beliefs. Every Irishman of the day knew that members of the constabulary were notoriously sympathetic to *The Crown,* and Barney's political sentiments stemmed largely from his affiliation with the long arm of the law, upon whose heads DeValera, the Old Man's hero, had heaped his own aspersions.

Born in a climate of hate against the English, the Old Man considered himself a bona fide Republican and had nothing but contempt for the forces of the Crown. Over the years, their differences had been drawn out and accentuated by well meaning, but mischievous friends. Of course, there was no evidence of hostility when the two men met in public.

"Morning Callaghan," the Old Man would nod.

"Morning Dempsey," from Barney.

But in the company of their private quarters, the stories told were different. There, Barney supposedly had been heard, on more than one occasion, to call the Old Man an upstart and an anarchist, and the Old Man refer to Barney as a no-good traitor, living on the proceeds of his treason.

So it had come as some surprise to Mickey to learn that the two men had been seen arm in arm on the Comer Road, following the political victory of the Old Man's candidate Jimmy Rattigan. Determined to cajole him into revealing all the facts, Mickey skillfully maneuvered the conversation.

"I see by the paper that Callaghan saved the day for us." The Old Man's eyes bored into him.

"Go on, go on."

"Well, you must have heard," said Mickey, commencing to repeat what he believed had transpired at Whelan's pub the previous evening.

"Whelan's! What's Whelan's got to do with anything? The count was made in the Deseart Hall." Mickey shrugged and held aloft the paper.

"Well, I'm only telling you what I read, and it says right here...." The Old Man interrupted.

"The paper! The paper! There ye go again. Is there any use in talking to ye?" He gazed about the room with a critical eye. It was his opinion that the truth could not be found in any newspaper, a fact he had mentioned many times to Mickey. "Just look at ye," he said, his arm sweeping in a circle, "your house is so filled up with papers, a man can't turn around without stumbling over them." This observation, I might add, had many times been made by others entering the Mulligan domain. Not a table or a chair was without a newspaper, or a written page of some description.

"Well don't go on about that again," sighed Mickey, "you know I like to read the papers."

"Aye, and every time ye do 'tis the same story. Ye believe everything ye read in them. Ye have to see what that lot has to say about everything, and the first thing ye do is tell it to me. If ye really want to know what's going on, all ye have to do is ask Gabby Hayes. He's the man that can put ye straight."

Mickey shrugged. "Maybe so, but I don't like having to ask him, he makes such a history out of everything."

"He'll tell ye the truth all the same." Mickey said he didn't care and that the Old Man had a mule's mind about the newspaper. He turned abruptly toward the fire and began poking at the grate. The Old Man eyed him warily. It wasn't that he disagreed with Mickey all the time about the papers, but he found it wise to pretend he did. He took a moment to relight his pipe, sheltering the flickering match with the cup of his hand. "And do ye blame me? When every time ye pick one up you see something like that?" He pointed to a picture of a man on the front page of the Independent. Mickey turned to look at it.

"And what's wrong with that?"

"What's wrong with it! I'll tell ye what's wrong. That fellow Mulvihill has no business there, or anywhere else in the news for that matter."

"And why not? Doesn't he have as much right to be there as anyone?"

"Not in my opinion, no. That fellow is nothing but a quisling. An agent of the Imperial Government, with a string of atrocities against his name longer than the Shannon." Mickey looked perplexed, asking to know how that could be since it said right there in the paper that not only was he a gentleman but a Republican to boot.

"There, ye see! What did I tell ye! A prime example! Just goes to show what *you* learn from the papers." He tore the paper from Mickey's grasp and held it out in front of him, rapping it with his knuckles. "I tell ye now, that fellow is no Republican, and ye can take my word for it." He asked if Mickey knew anything at all about the man and Mickey said he didn't, that they had never met.

"Well I do, and ye can take it from me his sympathies were never with this country. If ye ever heard him give a speech you'd know that. I heard him myself once at the Workman's Club, asking people to put aside their enmity and broaden their horizons. I never heard such treachery - England and Saint George and all that rubbish."

"Oh dear me!" Mickey laughed, "I didn't know that."

"Well ye do now, and you'd do well to remember it."

Unlike the Old Man who was intense and passionate, Mickey had but a superficial interest in political affairs and supported every candidate, a fact that irritated the Old Man.

"Why weren't ye at the meeting on Friday night and ye would have known all that?" Mickey insisted he didn't have the time for meetings and it wouldn't have mattered in any case because it wouldn't change his mind. People change, he said, and for all they knew Mulvihill could be a different man entirely.

"If I remember rightly, you weren't always keen on DeValera."

"Maybe not, but only because I wasn't sure then that he's the greatest politician of the century."

"Well maybe it's the same with this man Mulvihill. He's done a lot for the country from what I hear. Even wrote a book on it." He paused a minute before inquiring. "You haven't read it by any chance?" The question was deliberate, designed to raise the hackles on the Old Man's hide. A shuffling of chair legs on the hearth, plus a deluge of spittle on the grate told Mickey he had hit a nerve.

"Read it be damned! I'll see ye in hell. Haven't I seen more than that fellow could put into it?" Mickey grinned.

"Well, you needn't be profane about it. I only asked you a civil question. Besides, your man Rattigan had nothing but kind words for him. Called him a colleague and compatriot." The Old Man gave him a venomous look, at which point Mickey rose and walked across the room. He pulled back the curtain and looked outside. It was raining steadily, water rolling down the glass. Sighing, he walked back to the fire again, curious to know what the Old Man had to say about the news he had just sprung on him. He was aware of the camaraderie between the two men, and was eager to observe the Old Man's tactics in justifying his friend's behavior. After a short period of contemplation staring at the fire, the Old Man spoke.

"Well, if ye must know the truth, 'tis my belief that Rattigan has been misled as well as been mistreated. What else would ye have a politician say? He couldn't very well tell the truth and call the man a shyster. Give him time, he's learning." Jimmy, he asserted, was a clever lad who could put a crimp in Mulvihill's hair, the likes of which you couldn't remove with a rolling pin. "Moreover, he has had his head beat in enough times by certain members of the constabulary not to have that fellow's number."

"Speaking of constabulary," Mickey said, "I wonder what Barney will have to say about our friend Mr. Mulvihill?" The Old Man shrugged his shoulders. What did he care what either of them had to say?

"Only this morning I was running over in my mind about the two of them, and do ye know what it is I'm going to tell ye, they're well suited, the pair of them." This criticism of his friend didn't bother Mickey. In fact it was what he had been hoping for, the chance to bring Barney's name into the conversation. Feigning offence, he replied that it was all the same to him what the Old Man said about Mulvihill because he was no friend of his, but Barney was. He gave a sort of whimper that implied offence and pulled his head up in the manner of someone just insulted. The Old Man played along.

"Mind now, I wouldn't go so far as to say that Callaghan couldn't be a decent man if he worked at it." Mickey smiled and let him finish. "And talking of friends. A lot *you* know about yours when it comes down to it."

"And what's that supposed to mean?"

"I thought ye told me that Callaghan didn't drink?"

"He doesn't, except the odd drop on the occasion. Why?" His pleasure at having the conversation where he wanted it was not lost on the Old Man, who guessed all along what he was up to.

"Well, he had more than the odd drop taken the other night in Cassidy's."

"In Cassidy's!" Mickey feigned surprise.

"Aye, that's what I said. And ye needn't let on that ye hadn't heard, because I know full well that ye have." Mickey laughed, aware now that he had been exposed, and with no further need for pretence, inquired as to what had taken place.

"Tried to tell me it was lemonade he was drinking. Swore to it, he did. I wouldn't mind but ye could smell his breath with a peg on your nose."

"Arragh don't I know. 'Tis the way he is, worries about his respectability. Are you never to forgive him? Maybe it will turn out that he has been on your side all along."

"What! Callaghan on my side? Not a chance. You couldn't make a Republican out of Callaghan, and it would be a sorry day for Ireland if you could. Sure, the man has a sort of watery strain in him that makes him want to hop from one side to the other."

He stopped to let his words sink in and then. "Can you imagine him in the Dàil?" He depicted Barney bowing to the leader of the opposition and giving out secrets to the enemy.

"Dear! Oh dear!" said Mickey smiling. "Callaghan would never do a thing like that."

"And how would *you* know what he would or wouldn't do? I'd hate to tell ye the things he said to me on Friday."

"I'm sure you would," retorted Mickey, rising and going to the sideboard where he poured a drink and handed it to the Old Man. He poured a small one for himself before going once again to the window. The rain had finally eased off, though he could still hear the light tapping on the corrugated roof by the front door. Then he walked back to the fire again and sat down in his chair.

"Ye have a right to your opinion Mickey, but ye weren't there," the Old Man picked up the pieces. "Ye don't know anything only what someone is after telling ye."

"Then why don't you tell me and get it over with?"

"I will if you'll just shut up and listen." He cleared his throat.

"It was like this, see. Callaghan was already at the bar when I arrived, his hat pushed back on his forehead like he had been there all evening. He had a look of satisfaction on his face the likes of which I hadn't seen in years. I had got myself a drink and had started through to the other bar, when he turned around and saw me."

'Did ye vote Fenian?' ses he, the minute he clapped eyes on me.

"I did indeed ses I, knowing full well that he had a purpose in asking. 'And which one of the distinguished got your valuable suffrage?' The same one as has been getting it all along, ses I, when over he leaned and clapped his arm around my shoulder. 'Good man yourself so,' he grinned, 'tis a pleasure to have your company.'" Mickey gasped.

"The Lord preserve us! I wonder what came over him?" The Old Man chuckled.

"I'm asking myself the same question."

"You don't suppose he decided to go with Rattigan?"

"That's the funny part of it, he didn't say. But to hear him speak you'd think he had always been a fully-fledged member of the Cabinet. Either he has lost control of his senses, or there's more to that lad than meets the eye."

"What else did he say?"

"Oh! A lot of nonsense about changing his ways, and wanting to be more in touch with people."

"And you had something to say about that I take it?"

"Of course I had, why wouldn't I? I told him what I thought. That he might have better luck doing that if he went digging spuds at Clausey's."

"That must have upset him."

"You'd think so, but it didn't. 'Now, now Malachi,' ses he, "for he was calling me that now that I was his friend. Then he ordered a drink for the two of us."

"I don't believe it!" Mickey cried.

"Aye. It floored the others as well. I was on the verge of refusing, mind, when I caught a wink from Jack Molloy and quickly came to my senses, so I squeezed in beside him. All right so," ses I handing over my glass, "if your mind's made up, I'll not discourage ye."

"What happened then?"

"Nothing. A faint cheer went up from the others at the bar and things were grand for a while after. Rattigan hoisted up his banner with Fianna Fail Forever blazoned all over it, and Callaghan never said a word against it. But as the evening passed and a few of us began to remember who the other fellow was, Cassidy began to get nervous."

"Is that so?" Mickey's eyes were wet with laughter.

"Aye! Looked at me, he did, as though I were the culprit. And then ses he, before removing all the posters from around the bar, ''tis as much as a man's life is worth to have a vote in this Country'." Mickey slapped his knee with laughter, as both men coughed and spluttered in unison.

"Mind you, it could have got worse if it hadn't been for Callaghan, I'll give him that. He surprised us all. 'Look after my drink Malachi,' ses he to me when he saw Cassidy's face, and quietly left the bar. It wasn't long after when I heard him singing The Wearing of the Green, and the whole bar went silent. We had another drink after that. He can sing fine, I'll grant ye."

"He can begor. When he was a young lad he could charm the birds right out of the trees."

"Is that a fact? Ye wouldn't think it to look at him. 'Tis a sad thing to see a man like that so unpredictable, and we with a common cause."

"A common cause!" Surprise wrapped itself around Mickey's face.

"Aye, a common cause. Any fool can understand that." He gave a hard glare at Mickey. It was true he was a Republican, he said, and Barney one of the other sort, but when all was said and done, they were both against the Sassenach.

"The Sassenach!" Mickey shrieked, thoroughly elated and unable to contain his laughter. Mistakenly, he figured he had the Old Man exactly where he wanted him. "Well! Well! What do you know, you and Callaghan friends at last? I didn't think I would live to witness it." The Old Man frowned.

"Hold your horses a minute now. I never said that. When a man's in drink he has many a fine thought, but a friend of Callaghan's, never." Barney he said was too fickle for him and too fanatic about religion. "Thinks it's what brings people together, he does. And that's exactly where we differ. We'll never see peace again in this world, now that we've found religion. I could have told him that, but didn't." Mickey poured another drink while the Old Man went outside. The rain had finally given up and left the evening fresh and cool. When he came back in he endeavored to explain.

"Let me tell you something now that might surprise you." Life, he confessed, wouldn't be the same without Callaghan for his enemy. He had all the friends he needed, but a good enemy was difficult to find. "Sure I might have given up the grudge long ago if it hadn't been for that. I need him about to keep my blood pumping. He's the right sort for it, don't ye see. I dare not pass his house without fearing to be ambushed, and when we meet each other in the street, 'tis better than a shot of whiskey." It was the way they both wanted it, he explained. "Ye should have heard him the other night. Ten sheets before the wind he was when we left the pub, and do you know what he said as we were parting? 'Malachi, he ses, you're an honest man and tonight has been a revelation. But in the interest of the community I'll continue to regard you as a formidable foe, and I trust you'll allow me the same consideration.' I will indeed Callaghan," ses I, "you can be sure of it, and we both shook hands on it."

At this point, there was a welcome interruption as Mickey's wife burst into the room. Her face was red as though she had been running and she was wearing rubber boots. Her eyes looked out between layers of fat as she looked crossly at Mickey.

"Are you going to keep this man in here forever? Sure he must be starving, sitting here for hours without a bite to eat. Stir yourself now, and come into the kitchen." Gladly, the Old Man rose and followed her.

THE BETRAYAL

It was Sunday and a glorious sunny morning in mid May, signaling the end of the cold winter days. Not a cloud to be seen in the blue sky and the air alive with the sound of birds chirruping and church bells welcoming the Sabbath. My sister Jane, Maggie Murphy and I were sitting on the garden wall watching the boys hurling in the Green. We had been sitting there for what seemed like hours waiting for Maggie to make up her mind about coming with us to see the baby swans. It had been her suggestion to begin with, but then she decided she didn't want to leave until she saw her latest heartthrob, a lad by the name of Corkery. She had been watching out for him all morning so she could point him out to Jane, for he was new in town and only Maggie and two other girls had had the pleasure of meeting him.

"He said he'd be here for the game," she said, her eyes sweeping across the green.

"See. There he is. That's him, the one with the navy blazer, Kevin is his name." She pointed excitedly as two young men came through the gate on the far side of the Green and sat beneath the big oak tree just inside the wall. Kevin was the tall one we were told, as though we couldn't figure that out ourselves, the other one being Jimmy Doyle a lad well known to us. Jane had a serious crush on him, and I could never understand why, he was so conceited. He was a good-looking lad and knew it, and was never shy about letting everyone else know he knew. People thought him a proper gentleman, and so he was when elders were about, but it was a different story entirely when they weren't. I knew that because I had seen the *Mr. Hyde* in him.

One day as I was walking home from school I had come upon him pestering little Nora Brien, a shy, timid girl with a crooked leg and an ugly nevus on her face. He had torn the ribbons from her hair, muddied her dress and was in the act of pinching her. She was only eight or nine at the time and he in his early teens. He had skulked away when he saw me coming, and when I reached Nora she was crying. I never liked him after that, and tried telling it to Jane but she wouldn't listen.

Of Kevin I knew virtually nothing, but had heard that girls were drawn to him as a molecule is to a magnet. Jane and Maggie had begun to whisper but I heard Maggie say, "come on let's go," and they both jumped down and started off across the Green, leaving me behind. Resentment, simmering in my gut all morning, burst forth in a surge of rage, and all I could think about was getting back at Maggie. I clambered down from the wall and followed them.

"I would have thought you'd want nothing to do with that fellow," I sneered, "seeing as how he's great with Nancy Shanahan." That little titbit I had picked up on the street and wasn't sure about the truth of it. I was only saying it to annoy Maggie. Jane glanced at me with her eyebrows raised.

"Well, it's true. He's been spending a lot of time with her."

"You don't mean that girl from Walkin Street? The one with the frizzy hair?"

"They were even seen coming out of Collier's Lane," I added smugly, aware of the lane's notorious reputation as a hot spot for smooching couples. Maggie whipped her head around to glower at me.

"And how would you know that?"

"I have my sources," I replied saucily, and she gave me an icy stare.

"Well, for your information that's exactly why I want to talk to him. He deserves to know about that girl. She's a bad influence." Jane poked her teasingly.

"Oh! Come on Mag. Give the girl a chance. She's not that bad. Sounds like jealousy to me." Maggie tossed her head.

"Well I don't care. I'm still going to warn him. That one has no shame at all. You should have seen her the other day, perched above on Hogan's rail, her legs apart, and nothing but a flimsy knickers covering her blind eye." Jane looked at me but said nothing. We were used to Maggie's gutter talk, the low drop coming out in her.

"I know she can be a bit brazen at times, but I really don't think she's a bad influence," Jane persisted in her defense, and when Maggie didn't answer. "Who is this Kevin Corkery anyway, and what is he doing here?"

"How do I know? He doesn't talk much about himself. All I know is he's from Waterford, up here doing a job for the Corporation."

"So, he could be married, or going back tomorrow for all you know."

"No, he's not married, and he's up here for the summer. He told me so."

"Well okay then! Let's see what he has to say for himself," Jane tugged her along.

The boys stood up when they saw us coming, and Jimmy Doyle stepped forward to hand Jane a sweet. "It's the only one I have I'm afraid," he shrugged as Jane reached for it, her face flushing. Maggie paid him little heed, her interest solely in Romeo who was leaning leisurely against the tree, one arm extended to a lower branch. The nonchalant way he was standing reminded me of my brother Mikey and for that reason alone I felt drawn to him. Yet, he was not nearly as handsome as Maggie said, but he was good looking, with dark brooding eyes and shiny slicked-back hair. He was tall and muscular with broad shoulders, but his mouth had a downward curve that made him look unhappy.

Beneath his navy blazer he wore a clean white shirt, striped tie and grey flannel pants. His black leather shoes were highly polished. *All dressed up with nowhere to go!*

Maggie went and stood beside him. He greeted her with a friendly smile, but continued watching the hurlers. I slunk even closer, waiting for her to say something about Nancy Shanahan, but she didn't say a thing. She was grinning and gushing all over her face. It made me sick to look at her, with her tight sweater and enough perfume to drown a baby in. "Coo Blimey! Coo Blimey!" she kept chirping in that ersatz English accent she had picked up after two weeks holiday over there. I couldn't stand it any longer.

"Don't you have something you want to tell him?" I interrupted spitefully, but Maggie ignored me and went right on chattering and wiggling her hips. I wouldn't mind but she had no figure, had the I.Q. of a donkey, and could not arouse erotic fantasies in any man. I feel it only fair to mention that I was not usually as mean-spirited in my sentiments toward Maggie, for although we were never bosom buddies we normally got on well. Today was a different matter, though, for only a few days earlier she had played a rotten trick on me and I hadn't quite forgiven her.

It happened like this. There was nobody home at the time but me, and at Maggie's instigation I had stolen money from my mother's hiding place so we could both go to the pictures. Snow White was showing at the cinema and neither of us had seen it. I hadn't wanted to take the money because I knew my mother would be furious, but Maggie kept insisting.

"It's not stealing, it's only borrowing and I'll give it back to you the minute we get home." Her mother, she claimed, had gone out somewhere and forgotten to leave the money. She'd be back by the time we both got home and I could put it back without anyone knowing it was missing. Yet, when the movie ended I couldn't find her anywhere. She had managed to sneak away. Needless to say, I paid the penalty and suffered the indignity of a naked flogging in front of family and friends.

I had deliberately avoided bringing up the subject earlier not only to avoid her litany of lies, but because I didn't want to be the one to start a row and spoil the afternoon. I wished now I had. They both disgusted me, Jane clinging to Jimmy Doyle's hand like a drowning person, and Maggie chirping and chattering like a magpie on a perch. I felt awkward and embarrassed standing there alone, so in the end I left.

I didn't know whether to go straight home or continue to the river. In the end, I headed downhill toward the Ring Lane a favorite gathering place for children, with little commercial traffic to worry about. It was a narrow lane, lined with a few thatched houses on one side and a high wall on the other. Part way along, it widened and branched off to meet a wider lane, with a Brewery on one end and a Friary on the other. Behind the Friary one found the river where the swans liked to nest.

Today the lane was empty as I strolled along in my crepe-sole shoes making no sound at all. Except for Julia Breen shaking a mat outside her door, I saw no one. Without saying a word Julia looked at me before going back inside. A second later, she reappeared.

"Mind yourself going down there, there's a rabid dog on the loose." I thanked her for telling me and walked on a bit. But then I got thinking about the dog and decided to go back.

As I emerged from the lane I saw Liza Green, standing alone on the opposite path. It surprised me to see her out alone because from everything I knew about her, which admittedly wasn't much, she was seldom seen out without her mother. I had only spoken with her once before, and the only thing I learned was that she was a country girl of Protestant persuasion, and had moved to the city about a year before. She lived with her mother in Chapel Lane and I had heard that something bad had happened in their family but not what.

A bookish-type girl, tall and painfully thin, with short blond hair of the type that always looked unkempt. She had big dark circles underneath her eyes that I thought strange for a girl her age. I knew she was a few years older than myself, because she had already left school, so I marked her age at around fifteen but I couldn't be sure about that.

I saw her watching as I left the lane and then, having glanced around her cautiously to make sure no one was watching, she motioned me across.

"Hello there," she called, as I walked up to her, her smile wide as though we were already friends and she had been waiting there for me. "Out for a walk are you?" The question, being rhetorical, required no reply, but then she asked something that took me aback. "Do you mind if I walk along with you?"

I tried to conceal my astonishment for it was the first time she had made an attempt at friendship. Many times we had passed each other on the streets but usually with Liza's eyes downcast, as though she considered it a liability to be even seen with me. She had told me when we first met that her mother was a *general factotum* at St. John's Protestant College and I, thinking that to be an important teaching job, assumed it the reason for her snobbery. The fact that they lived in a council house like the rest of us poor folk had escaped my mind entirely.

Liza didn't have much to say at first, allowing me to do the talking, and when she did speak there was little said, just certain subjects hinted at but never quite revealed. I asked how she liked living in the town and she gave me a withering look. How would I like living in a place where people looked down on country folk?

"You'd need four legs and a tail before anyone here would welcome you."

That wasn't entirely true, though I had to admit we city folk did have a few preconceived notions about the cerebral quality of country folk.

"Do you always go walking by yourself?" she asked.

"No. Not always. But I like being alone." I had always been the sedentary type, enjoying the solitude of my own company and, unlike most girls my age, preferred to keep my feelings hidden. So I wasn't at all sure that I wanted Liza's company. I said nothing, though, and we continued walking. We had walked the length of the street before she spoke again.

"Were you going anywhere in particular?" she asked, as we neared the corner of Dean Street, and I shrugged, ready to relate my disappointment earlier but saying only, 'not really'.

"Good! You won't mind coming this way then," and she shuffled me around the corner. For some reason she had quickened her pace and began trotting off in front.

"Wait a minute Liza! I'd like to know where we're going first?"

"To the graveyard."

"What graveyard?"

"The one at the top of the Deanery Hill. Do you know where that is?" *Do I know where that is? What a silly question, and I born and bred here!* When we reached the bottom of the Deanery Hill, she stopped and looked up.

"That up there is our church?" she said, "It's the oldest and most historic building in the city, wouldn't you agree?" I wasn't sure what the answer was to that, so all I said was 'I suppose,' and followed her gaze to the top of the hill to the ancient Cathedral of St. Canice, it's heavy, leaded windows gleaming in the sun. Beside it, on once a point of tactical importance, stood the ancient tower of O'Connell.

Built in the ninth century as a lookout against invaders the tower, having stood the ravages of time, had witnessed the triumphal march of Cromwell into the disease-ridden city. Both the Cathedral and the tower, were at that time the property of the Catholic diocese of Ossory, but had long since passed to the Protestants, whose dislike of anything Catholic could be tempered only by the acquisition of their property.

One doesn't ordinarily prod dead dogs in the ribs I know, but something in the way Liza had said '*our church*', as though it had belonged exclusively to them, sent a ripple of resentment up my spine. All at once I found myself reciting the church's history. Of course Liza didn't believe a word I said and made no effort to conceal the fact.

"Tell me," she said, with a cynical smile, "what school is it that you go to?"

"Why? What's that got to do with anything?"

"Well it must be to the Liars School, mustn't it, for you to be able to lie like that."

"I'm not lying Liza. It's a well documented fact," I insisted, not one bit certain that it was.

"Typical papist propaganda if you ask me," she replied indignantly. "A total fabrication designed to suit the situation."

"No, it is not." I was angry now. "That church did once belong to us and for your information a massacre took place there at the time of its appropriation."

"Good grief! Now I've heard everything. Just because you've lived here longer than I have, doesn't mean I should believe that nonsense."

"It's not nonsense Liza." I was insistent and repeated the story as it was told to me. How a group of terrified villagers, fleeing from Cromwell's army, had come at night to the city for protection. But the city, in the grip of a terrible plague, could offer no suitable shelter. So they had taken refuge in the Cathedral grounds, planning to return to their homes the following day when a treaty was to be signed. The following day, however, with the treaty signed and the city given up its arms, Cromwell brazenly seized the church and butchered all its occupants.

Liza didn't say anything, just stared at me, whether in admiration or irritation I couldn't say. Believing I had made my point gave me the confidence to continue. "Did you know this hill is haunted?" She rolled her eyes.

"Good Lord! Not another superstition! The Headless Coach you mean? I've heard about it, and I'd certainly like to know how that story came about?" I was only too glad to oblige.

"Well, I don't know all of the facts myself, but according to legend the ghost is that of a man called Wade, who on witnessing the carnage in the church had tried to alert the mayor by leaping into the driver's seat of an open coach nearby. But no sooner had he whipped up the horses than a soldier spotted him and lopped his head off with an axe." Here I took a moment to reflect, and to see how she was taking it

"So," she urged impatiently, "what happened then."

"Well, from what I understand, the terrified horses bolted and galloped off into the night with the headless man still clinging to the reins. They had run the length of the hill before anyone caught up with them and took the body down. The man's head, of course, was never found and that is why his ghost returns each night on the stroke of twelve."

"Looking for his head I shouldn't wonder," Liza said, pulling a spooky face and we both laughed simultaneously.

The historical fact of the plague and the disregard for the treaty I knew to be correct, but the rest I had gathered on the breeze. Many times I had heard about the spectre on the hill, but am happy to say I was thankfully spared an encounter.

We had reached the top of the hill by now and Liza, once again in a serious mood, pushed open the heavy gate that led into the church grounds. I did as I was told and followed her, my eyes fixed on the back of her head as she moved along the gravel path. A wheelbarrow filled with bricks, left there by the caretaker I imagined, was parked in the middle of the path and so she maneuvered around it, in and out between the graves, stopping every now and then to comment on a certain grave, the person buried there and his progenitors before him.

"What exactly are you looking for?" I asked, when she continued walking, and she flicked her hand impatiently for me to keep quiet. Reaching a spot at the outer limits of the grounds, where the neatly clipped lines of the grass verges ended, she said.

"Over there. That's where they buried him." She was pointing to an untended plot overrun by weeds and grass, with only a vague outline to indicate a grave. There was no headstone or marker of any kind and deposited in one corner was a pile of rubble.

"Buried who?"

"My dad. Or what was left of the man I used to call my dad." There was an unmistakable note of bitterness in her voice that caused me to look at her.

"You sound as though you hated him?" I said, wondering what terrible thing he could have done.

"No I didn't hate him, though I had every reason to." An unasked for explanation followed. "He ran off when I was six. Didn't even say goodbye to me. I remember it quite well. He was there when I went to bed, and in the morning he was gone. My mother told me he had left, but that he would be back. I was a lot older by the time I realized he wouldn't." The terrible thing was, she said, her brother Harry had just died of pneumonia and her mother was still in shock. Yet she never gave up hope of him returning and had tried for ages to locate him.

"She used to lie awake at night listening for his footsteps on the stairs, until one day a letter came to say that he was dead and was buried in these grounds." She gazed about her silently before continuing, as though trying to decide whether she should tell me. Then when I didn't ask, or offer encouragement, she said.

"We had been living out near Comer at the time and she had to walk the whole nine miles to Kilkenny to try to find out more. It was then she learned he had been living in the city all along, but using a different name and living with another woman."

When I asked her who the woman was, she claimed she didn't know and couldn't remember her name. Suspicious, I tried to press her on that point but she became so agitated that I let it drop. Considering the harshness of her tone a moment earlier it surprised me greatly when I saw her eyes brim up with tears. I was at a loss for words to say to her as I stood there contemplating everything she said, and wondering whether I should surrender to unsatisfied curiosity, or simply wait for her to tell me more. When it looked like she wasn't going to, I said.

"Looks to me like he paid for whatever hurt he caused. What happened to him, do you know?" There was a long pause before she answered.

"Got run over by a train, is what we were told. I don't know the details, only that he lost his legs and part of his lower body." At least that was what she had overheard her mother say.

"My God! That's punishment enough for anyone."

"I suppose." She gave me a weak smile and wiped her eyes with the heel of her hand. "The strange thing is I miss him, while at the same time I'm glad he's dead." Her statement, so contradictory, together with a slight inflection in her voice set me to wondering if she might be lying, or just putting on an act, though for what reason I couldn't say. It all sounded like a fairytale to me and I was tempted to ask what school she had attended.

Yet on the heels of that thought had come a twinge of sympathy. So all I did was shrug, though it was hard for me to understand why anyone would leave a loved-one's grave in such a sorry state. It was all her mother's fault, she decided, for not telling her the whole story, but allowing her to create her own version of events. Tears had gathered in her eyes again and so I quickly said.

"It's not that I don't believe about your father Liza. It's just that ..., well, how can you be sure this is even a grave? It looks like an empty plot to me. That's all I'm saying."

"Honestly!" she snorted, brushing me aside like a troublesome gnat and stomping away in the direction of the church.

On my way home from school, I had many times walked through the grounds of this old church, but had never gone inside the church. Now as I followed Liza through the heavy wooden door, I saw for the first time its attraction. It was more awesome than I had imagined, like a great mausoleum. A silence like the silence of death hung over it, and though the air reeked of dampness and decay, it was circumvented by a certain epic grandeur. The huge lead-glass windows, catching the rays of the morning sun, flooded the walls with prisms of light that enveloped the white life-sized statues and brown tile floor in a kaleidoscope of colour.

The walls themselves reached into the sky, supported by huge granite pillars adorned with Argus-eyed images carved into the rock. Covering almost the entire floor space inside the door were the burial places of some of the architects and craftsmen involved in the building of the church, each space lavishly inscribed with medieval crosses and various symbols interlaced with birds and animals.

We moved up the aisle to the middle altar, where a golden spread-winged eagle kept vigil over the tombs of the more illustrious dead, huge life-sized figures lying on top of an impressive vault.

"Read what it says," Liza urged, and I clambered up on the base of the vault to get a better look. The large strange lettering on the upper edges meant little to me, but the smaller more recognizable print along the side told me it was the tomb of the eighth Earl of Ormonde and his Countess. I had never in my life seen anything like it and I wondered about the power and wealth of the people who commissioned it. Though I had little affinity with the sentiments of these erstwhile gods and their marble tombs, my heart was filled with pride for the humble craftsmen whose undisputed superiority was revealed in every stroke of the chisel. Endowed with an immortal genius, they had carved out every minute angle with a sharpness of detail that defies imagination. Stand with me now and I will paint for you a picture.

One end of the tomb is raised in the likeness of two pillows, on which rests the heads of the deceased. The Countess' gown with innumerable folds ranged row upon row, drapes about her body. The sleeves, cupped tight about the wrists, billow out around her arms and sides, and her bare hands rest gently on her breast. On her head there is an elaborate headpiece, held aloft at each side by an angel. In his place by her side the Earl, as formidable in death as he must have been in life, is arranged in a suit of armor. His head is encased in a sort of heeled cap while a tunic of mail covers his neck and shoulders, and fitted to his waist a skirt of pleated armor. His arms and hands are encased in heavy armored gloves and standing vigil on each side of the pillows is another spread-winged eagle.

As I ran my fingers slowly over the highly polished surface I was whisked away to another world, a world of orchestrated ballrooms and glittering chandeliers, of white-wigged men and powdered women, riding in carriages drawn by splendid horses.

Stories of the spoils of British conquered lands had been told to us at school; of India, the golden Empire of elephants and jewels, and Australia with its mines and minerals, and for a while I was carried away with the grandeur of it all. Until with a stab of guilt I remembered the words of my old friend Mr. Dempsey, *"caterpillars of the commonwealth eating up the lands of the impoverished,"* and behind the dead but open eyes of the lifeless form before me I caught a glimpse of another world. A world of famine and death, of innocent people crushed by the weight of poverty and strife, their lives ruined by sickness and despair, and it was all I could do to keep myself in check.

I gazed in anger at the lifeless form, still stubbornly contesting his foothold on the sacred soil of Ireland. In the blink of an eye the faint smile on his lips had become a sneer, and I could almost sense the hatred smoldering behind his battle eyes. Every innocent and good-natured thought I ever had slipped away from me as I prayed for his eternal damnation. I turned away at last and looked around for Liza who was standing motionless in front of the middle altar, her face fixed in a grim expression, her eyes focused firmly on the floor. I could have sworn I saw her talking to herself.

"Liza," I called, and she spun around, her eyes wide and startled. I walked across to her. "Are you okay?"

"I'm fine, why wouldn't I be?" Yet I could tell there was something troubling her.

"Well, for a moment there you looked a little ...., weird is what I was going to say, but altered it to pale." Liza grunted.

"I'm fine. I was just thinking."

"About what?"

She threw her head back with a sneer, flicking her fingers at the altars and the numerous lighted candles.

"All this. Just look at it. What good does any of it do? Spit and polish, that's all it is, because prayers don't do a damn thing for anyone."

The heavy sound of footsteps from the other side of the door announced the arrival of someone else, as Liza took me by the arm and ushered me out through another door. Outside in the clean air again, we made our way back to the gate and out into the lane, intending to avoid the hill and take instead the age-old steps leading down to Vicar Street. So preoccupied had I become with Liza's company that I forgot entirely about the dog until I saw one coming toward us down the lane. It was a little wire-haired terrier with a black patch on its back and another covering one eye.

At first I thought it an ordinary dog, out for a stroll from one of the little houses in the lane. But on closer examination I realized there was something odd about it. Something in the way it held its body, sideways and sort of tense. Once or twice I saw it bump against the wall, before weaving into the middle of the lane unable to keep its balance. I told Liza what the woman in the other lane had told me and she began to panic. "No, don't run, don't even move," I said, as we flattened ourselves against the wall and watched the dog go by. It seemed oblivious to our presence, its eyes fixed on the ground ahead. We watched it move along the lane and turn the corner at the brow of the hill, before we both ran back to see where it had gone. We reached the corner just in time to see the accident.

At the bottom of the hill a young lad on his bicycle had swerved to avoid the dog and landed in front of a horse and cart carrying an assortment of wooden crates filled with empty bottles. The startled horse reared up in panic, backing the cart onto the path and sending the crates flying and smattering glass all over. The dog went skidding underneath the cart and we lost sight of it.

We switched our attention to the pedestrians on the path, a woman and a little girl about to step into the road. They had pulled back onto the sidewalk for security, when one of the cartwheels hit the girl and knocked her to the ground. We heard the woman scream before picking up the girl and carrying her across the road.

The driver, his attention focused until then on quieting the horse, responded with a yell and leaped down from the cart. We could see him talking to the little girl who was obviously shaken but otherwise unhurt, because some seconds later she and the woman continued down the street.

We arrived on the spot just as the driver was speaking to the young lad with the bicycle. "Are you okay son?" we heard him ask and the boy said yes but that he'd bent a spoke in his bicycle. "Well, if that's all that's broken....," the driver laughed, ruffling his hair and bending to take a look at it. When he had finished and the young lad cycled off, we helped him put the crates back in the cart. He looked apologetically at the broken glass, but there was nothing for it but to leave it there, so we kicked it to one side. Then we told the man about the dog and though we all looked up and down the street, it was nowhere to be seen.

I left Liza at the corner of Abbey Street with a sworn promise never to reveal what she had told me. My lips were sealed in perpetuity I assured her as we said goodbye, not for one moment suspecting they were the last words I would ever say to her. Unknown to me Liza had Leukemia and was soon to be admitted to a hospital in Dublin. It shocked me when I heard it some weeks later. She hadn't said a thing about it. Yet looking back on that day I did remember thinking how pale she looked and wondering if she might be ill.

By the time I got back to the Green again the game was over and the hurlers gone. The place was almost empty, except for Jane and Maggie strolling idly across the field. I waited by the gate until they arrived. They looked a sorry pair. Maggie looked like she had been crying and her hair was mussed. When she saw me, her expression hardened and she gave me a wicked look. As we were leaving the Green we bumped into Maggie's brother, and Maggie moved ahead to walk with him. That was when I turned to Jane.

"What's wrong with her?" I asked, and Jane said.

"She got a smack around the face from Nancy Shanahan for telling Kevin Corkery to keep away from her."

"Oh! So she did tell him then."

"Yeah. Just after you left. I warned her not to, but you know Maggie, she couldn't keep her mouth shut."

"What did he have to say?"

"Nothing. He just grinned and turned away."

"And how did Nancy Shanahan find out?"

"Kevin told her, didn't he?"

"You've lost me now?" I said, and Jane explained how they had stayed where they were until the game was almost over, when who should come along but Nancy Shanahan, evidently with a prearranged appointment to meet Kevin there.

"She was all dressed up in her Sunday best and if I do say so myself, she did look nice. I never realized she was that good looking."

"And how do you know they had planned to meet?"

"Because I heard Nancy saying, 'let's go then Kevin or we'll be late'. She didn't say where they were going, but I'm sure she meant the pictures."

The way Maggie glared at Nancy while clinging to Kevin's arm, Jane thought, may have been what prompted him to play the oaf and say he couldn't go because Maggie had told him she was a slut and he should keep away from her.

"That was when Nancy hit her, a really hard blow to the side of her face. She was absolutely livid. I thought she was going to murder her." I was elated. It was the best news I had had all day.

"Well I'm not one bit sorry for her. She got what she deserves. Now maybe she knows what it feels like to be the victim of someone else's trickery." Jane gave me one of her matronly looks.

"Well, you needn't look so smug my girl, because if I know Maggie she'll make you pay."

"Make me pay! Why me? What did I do?"

"You know very well what you did, telling her that story about Kevin and Nancy coming out of Collier's Lane. If you hadn't told her that she might never have said anything."

"So I'm to blame! And how was I to know she'd take it seriously," I snorted, not willing to admit that yes, I had deliberately tried to goad her. "Besides I only made it up to annoy her."

"Maybe so, but you were closer to the truth than you imagined."

"How come?"

"Turns out that Nancy and Kevin have indeed been seeing a lot of each other, but only because Kevin is Nancy's mother's nephew and is staying at their house for the summer."

What was I to say to that! What goes around comes around!

HARRY'S PITCH

Harry gazed idly through the dusty window of the train taking in the scenery beyond, the hills, the fields, the meandering streams, and here and there a sprinkling of small farms. He saw the cows grazing in the meadows and the sheep wandering aimlessly in the fields. Everything looked as he remembered it, so green and fresh, with no high-rise buildings, and no noisy traffic. He loved this country and never should have left it; at least that was what he kept telling himself. For in his youth he couldn't wait to get out of it and had put a lot of effort into that pursuit. He wanted a taste of city life like all the young lads of his day. Yet, the truth was he had never really taken to big city life, despite spending the last fifteen years in one. New York, with its eclectic offerings of wine women and song, had been more than good to him and he would not forget that. Yet, over the years he had tired of it, had had his fill of parties, of women and of bars. Where he was going now was where he wanted to be, the village of Rathdowney where he was born and bred.

He began to think about Bridie, the girl he had left behind. Would she be happy to see him, or would she turn her back on him? He couldn't blame her if she did, the way he had gone off and left her. But at the time he didn't know what else to do. Her anger when he told her he was going had caught him unawares, leaving him speechless and unable to explain.

"And I'm supposed to sit home like a faithful little dog while you're off gallivanting! Is that what you think? Well, you can think again my lad, because I have no intention of sitting home alone, waiting for Sir Galahad." He had never seen her in such a rage and wished then he hadn't told her. They had been friends since childhood, sweethearts in their teens, and shared in the village prophecy that one day they would wed. A few days later he had written her a letter hoping to make her understand but she had torn it to pieces in front of him. The one time he had come home on holiday, she was in the Isle of Man. According to his mother, she had never married, and though his mother never had a chance to speak with her, she had caught a glimpse of her once or twice going into Mass.

Harry felt in his heart he still loved her and never should have left, but what else could he have done? He couldn't have stayed in that village another day. Condemned to a life of drudgery on the farm. *The farm* was what his father liked to call the place, a piece of land no bigger than a postage stamp. Day after day, from sun up to sun down they had worked their fingers to the bone, trying to coax some goodness from that useless bit of earth.

The only thing that would grow on it was a weed. It had driven his father to the drink and himself to the edge of madness. Were it not for the two cows in the barn, the horse and a handful of laying hens, they might very well have starved. Night after night he had lain awake planning his escape, but every time the subject came up his parents talked him out of it. They had lost two children to Diphtheria when he was still a child and he could understand their fear, but he didn't have the same attachment to the land his father had, and he knew he never would.

"We've talked about it enough times now and you both know how I feel. This is no life for anyone and it's not going to get any better if I stay."

"It's good enough for me," his father rasped, his heart as calloused as his hands.

"Your father is right son. It's a rash decision. To leave the comfort of your home and take a chance like that! What will happen if you can't find work?" And so it went, each one doing their best to talk him out of it. Yet, despite the worry gnawing at their hearts and their sincere efforts to dissuade him, he had made up his mind to go. What he hadn't told them was he had already found work on a shipping line, on a freighter bound for Canada, leaving in seven days. Question was whether to divulge that information or simply steal away and avoid the inevitable row. "Well maybe he will find something over there and make something of himself like he says," his mother tried to reason when he finally confessed. His father wouldn't budge.

"Don't expect a welcome here when all fruit fails over there," and he stomped out of the house. On the day of departure his mother looked so desolate that Harry almost changed his mind.

"Promise me you'll write son. You won't forget us, sure you won't?"

"Of course I won't forget you. How could I?" He hugged her tightly, knowing he had her blessing, a compensation for his father's grudging handshake.

Later he would say those first years in Canada were the hardest he had ever known, breaking his back on the railway line, the winters cold and crippling. But the pay was good and he had stuck it out and saved enough money to buy a car. After the first unbearable winter, he made up his mind it would be the last manual labor he would ever do for pay, and two years later, with a hopeful heart and money in his pocket, he landed in New York. The following years were the halcyon ones for him when he landed a job at "Sammy's Place" a popular restaurant and bar, where he worked hard to get ahead. The owner liked him, admired his ambition to succeed, to accept advice and welcome responsibility. At the end of his second year he had handed him the reins.

From that moment on Harry never looked back, and a year or so later, when given the chance to buy the place he didn't hesitate. Admittedly, it had come at a lucrative price, though he had to borrow money and save like a miser to pay for it. With the help of a loyal staff and a steady clientele, the business thrived. As promised he had not forgotten his parents and sent money home as often as he could, but when his mother wrote to say his father had died, he was so immersed in the business he couldn't travel home for the funeral. He felt bad about that but what could he have done? At least it wouldn't be the same story this time.

The letter lay open on his lap. He picked it up and looked at it, the words leaping out at him. *"...bearer of bad news.....mother dying."* He had read it over and over unable to believe it. Why couldn't she have told him she was sick? Her letters never even hinted at ill health. Cancer of the throat the letter said, *and she a non-smoker all her life.* The rotten thing was, he had been planning this trip for ages and had deliberately not said anything, wanting it to be a surprise. Only weeks before he had decided to sell the restaurant and use the money to renovate the house and set himself up in business back home.

He couldn't wait to see the place and when the train stopped at the station, the first thing he did was look around to see if anything had changed. But no, it was the same little station with the same wooden bench outside the door, and the wildflower box on the window. When he was a lad he used to spend hours sitting on that bench watching the butterflies sip nectar from the flowers and waiting for the train to pass.

Today he was the only one off the train. He stepped out onto the platform and walked around the corner to the other side where a black four-door sedan was waiting. A tall, skinny fellow with deep-set eyes and dark wavy hair opened the door and stepped out. He was wearing dirty overalls, smeared from top to bottom with stains of oil and grease.

He started walking toward him, then stopped and turned back to the car. Harry watched him lean in through the open window and withdraw something from the front seat. He came toward him again.

"Harry Gorman I presume," he said, looking him up and down, while wiping his hands with a grimy rag.

"I was expecting Jerry Boyle," Harry said, looking around him.

"I know. I'm his cousin Ned Larkin. He couldn't come himself, he's away in Dublin don't you see, and since I'm the only one with a car in these parts," he shrugged. Harry put his suitcase on the ground and took the outstretched hand.

"Sorry about this, by the way," Ned added, indicating his attire, but I got involved with the mechanics of the car and lost track of time."

"I see," Harry said, picking up his suitcase.

"Jerry told me all about you, so I feel as though I know you. Sorry to meet you under such sad circumstances though," he said with a warm sincerity that Harry liked. He piled Harry's bags into the back seat and held open the front door.

"There you are now, hop in." Harry thanked him and stepped inside, admiring the interior.

"Nice car," he said, as they left the parking lot and pulled out onto the road, "what is it?"

"A Standard, top of the line," Ned replied proudly, evidently pleased that Harry had asked. He described how he had bought it at an auction in Liverpool and had it shipped home.

"I'd say it costs a few pence to run?"

"Not that you'd notice, no. With the war behind us two years now and petrol plentiful again I have no room for complaint." As he moved his hand across the steering wheel Harry noticed the ugly mutilation just above his wrist and the absence of two fingers of his hand. Curious he asked.

"What happened to your hand, if you don't mind my asking?"

"I don't mind at all, sure everyone wants to know that. Happened in Dublin of all places. I was there when the bombs fell on The Strand. Passing through is all I was at the time and decided to stay over with some friends. Couldn't have picked a worse time."

"That must have come as something of a shock, the bombing I mean."

"Ah whist! A whole neighbourhood demolished, men, women and children all blown to bits. My own people lost everything that night. The house wasn't hit directly, mind, but the one next door was blown to smithereens and took half of ours along with it."

"You don't say. I think I remember hearing something about it at the time."

"I shouldn't wonder. Sure wasn't it in all the papers over there, if not a mention of it in the British Press. We had a lot of bombs dropped on us that the world never knew about. Not only in the North but in the South as well."

Harry couldn't believe it and wondered why his mother had never mentioned it. Maybe she had and he'd forgotten.

"You can think what you like," Ned continued, "but in one way for me it was a blessing."

"How's that," Harry asked.

"Well, it's like this. I used to be a postman back then, out in all kinds of weather toting that heavy bag, but after I lost the fingers, trying to rescue a young lad buried in the rubble, they found me a cushy job inside. It was supposed to be temporary, but I'm still there. So you see, some clouds do have a silver lining."

No more was spoken between them after that, Ned clearly not inclined to further conversation, his concentration devoted to negotiating the narrow corners while stuck behind a rickety, overloaded lorry. The drive through the village proved uneventful with little to see but the tiny row houses with the low stone walls and small front gardens. There were few people on the streets. The sound of an accordion playing somewhere brought memories of happy times. As they drove in silence along the narrow streets, Harry kept his eyes alert. He remembered Bridie lived on Moore Street, and wondered whether he should call in at her home. For a moment he thought about asking Ned to stop, but decided against it.

They left the village and drove in silence along the narrow road, surrounded by thick hedges of Hawthorn, Celandine and Lilac, pockets of their aromas still lingering in the air. Beyond the hedges were the rich green fields reaching all the way to the fairies' wreath and the ruins of the old castle with its gaping mouth for a door and black holes for windows, where he and his buddies liked to play.

"I won't come in," said Ned, interrupting his thoughts as they approached the house, "I'm already late for an appointment in the village. "

"Well, if you're sure." Harry thanked him and removed his bags from the back of the car. He pulled his wallet from his pocket, but Ned waved him off.

"Don't worry about that at all, at all. Sure 'tis only a short run and who knows when I'll get the chance to do you another kindness." He started back along the lane. "See you around Harry," he called through the open window, and was gone before Harry had a chance to speak.

His mother's sister Kate met him at the door. He had only met her a few times before but recognized her right away, though the years had worn deep furrows in her face. If he remembered rightly, she was about ten years older than his mother, which should make her eighty-two. She came forward to embrace him, her arms outstretched.

Theresa Lennon Blunt

"I'm sorry I couldn't come sooner," he said, "but I had no idea she was so sick. I came as soon as I got the news."

"That's okay, nobody knew. She kept it to herself. She's been hoarse for the longest time but insisted it was just a cold. Only when she couldn't swallow did we suspect there was something wrong and by that time she couldn't speak. We only learned about the cancer when the doctor put her in the hospital, but there was nothing he could do. She refused to stay there, insisted on coming home." Harry left his luggage on the floor inside the door and hanging his coat on a peg nearby, followed her into the front room.

"I'm glad you're here in any case," she said, sitting on the soft chair inside the door, "she'll be glad to see you when she wakes. She never talked about anything else, when she could talk." Harry took the chair opposite.

"How is she anyway? Is she expecting me? Will she recognize me do you think." The old woman's face went serious and she seemed not to know what to say to him. Her voice fell almost to a whisper.

"I think so, but it's hard to say. She drifts in and out of it. To be honest, I don't think she'll last much longer, but she's in no pain. They've got her on medication now. You just missed the nurse. She usually comes in later to settle her for the night, but today she was early." She paused a second and looked about her silently as though listening for a sound, and then turned back.

"Will you be wanting a drop of anything to drink?" she asked, "only there's nothing in the house, but I could get Tommy Whelan to go and fetch you one." Harry smiled, remembering how his mother frowned on alcohol and refused to have it in the house.

"No, don't bother. I'm all right. I'll have a cup of tea if it's no trouble."

"No trouble at all. I'll make one so." She got up and left the room, and Harry followed her to the kitchen. He seated himself

80

in his usual place beside the table. "You'll have a bite to eat with it won't ye?" she said, and disappeared inside the pantry. She returned with a plate of cold roast beef, some cheese and a loaf of bread, which she set out on the table. Harry looked at the food but didn't touch it until she poured the tea and sat opposite. He didn't really feel like eating, but didn't want to seem ungrateful.

"A nice bit of beef that," he said, chewing on a chunk between slices of bread. She nodded but didn't speak and he watched her tip her cup to fill the saucer and then blow on the surface to cool the tea, drinking it in small soundless sips. The action evoked a memory of his mother doing the same. When she put the saucer down and looked at him she asked.

"Are you planning to stay or what?" The question caught him by surprise and Harry acted as though he hadn't heard. He had been overjoyed at the thought of coming home, couldn't wait to get there. Had felt so confident about everything, renovating the house, opening the restaurant and settling down with Bridie. But now that he was there, sitting in the kitchen, he wasn't sure of anything. He looked awkwardly around.

"Would she be awake now do you think?" he asked, neatly side-stepping the question, "because I'd like to go up and see her." He attempted a smile but the effort failed as the old woman gave him a fishy look and leaned back in her chair.

"We'll know when she is, don't worry." Harry leaned over and touched her arm.

"I'll go up anyway, if it's all the same to you."

"Of course it is, why wouldn't it? You go ahead and I'll clear up here."

He climbed the few steps to the landing and walked along to his mother's room. The scent of Lavender came to him as he stepped in through the door and saw his mother in the bed. She was lying on her back, her head tilted sideways on the pillow, her eyes closed, her lips parted. The corners of her mouth looked red and sore, and a dried up trace of saliva trailed across her chin. He couldn't believe she had gotten so thin, her cheeks sunken, the skin drawn tight across them. Her breathing sounded horrible and there was some sort of cylinder standing in the corner, oxygen he thought. The bed covers were tucked in neatly at the sides, but both her arms were outside the covers. He saw that she was wearing the pink cotton nightdress with the little lace collar and fancy pearl buttons he had sent her years before, and the memory saddened him. He took her hand and held it and then bent and kissed her forehead.

In that instant she opened her eyes and looked at him, eyes that were once of the clearest blue now blurred and scarred with cataracts. Puzzled, she stared up at him with no sign of recognition. "It's me Ma. It's Harry," he began, when he saw her eyes widen and realization come to her. "Hello Ma," he said again, and she smiled up at him in exactly the same way that he remembered. Instantly, tears flooded his eyes and he wrapped his arms around her not wanting her to see.

What maddened him was the thought that she, who had worked so hard all her life with never a complaint or harsh word about anything, should be the one to suffer. While his father, a sour-tempered man with never a grateful word should drop off quietly in his soft armchair.

"I'm here to stay now Ma," he mumbled softly in her ear and thought he could feel her trying to respond. But the effort proved too much and she lay still, closing her eyes again. Harry kept talking, wanting to keep her with him, telling her the things he had been telling himself about opening a restaurant and settling down with Bridie. "If she'll still have me I'm going to marry her," he declared determinedly, reaffirming his intention to settle down and start a family. The words gushed unhindered from his lips as he went on and on, meaning every word he said. For the more he spoke the more the dream became reality, its conviction gathering momentum like a breaker on the surf and he an eager rider on its crest.

A noise at the bedroom door caught his attention and he looked up to see Kate standing there. He wondered how much of what he had said she might have heard, and knew that if she asked he would repeat it all again. She walked to the bed and looked down at her sister, tracing her fingers lovingly around the hairline of her face.

"She's sleeping peacefully I see, so I doubt if she'll wake 'til morning. Every now and then she gets a wee bit restless, but most of the time she sleeps." She placed her hand on his shoulder. "Your bags are in your room. Try to get some sleep why don't you. You must be tired after your journey." Strangely enough he didn't feel tired.

"I'm okay here for a while Aunt Kate, I'll be down in a little while."

"Right so," she said, and left the room.

By the time he came downstairs again she had cleared the table, washed some linens for the following day and was at the window pulling down the blind. She turned around to him. "There's a meat pie in the oven if you feel hungry and failing that there's plenty of food in the pantry. You know where everything is." She walked into the hall and returned with her coat across her arm. "There's nothing left for me to do here, so I might as well be off," she said, pushing her arm through one sleeve of her coat. Harry stared at her astonished. It hadn't occurred to him she might be going home and leaving him alone with a dying woman. Seeing the alarm so clearly on his face, she paused. "You'll be all right on your own, won't you? You're not afraid or anything? Because if you feel...." Harry stopped her.

"No, no of course not. You go ahead. I'll be fine." He picked up her purse and scarf and held them out to her.

"Should I come with you or what," he asked, not sure of the proper etiquette, "only I see it's getting dark outside."

"Not at all, not at all. I'll be fine. The dark doesn't bother me. I know the road like the back of me hand, and sure I only live a few fields away. I'll be here first thing in the morning and in the meantime you know where to find me if you need me."

Harry assured her he would manage and walked with her to the door. He heard the crunch of her shoes on the gravel and saw her wrap the scarf around her head as she headed down the lane. After she had left he took himself into the small front room and sat down on the sofa. He looked around him wearily, amazed at how small everything looked compared to his boyhood memory. The shabby grandeur of things he had once imagined lovely disappointed him. Big upholstered chairs, lamps with fringed edges and scratched hardwood floors. Some effort had been made to make it look more cheerful with lace curtains on the windows and a small rug covering the center of the floor.

His eyes scanned the pictures still hanging on the walls, a large one of the Sacred Heart with a gold-leaf frame, hanging above the fireplace. On the opposite wall, hung a picture of The Angelus, and below it a row of old sepias of Irish towns and patriots. Except for a solitary photo of his parents on their wedding day, there were no other pictures of the family. That saddened him for he couldn't remember his father's face and wanted so much to see his mother's as he remembered it and not as it was now.

The picture on the wall was of another time, taken years before he was born and the faces there unknown to him; faces frozen in the blink of a camera's lens that had no connection with his world. Yet, the smiles on both the faces intrigued him. Why was it, he wondered, that he had never noticed it before. From as far back as he could remember he had never seen that look on either of their faces. The only time he remembered his mother smile like that was when he was selected for the Soccer team. In fact now that he thought about it, he had never ever seen his parents show affection to each other. *But that's how it was with people of their day. It didn't mean there was no love, or that they weren't happy. Or did it?*

A vague memory stirred in the attic of his mind as a door to the distant past creaked open and he saw himself as a little boy sitting on the floor beside the stairs playing with his tin soldiers. He heard a noise above him and looked up to see his mother standing on the landing looking down at him, her face wet with tears. Only minutes before he had heard the front door bang and his father leave the house.

"What's wrong Ma? Why are you crying?" He remembered feeling frightened and running up the stairs to her. She had picked him up and held him, crying softly into his hair. To this day he didn't know why she had been crying, but the memory of her soft breath against his ear triggered another memory. He couldn't get the image clearly, but he's in his mother's arms again and this time he is crying. Something has hurt or frightened him. He turns his head and sees his father by the kitchen door, his face contorted in an angry scowl, a leather belt clutched in his hand. Harry tried to remember the events leading up to that moment, but nothing came. Better to let it lie, he thought, and turned sadly away.

He left the room, and went again to his mother's. She was sleeping peacefully. He stood for a moment looking down at her, and then crossed the hall to his own bedroom. At some point his head had begun to hurt and he wondered if a drop of whiskey from his flask might not remedy it, but then he remembered his mother's rule about liquor in the house, and took an aspirin instead. He lay down on the bed, and looked around the room. No changes had been made here. Still the same old metal bed, the same mirrored wardrobe and matching chest of drawers. Even the bookcase underneath the window was the one he had made himself. He was amazed to see his old school books still sitting on the bottom shelf. *Tomorrow I'll have a look through them.* He was too tired to bother now. The silence of the house closed in around him as he pulled a blanket up around his chest.

Sometime later a sound from outside the house awakened him and he sat up in the bed and listened. He felt surprisingly alert and rested, the pain around his temples gone. Though the room was still dark, a faint light coming through an opening in the blind told him it was getting on for morning. He was sure he heard the front door opening and guessed it must be Kate. He listened for a moment longer, and then heaved himself off the bed and crept across the landing to his mother's room. She was sleeping soundly, her head in the same position on the pillow. She looked so pale and peaceful that for a moment he panicked, thinking she was dead. He leaned closer to check her breathing and was relieved to hear the slight wheezing in her chest. He spent a few moments lingering, trying not to make a sound, yet at the same time wanting her to wake, to open her eyes and look at him and know that he was there. Quietly he tiptoed across the room and headed back downstairs.

Kate, busy in the kitchen trying to light the fire jumped quickly to her feet. "Oh 'tis you Harry. You gave me a fright. For a minute there I thought...." She shook her head, and then as though sensing something in the tightness of his face, her voice rose in alarm. "What is it? What's happened? She's all right isn't she, your mother? I mean...she's not....because I was just going up to check on her." She dropped the bellows she was holding and started to get up. Harry held her back.

"I've just been in to see her and she's fine." Kate sighed in relief.

"Thank God for that. For a minute there you had me worried. I'd never forgive myself if...." She left the sentence dangling and picked up the bellows. Harry took it from her hand.

"Here I'll do that," and he lowered himself onto one knee and began to fan the flames. In no time he had the embers glowing. He gave it another pump for good measure and then stood. Kate, in the meantime was sitting at the table her head resting on her arms. He walked over and stood behind her, laying his hands gently on her shoulders. "Are you okay Aunt Kate," he asked, and she looked at him across her shoulder, giving him a tender smile.

"I'm fine son, I'm fine," she laid her fingers on his hand. "It's just that it's been hard for me these last few days watching the life ebb out of her. I always thought I'd be the first to go, what with being older and a weak heart an all. After she's gone I'm all that's left of the family." Harry didn't know what to say. He felt totally ineffectual, coughing awkwardly and wishing he could do or say something positive.

"I didn't know you had a weak heart," he managed finally and Kate shrugged.

"Well how could you? Sure we hardly know each other. I didn't use to live around here until five years ago. I only moved here after your father died."

"Does it bother you much? Your heart I mean."

"Not much, but you know how it is, some days are better than others." Two places had been set out on the table. Beside each plate was a cup upturned on a saucer.

"I won't make breakfast for a while yet, it's still early, but I like to have a pot of tea ready when the nurse gets here. She'll be here at seven." Almost an hour had passed since she said those words and it was now seven thirty, and still no sign of the nurse.

"I can't understand it," Kate moaned, going to the window, and pulling back the curtain. Something must have happened.

She's usually here on the stroke of seven." No sooner had she said the words than the front door came open and a breathless woman almost fell into the hall. Kate went hurriedly from the kitchen and Harry listened to the nurse explain, though he couldn't hear precisely what she said.

"I'll go right up so" was what he did hear before he heard the footsteps on the stairs.

"Wouldn't you know it, it never rains but it pours," Kate complained coming back into the kitchen. "She took a tumble from her bicycle."

"She isn't hurt is she?"

"No she's not hurt, but it gave her a bit of a fright."

She could understand that, Kate said, and began to describe a fall she had taken herself some years before. She stopped when she heard the footsteps at the kitchen door. They both looked up surprised as the nurse entered.

"Finished already?" was the question on both their lips.

"I've done all I can do for now, she's not fully awake and it's not worth upsetting her. There's no real change that I could see, but to be honest I don't think she has much time left. Her pulse is very weak." Harry began to rise but the nurse held his arm. "There's no emergency sir. It'll be a while yet." She looked quizzically at Kate who made the necessary introductions.

"Nora, this is Harry, Annie's son, home from America. Harry this is Nora Cassidy, your mother's guardian angel." Harry felt embarrassed. Somehow he had expected a much older person, but the woman standing before him couldn't have been more than twenty-five. She had the figure and face of a Hollywood star, but without all the makeup. For the first time in ages, he was lost for words. Evidently accustomed to the male reaction, Nora smiled.

"So!" she exclaimed, "the prodigal returned is it? I feel as though I know you, your mam spoke of you all the time." She took his outstretched hand. "Pleased to meet you indeed. I only wish it were under happier circumstances." She looked hurriedly at Kate who was scouring out the teapot with hot water from the kettle.

"Don't bother about tea this morning Kate, I can't stay. I've another call to make." To Harry she said, "Sorry to run off like this. I'd love to stay and chat but you know how it is." Disappointed, Kate put the kettle down and saw her to the door. Harry listened to them talking, but couldn't hear what was being said. He wondered why they were whispering. Talking about him most likely. An uneasy feeling began to settle in his stomach. When Kate came back into the kitchen she looked visibly distressed. Her face looked grey and long strands of hair had worked loose from her bun.

"Why don't you sit down and take a break," Harry said, "I'll see to breakfast. Just tell me what you want and what to do." Kate sighed.

"That'll be grand lad. A cup of tea and toast is all I want, but there are eggs, sausages and rashers in the pantry."

After he had fried a few sausages and an egg he poured the tea, made some toast and sat back at the table. Kate joined him, pouring her tea into the saucer as she had done before. She was curious about his life in America and asked him many questions. She didn't seem to be able to tell him much about life in Rathdowney. She seldom went into the village, she said, the walk was too hard on her legs.

"From what I hear, all the young people have left the village anyway, and those that haven't soon will."

"Is that so? How is it that Nora is still here then? Is she married or what? Because a girl with her looks could go far in a big city." Kate took her time answering.

"You noticed that did you?" she said with a sly grin. "No she's not married, though she could have her pick of any man around these parts. And yes, she's a fine lass, the spitting image of her mother who was a beauty in her day. Won all sorts of competitions, so she did."

"Is that a fact? I can well believe it. Is she from around here then? Only I don't remember ever seeing her before."

"Well, you wouldn't, would you? She grew up in a small place just outside Kilkenny where your own mother lived for a while after she was wed. I don't remember the name, though I'd recognize it if I heard it. It's a small place, Bally something or other, a remote little place in the back of beyond. That's how they got to know each other. A few years back Nora's mother went funny in the head and had to be admitted to the Asylum. She didn't last long there and died a year or so later. Nora couldn't get along with the old man, a miserable auld devil by all accounts and a terrible man for the drink. She met your mother for the first time when she moved here, and when she learned that they were both from the same place, she made a point of visiting her. Then when your father died, she took to dropping in more frequently, and has been doing it ever since. If not for that, your mother would have had to stay in hospital."

With breakfast over, Kate rose from the table. "I think," said she with a heavy sigh, "I should be looking after me chores. It's time I got them done." She began to clear the table.

"Is there something I can do to help?" Kate smiled appreciatively.

"Not at all. You'd only be in the way here. Why don't you take a walk into the village and have a look around? I'll be finished here by the time you return and she'll be well awake by then." Harry said he'd rather stay. It was a long walk to the village and he felt too weary to tackle it.

"I could do with a wash and shave, though." He fingered the stubble around his chin. Kate handed him the kettle.

"Take this with you so. The water won't be hot enough up there yet."

At the top of the stairs he heard the noise. It seemed to be coming from his mother's room. He left the kettle on the floor and went to investigate. He found her tossing restlessly, her body jerking as though trying to dislodge something in her throat. Quickly he ran to her, threw the covers aside, and held her upright against his chest allowing her to cough more freely. Her frail, wasted body was like a feather in his arms. When the coughing passed he eased her back onto her pillow, pulled a chair up beside the bed and taking her hand in his began again to tell her of his plans. For several seconds there was no reaction. Then all at once her eyes fluttered open and she looked at him, lifted his hand in hers and brought it to her lips. Then she closed her eyes again. Overwhelmed with emotion Harry cried. If only she would stay awake and talk to him. Say something. Anything. He fought the urge to shake her. Instead, he took a deep breath and started talking again, telling her all the things he had told her earlier, only now that he had started he couldn't stop.

"Does she know you're here?" Kate asked, stepping quietly into the room and Harry told her what had happened.

"That's good to hear. She's content so. It's a great comfort to her to know you're here." She wiped a tear from the corner of her eye. It gladdened her heart to know that her sister might die happy. There wasn't much time left now, the shallow breathing told her. Later that afternoon the priest came and Harry stayed beside the bed long after he had left. By late afternoon his mother's life was waning, and as the last rays of the evening sun slanted into the little room she drew her final breath. Only Kate and Harry were present by her bed.

"She's gone son. She's at peace finally," Kate whispered in a shaky voice, tears streaming down her sorry face. "Macushla! Macushla!" he heard her whisper as she bent and kissed the haggard face. Then she put an arm around Harry's shoulder.

"At least she went peacefully knowing you were here, if that's any consolation." She ran her fingers through his hair, and then turned abruptly and left the room. Harry remained beside the bed. He laid his head into his hands and let the anguish flow. In that position he remained, clinging to his mother's hand long after death had taken her.

With an urgent need for solitude, he pulled his jacket on and went outside. The yard looked bleak and empty, the barn in need of paint. It was uninhabited in any case, the animals long gone. Beside the barn was the paddock where they used to keep old Ned. Harry remembered the first day his father brought him home, he was just a young colt then, and Harry had helped build the barn that housed him. He too had gone to his eternal rest, his body wasted with the burden of toil and loneliness.

Outside in the lane he saw the wooden post that marked the turning into their house. Even when he was a boy there was no gate there, just a gap in the bank and a widening of the lane into the small cobbled yard. The house itself was small but sturdy, with three rooms upstairs and two down. There was a walk-in pantry and a cellar. One of the first houses in that area to boast a slate roof, it stood alone on a bare scalp of hill that the neighbors called The Rock. Below that was the Kelly farm, separated by a stand of trees and gorse. From where he stood he could see it clearly. Discarding the half-smoked cigarette, he began to stroll along the lane, looking for the spot where the stile used to be, and where as a lad he used to pass through to the Kelly farm. It was then he heard the dogs.

"Good day to ye sir," a voice hailed as a man, one arm pushing through the stile the other holding a rifle, stepped out into the lane.

"Good day," Harry said with a look of surprise, and wariness about the dogs that were barking loudly about his legs. The man assured him they were gentle. *A farmer*, Harry thought, *dressed for hunting.* He was gaunt and gingery with bushy eyebrows and protruding teeth.

"My name is Kelly, brother of the man who used to own this land. He pointed to the surrounding area. "I'm fairly new to this part, though I know most people in it. Came up here a year ago when Joe died. Can't say as I recognize you though." Harry smiled.

"Well you wouldn't, would you? I've been gone a long time. I'm Harry Gorman. I used to be Joe's neighbor." The farmer thought a second.

"Ah! You must be auld Ned's boy. The one who was sweet on Bridie Malone?"

"The very one," Harry said, holding out his hand. "I arrived here a few days ago." The farmer took his hand and shook it heartily.

"I had heard you were coming right enough, and I don't mind telling you it gave me a shock to learn about your mother. How is she anyway?" Harry told him, and the man's face went sad. "Well, I'm sorry to hear that. She was a grand old woman, your mother. I didn't know her all that well, but I heard a lot about her."

"She was that," Harry said.

Harry told him of his plans to settle down as they chatted amiably, before the dogs became impatient and began to nudge their master. He patted them apologetically.

"All right lads. All right, I'm coming," and he continued down the lane. Harry started back.

The wake was held in the room downstairs and many of the villagers called to pay their last respects. Most of them were farm folk from around the area. Some were strangers but a few remembered Harry and wanted to talk.

"Ah sure 'tis grand to see ye, your looking great. How long are you away now Harry?" and before he had time to answer, "ye came by boat I take it? Did ye have a rough crossing? They say that Atlantic can be a brute." A man he should have known but couldn't place came up to him.

"Is it true there are more Irish in New York than there are in the whole of Ireland?" he asked in all sincerity. And so it went. Harry did his best to answer graciously, going into details about New York he thought they might want to know. He listened patiently to the stories of their own lives, their trials and misfortunes, though he found the talk depressing. *Why can't people just sympathize and go quietly on their way!* He was trying not to show his irritation, while all the time wondering why Bridie hadn't come. Surely she knew that he was home and had heard the news about his mother's death. He ached to see her.

Nora approached to offer her condolences. She looked tired and weary, obviously finding the whole thing a strain. Her eyes were red and watery, and Harry suspected she had been crying. "How are you holding up?" she whispered, and Harry replied that he was managing but wished he were somewhere else. "I know what you mean," she responded knowingly, giving his arm a squeeze before returning to the kitchen to help Kate organize the food. *How fortunate we are to have her,* Harry thought, as he watched her passing through the door, a strange sensation of excitement passing over him. He saw his aunt Kate come into the room, cups chinking noisily as she passed around the tea, while explaining apologetically about the lack of liquor. To Harry's delight, her announcement produced some extraordinary results, as one by one the greater part of the gathering quickly vanished.

The following morning around ten o'clock the same group of people attended his mother's funeral. Bridie was not among them. Like a man possessed, Harry stood beside the grave trying to concentrate on what was being said. But his mind kept coming back to Bridie, he could not drive her image from his head. When the service ended, Nora offered to take Kate back to the waiting car as Harry, unwilling to leave when the others did, lingered in the graveyard looking at the graves. One or two mourners from the night before were hanging around outside the gate, and Harry not wanting to be drawn into conversation, moved back along the path, making his way in and out among the graves.

Apart from two old ladies removing weeds from a loved one's grave, their heads bowed, Harry was alone. They both glanced up as he approached, but Harry kept his head down and hurried by, all of his attention focused on one question. Why hadn't Bridie come? What could have happened? Not even a card or a note from her. He refused to believe she was avoiding him. That wasn't Bridie's way. Of course she had been angry when he left and even said some wicked things, but that was a long time ago, and if he knew anything at all about Bridie it was that she could never hold a grudge.

"I see no virtue in that kind of behavior," she always used to say. Sure, hadn't she even asked about him after his father died, and wished to be remembered? He should have written to her then when he had the chance, but he had put it off, too busy with the restaurant. Well it wasn't too late; he would make it up to her. He would take her to New York on their honeymoon. Take her to all the theatres and museums. Places he had been to himself. The very thought excited him. He imagined them arriving in New York and the excitement on Bridie's face when she saw his restaurant. How proud she would be of him. She would want to know everything about it and maybe admit that she had been wrong about him leaving all those years ago.

The more Harry thought about it, the more excited he became. *I'll do it now,* he decided. *Right now. I'll go directly to her house and ask her to marry me.* He glanced quickly at the sky, which had begun to darken, the sun gone in behind the clouds. Harry thought it might even rain. The crows that had been making a disturbance earlier had fallen silent now as he started back along the gravel path. He was passing out through the cemetery gate when he heard the voice, and turning saw two people running up behind him.

"Harry! Harry! Thank God we found you. Listen Harry, I'm so sorry about all this, I really am. I should have been here. We did make it to the church but we were late. We had trouble with the car coming down from Dublin. I'm really sorry, I had no idea..."

Bridie left the sentence dangling as she turned to introduce her friend. "This is Jerry Boyle, I think you know him. We were married yesterday."

A TRAGIC CASE

It was Saturday, November 21,1953

Big Bill Brennan swallowed the piece of bread he had been eating and washed it down with a gulp of tea. He was still grappling with confused reaction to what Denny Hayes had told him the night before in Ryan's bar. Normally they didn't talk about Eileen, Bill's estranged wife, because Denny knew Bill's feelings on that subject. Besides, in a way he felt responsible for what had happened, for it was he who had brought the two of them together. Yet despite all careful efforts, there were times in their conversations when the mention of her name was unavoidable, and last evening proved to be one of those times.

They had stopped off for a drink on their way home from work and Bill could tell by Denny's mood that he had something on his mind. He listened to the talk around him for a while, but as the minutes passed and Denny hadn't said a thing, Bill finally asked.

"What is it Den? What's on your mind?" and when Denny hesitated, "come on man, out with it."

"Well, there's something I think you ought to know," and Denny told him the sad news about Eileen. She had Pancreatic cancer and didn't have long to live. Bill felt a chill pass over him.

"How long is long?" he had asked. Denny didn't know but thought it could be any day.

Good God! As soon as that! He had put on a show of listening to what the other men were saying, while all the time thinking about Eileen. He hadn't laid eyes on her since she buried the baby, almost eight years ago. *Where in God's name had the years gone?*

On the way home he had made up his mind to go and try to make things right with her, and cursed himself for not doing so earlier. It was what he had wanted, at least at the beginning, but could never put aside his bitterness long enough to act. Yet, in those first months after he had left her, he had waited in daily expectation of a visit, or a message of some kind. That was all he needed to bring him back to her. But it never happened. No message came and no one tried to contact him. Eventually, his own will had weakened and before he knew it, the months had quickly turned to years.

He emptied the last dregs from his mug and got up from the table, washed his face in the scullery sink and ran a dry towel over it. He had made up his mind to go, in spite of the bad weather, for he knew if he didn't go tonight he'd never go. As he stood before the mirror, running his fingers through his hair, he tried to focus on the journey ahead. It was a fair ride to Eileen's house from where he lived on the other side of Bennetsbridge, and the clock on the mantel said five to six. With a bit of luck he could make it there by seven.

He pulled on his heavy boots, his overcoat and cap, and hurriedly left the house. The cold air hit him when he opened the front door. The rain that had been drumming down relentlessly all day had finally stopped. But it was already dark, the sky black and threatening, with a watery moon showing fitfully between the skidding clouds. In the shed out back he found his bicycle and pulled it out. The brakes weren't what they used to be, but they would have to do. Good thing he had the Dynamo, he would need it now. With his mind on the long, dark journey ahead, he mounted the bicycle and pedaled off into the night.

Many a night in the old days he had cycled this same road. He knew it well, every twist and turn of it. But he was younger then and thought nothing of the journey. Now he was a man of thirty-eight with a steel pin in his knee, and a face already creased with the prominent signs of stress. The memory of those earlier nights came back to him and he thought about Eileen and the very first time he saw her.

It was St. Patrick's Day, March seventeenth 1943, and Denny Hayes and a few of his friends had asked him to go with them to the Mayfair Ballroom in Kilkenny. Though all of them seemed keen to have him go, he had at first refused; not only because he was older than the others and didn't share their love of dancing, but also because he felt awkward and embarrassed in the company of girls.

Tall and lanky with a pitted face from Chickenpox and a slight limp in his left leg, he didn't think much of his chances with any girl. To make matters worse, he had never been inside a ballroom and the entrance fee of half a crown had seemed extravagant. In the end, though, he yielded and once inside the ballroom, listening to the band and watching the couples dance, he forgot about the money and relaxed. He had stood alone for the first half hour watching the others dance, and was glancing around for a place to sit when Denny Hayes approached.

"See that girl over there? Her name is Eileen Farrell and she's been looking at you since we came in? Why don't you go and ask her out to dance?" He looked in the direction Denny pointed and saw a short, plump girl with light brown hair and hazel eyes. Her hair was short and framed to her face in soft, loose curls. Bill thought she was the loveliest girl he had ever seen, her smile so warm and inviting. When the next dance was called, he worked up the courage and strolled over. He introduced himself.

"I'd like to ask you out to dance, but I'm afraid," he said, explaining his ineptness and reluctance to embarrass her. Eileen laughed and told him not to worry, that she wasn't much for dancing anyhow and was mainly there for the company. She was gentle and shy and didn't say much, but when she did she made him laugh.

"Do you come here often?" he asked, and pulling up her shoulders in a shrug, "now and then," she said, her eyes drifting past him to the dancers waltzing by.

"Well, if you're willing to chance it, so am I," he said, as the waltz continued. She laughed and stepped onto the floor, laying her hand against his shoulder and looking up into his face, her eyes shining. The highly polished floor had worried him at first, he felt sure he was going to fall, but he soon got used to it and managed to complete the waltz. They tried a second dance and when the next slow dance was called, Bill wrapped his arms around her and led her to the floor. When that dance ended they sat together on the wooden bench arranged along three walls around the dance floor.

Bill could not remember ever being so happy. That night had become a dream night in his memory. When the evening ended he had walked her home, his arm around her waist, and she had kissed him tenderly before parting. He knew right away that he was smitten, but didn't dare tell the others for fear they'd laugh and jeer at him. Yet, the following week he had sneaked in almost every night to see Eileen, and before the month was out they were going steady. Soon she introduced him to her family. They were warm and friendly and Bill enjoyed their company and before he knew it there was talk of marriage.

As they had only known each other a few months Bill thought it a bit premature, but Eileen was sure they were doing the right thing. They could live rent free with her mother, she said, until they found their own place. It sounded so romantic that Bill didn't have the will to disagree. Besides, he had saved a tidy sum, having worked since he was fourteen, seldom drank and never smoked.

If the truth were known he couldn't wait to leave his home and get away from a drunken father. It hadn't always been that way of course. There was a time when he had been happy, working at the mill alongside his dad and bringing home a wage. Then had come the galloping consumption that robbed his mother of her life and not long after, his father started drinking. Within a year he had developed a proclivity for the taste of Power's whiskey.

The last of the streetlights dropped away and he had crossed the wide stone bridge that spanned the river Nore and was cycling out onto the main road before he noticed the mist coming off the fields. It had gathered in tight pockets on the road, light in some spots, hanging like a dense cloud in others. Bill wondered whether he should turn back. The further on he went the denser it became, his vision extending to the few yards within the arc of his Dynamo.

At times he couldn't judge where the roadside ended, and once or twice rode up onto the grass. Peering ahead he could see only vague shapes and the tops of tall trees. Nevertheless, he decided to keep going, straining his ears for any sound that might warn him of movement ahead. Normally, he knew, the road saw little traffic and he most likely to be the only one abroad. Though in recent years the use of automotives had increased substantially, bicycles were still the main mode of transportation.

The ride went quicker than he expected, in spite of a dug-up section of the road that he failed to see until he rode right into it. Workmen had placed a Davy lamp and some wooden planks around the void as a warning to unwary travelers. But the heavy winds of earlier had tipped over the lamp and Bill didn't see the barricade until it was too late. The fall jolted him out of his reverie. *It's a wonder I didn't break my neck*, he thought, as he floundered in the dark searching for his cap. He found it and picked it up, the back of his knuckles stinging where the skin had been scraped away. The recent rain had muddied the road and he could feel the wet slime on the edges of his cap. He wiped it off with the sleeve of his coat. Luckily his bicycle was undamaged. He rolled it back and forth just to be assured and the wheels moved easily. How he had escaped worse injury was a mystery.

Across the fields to the left of him two dogs had begun to bark and he heard someone shout a warning. He guessed it was Matty Connelly who had a farm close by. He remounted the bicycle and continued. He had covered half the journey before the road began to rise and he had to push hard on the pedals to climb the first few hills. He shifted his body on the saddle, his behind numb and the steel pin in his knee beginning to make its presence known.

Even in the old days he had had to take the last hill standing on the pedals. This time he got down from the bicycle and took the rise on foot, all the time thinking about Eileen. It was useless thrashing through it all again he knew, but he couldn't help himself.

The first few weeks of marriage, he remembered, had been heavenly. He had never known such bliss and when in a month Eileen informed him she was pregnant he was ecstatic. The fact that the baby wasn't his, had been conceived two months before the marriage, and its mother still consorting with the father had remained unknown to him. All these things he would learn later, though in retrospect the signs had all been there, had he but had the sense to recognize them. That very first night of the honeymoon for instance, sitting on the bed watching her undress he remembered thinking how completely at ease with nudity she was, displaying not a hint of modesty or embarrassment.

Again, in his eagerness to consummate the marriage he had sensed a certain restraint in her, a kind of reticence of which she didn't speak and which he was too shy to mention. There had been other indications later, though at the time he had made no connection. Of course it had been an easy task to fool him, for the truth was that before Eileen he had absolutely no experience of carnal love. Had believed, as any man would, that love had driven Eileen into his arms, and never suspected for a moment he might be serving a purpose, or filling a need in some shameful way. He had always been a sensible type, so how in the world had he allowed it all to happen? Only a fool would not have realized there was something wrong. He recalled that day he had stumbled in on her in front of the wardrobe mirror, both hands caressing her abdomen. They had been married barely a month then and she had turned away abruptly, and flown into a rage when she saw him in the door. Her reaction had confused him, but it wasn't until later, when he looked back on it, that it had occurred to him the reason for her anger was not the fact she had been observed, but the fact she might have inadvertently drawn his attention to the size of her growing belly.

"Oh! What a tangled web", he sighed, thinking about it now as he reached the crest of the hill and got back on his bicycle. A sharp breeze had risen and the mist had all but gone, and by the time he reached the bottom of the hill he could actually see the sky; light flimsy clouds scudding across the pale face of the moon, with a few bright stars peeping in between.

Ahead the road was straight and flat with progress less restricted, yet his mind remained cemented to the past, the memory of one incident leading quickly to another. He could almost pin point the date when the marriage had begun to fall apart. Beginning with a rainy day in August when he had come home unexpectedly and found Eileen bent double on the kitchen floor, a white enamel basin on the ground between her feet, blood streaming down her legs. Her older sister Brede had emerged from the scullery carrying a wet towel. They had both reacted to his presence like children caught in the act of some forbidden deed. Bill had caught the glance that had passed between them but could not interpret it.

"Miscarriage"! Was what he thought he remembered someone saying before he rushed back out. Brede had hurried after him and grabbed his arm. "It's all right Bill, there's no need for the doctor, the bleeding's stopped." Bill wanted to know what had brought it on but couldn't get a direct reply, just a skirting around the subject.

"A false alarm! No need to worry," Eileen had brushed aside his questions. It never occurred to him that she might be lying, or that something far more serious had occurred. Had it not been for Mona, her next-door neighbor and closest friend, he might never have learned the truth. He had overheard them quarrelling.

"A hussy, is that what you want people to think you are? Wake up Eileen, he's a married man, and you're probably not the first girl he's put in the family way." Shocked, he heard Eileen beginning to reply, her voice low, but before he could make out what she was saying, Mona spoke again. "I know what I saw Eileen. Don't try to tell me different. I'd know that fellow anywhere with his mop of ginger hair. Don't you realize if I saw you others did?"

Bill couldn't believe his ears. From what he could make out she had known about Eileen's pregnancy all along, and had since seen her in the company of the man responsible. He had stood in the hallway listening, his heart stopped, waiting to hear Eileen refute the allegation, but all he heard was her sniveling voice wanting to know if her friend had all at once become her enemy, and pleading with her to keep a quiet tongue and not involve the family.

There was a lengthy silence before Mona answered. "All right then, but promise me it's over and you'll not do a stupid thing like that again. You could have killed the baby." Eileen sighed.

"I know. I know. But at the time I wasn't thinking straight. I had so much on my mind and somehow it seemed the best solution." Bill had heard enough. The admission dulled his senses. Usually, a quiet, soft-spoken man who hated the sound of raised voices, he would rather walk away from an argument than become embroiled in a shouting match. He knew he should feel anger, if not unbridled rage, but all he could feel was a numbness. The thought of an angry showdown defeated him.

From the time he was a baby he had feared his parent's arguments, with frightful accusations and cruel, callous words, words that had driven both his siblings from the home. For a moment he considered leaving and avoiding a confrontation, but what good would that do? Coughing to announce his presence, he had walked into the kitchen. Eileen was standing by the table, an apron wrapped around her waist, her friend seated in a chair nearby. Some eggs lay broken in a china bowl and sausages sizzled on a pan. She was preparing the evening meal. She raised her head when she heard him enter and gave him the usual welcome.

"Just got in ahead of you," she said, with a forced cheerfulness, before picking up a fork and beginning to beat the eggs. He knew she knew by the strained look on his face that he had heard the argument. Mona rose from her chair.

"We didn't hear you come in," she said, apologetically, glancing anxiously at Eileen while at the same time engaging him in conversation. Bill did his best to be polite, returning her small talk, while finding her presence irksome and wishing she would go away.

"Why didn't you tell me about the baby?" he asked immediately she did and, without removing her attention from the task at hand, Eileen replied.

"So you heard. I thought you did. Well, there's not much left to tell then, is there?"

"Probably not but I'd like to hear it anyway." Bill replied sarcastically "and you can begin with the fellow's name." Eileen gave an exasperated sigh, laid down the fork she was holding in her hand and came directly to the point.

"Listen Bill, what you heard is all there is to hear and I'm not saying more. What good will my telling you all that do now? Be sensible for heaven's sake. What else could I have done? I was desperate. I couldn't bring shame on the family. It would have broken my mother's heart, so soon after losing Dad." She retrieved the discarded fork and began again to beat the eggs, while Bill traversed the kitchen like an angry lion. All he could hear were Mona's words going round and round inside his head. The truth about the pregnancy was hard enough to swallow, but the thought of a continued friendship with the father was insufferable. In a way he blamed himself. He had known from the start they should never have married, and she but a girl of nineteen, almost ten years younger than himself. Any anger he did feel was with himself, at his colossal ignorance and inability to see what was going on. Why couldn't he have paid more attention, maybe picked up on the nuances? *A more observant man would have noticed.*

The last thing he wanted was a breakup of his marriage, but this was not a situation he wanted to be in, and could hardly pretend otherwise. "How long has it being going on?" he asked through clenched teeth, bringing his fist down on the table and inadvertently knocking a cup and saucer to the floor. Eileen hastened to pick them up, but Bill kicked the pieces from her reach. His action, unexpected, startled her and she became enraged. A fierce row erupted, with each one heaping insults on the other. At one point an accusation from Eileen momentarily took his breath away. He had almost struck her then, had it not been for the fact that she was pregnant, and her face so flushed it frightened him.

"All this is making me ill," she cried, gripping her swollen belly, "can't you see what you are doing?" Defeated, Bill dropped his head into his hands and sank into a chair. His whole world was falling in around him. This woman to whom he had pledged his troth barely six months earlier had become a stranger, a paragon of lies and prevarications. For all he knew she was still consorting with her lover, though she vehemently denied it. Silently he wept into his hands, unable to raise his head and look at her. After several moments she came and knelt beside his chair. "Look Bill," she began in a more conciliatory tone, "there's no use pretending. What happened, happened and I can't change that. But surely we can work things out? I never meant to hurt you. You must know that. I didn't want you to know. That's why I did what I did earlier." At this the tears came to her eyes and she made no effort to restrain them. Bill pushed her angrily away. All he wanted now was to be left alone.

"I'll leave first thing in the morning," he said, rising and heading for the door. Eileen blocked his passage.

"For God's sake Bill you can't leave now. Stay. If not for my sake, then, for the baby's."

Talk about the straw that broke the camel's back! Bill couldn't believe she had said it. It was incomprehensible. *She must take me for a real stookawn,* he thought, as he swung around to face her. "The baby that isn't mine you mean? The one you tried to get rid of?"

Rain had begun to beat against the windowpane and the wind howled around the eaves as the front door was heard to open and Eileen's mother stepped into the hall. The quarrelers fell silent. The only sound now, that of the sausages sizzling on the pan. After a brief exchange of pleasantries with the mother, Bill quietly left the house.

Later that same evening Eileen went into labour and next morning for the first time he saw the baby. A little boy, lying in his crib beside the bed, and he knew the moment he looked at him there was something wrong. A wizened little creature, with a tuft of red hair on a head too big for his tiny body, he had arrived too early, the wrong way around and was almost dead by the time he came into the world. Bill had hoped for Eileen's sake that he would live, but by the following morning it was obvious he would not. He didn't wait to see him buried, and had no reason to hang around. At the first suitable moment, he packed his things and left.

Such were the thoughts that inhabited his mind as he drew nearer to the city. All around him the land was in darkness, broken here and there by the glow from a farmer's lantern or the light from a farmhouse window. Way ahead, the town lay out in front of him, the streetlights blinking in the distance, and the turrets of the Ormonde Castle coming into view. His legs felt tired from pedaling and he sighed with relief as he coasted down the hill to Grand Parade and onto the city streets.

All of the shops were closed by now, but some windows still had light in them. People strolled unhurriedly along the sidewalks, or stood in small groups chatting on the corners. The glow from the street lamps was comforting. Eileen's house was located on the Comer Road, the other side of town, and one of the nicer parts of the city where the people were more affluent and owned their own homes.

As he neared the house he felt a growing panic, wondering what kind of welcome he would get. Would they be glad to see him? Would they invite him in? Maybe Eileen would refuse to see him, and then what would he do? He was filled with a mixture of uncertainty and shame as he tried to imagine the reaction. But it was no use, he should have thought about it earlier. Right now he was too tired to think. His legs were stiff and heavy, and every turn of the pedals an extra effort. It had become very cold, and by the time he reached the house he was shivering. He left his bicycle by the gate and walked up the garden path to the door.

Eileen's brother Tom opened it. A big broad-shouldered man he was, with a beak nose and a slightly wedge-shaped head. His sleek, black hair was heavily oiled and glistened in the light. At first he looked confused, his face taking on an inquisitive expression, unable to put a name to the face outside the door. Then all at once the penny fell. "Good God Almighty! Speak of the devil and he's sure to appear." He stomped back inside, leaving Bill outside the open door. After a moment of indecision Bill followed him in to where the family was gathered in the kitchen. They all grew silent at the sight of him. Eileen's mother, much older now, and slow to observe the niceties of civility, was huddled in the armchair beside the fire, a shawl covering her shoulders. She darted a vicious glance at him, half rising from her chair. "Bastard," was the word he thought he heard before she spat into the grate, her angry eyes blazing in their sockets. Her reaction startled him, for he had known her as a warm, congenial woman incapable of profanity. He remained standing inside the door, feeling awkward and uncomfortable and unable to think of a word to say until brother Tom, preceded by an arsenal of invective, decided to confront him.

"What are you doing here anyway? Who asked you to come?"

Bill struggled to keep his composure while attempting to explain. "Well, you can turn around and go right back to where you came from, you're not wanted here." He raised his fist as if to strike, giving Bill a push that sent him staggering back against the door. The action, unexpected, sent a bolt of anger through him, causing him to ball his fists. Yet he resisted the urge to retaliate. Instead he offered Tom his jaw.

"Go ahead then if it will make you happy."

With those words Brede, who had been fluting the crust on an apple pie, dropped her fork and came between them.

"Now you two," she scolded, glancing sideways at her mother, "leave the man alone he's not hurting anyone. He came of his own free will and the least we can do is be polite to him." She held her hand out. "It's nice to see you Bill. How are you anyway?"

"I'm fine thank you," Bill managed a grim smile and clasped her outstretched hand. With a warning glance to the others, she took him firmly by the arm and shuffled him out into the hall.

"Don't mind them two at all," she said in a lowered voice, "they don't know the truth. Eileen never told them anything. They still think you brought disgrace on her and then ran off and left her. But Eileen and I were always close and I know the truth." Bill thanked her for her understanding and asked about Eileen. It was a hard thing to ask but he had to know, how much time exactly? Brede's grave face grew even graver.

"It's hard to say. It could be weeks, or it could be days. We can only wait and see." It was good of you to come. She'll be glad you did."

"Where is she now? I'd like to see her if I it's possible?" Aware of movement by the kitchen door, Brede nudged him hurriedly toward the stairs.

"She's in bed. She has to get as much rest as possible." She started up the stairs in front of him. "She may be sleeping, but we'll take a look," she whispered as they neared the door, "we won't wake her if she is. It's best if she can sleep." She pushed the door in quietly. The room was in semi darkness, the only light coming from the fireplace where several logs were burning in the grate. More logs were stacked in a bucket on the hearth and Brede picked one up and laid it on the fire. "This room gets very cold at night," she said, giving a little shiver.

It was the same room he had shared with Eileen when they married, the same bed and mirrored wardrobe. Eileen lay on her back beneath the covers. She had her eyes closed, the covers up around her neck. A heavy army blanket was draped across her feet. "Are you awake love?" her sister called and Eileen's eyes came open. Brede switched on the small lamp by the bed.

"There's someone here to see you," she said, and Eileen raised her head to look, unable to believe what she was seeing.

"Bill! It is you! You came! I hoped you would." She raised herself slightly on her pillow, evidently pleased to see him. Bill smiled and nodded, unable at first to find words with which to answer, so shocked was he at the sight of her. She looked old and withered. Her once rosy cheeks had a sickly yellow pallor, as did the whites of her eyes, and her beautiful golden hair hung limp and dull. Raw, ugly sores had formed around the corners of her mouth. He found it hard to look at her.

"I only found out about it yesterday, or I might have been here sooner," he said finally.

"Denny Hayes told you I suppose?" Her voice was close to a whisper.

"Yes, he did."

"I thought he would." She reached out and took his hand, feeling its icy touch against her fingers.

"Good Lord! Your hands are frozen! Go warm yourself beside the fire."

"No really I'm grand." He reached for the chair at the bottom of the bed, while from the corner of his eye he saw Brede whisper something into Eileen's ear.

"I'll leave you two alone so," she said, walking to the door, "but don't stay too long, she tires easily." She pulled the door shut behind her.

"It's good to see you anyway," Bill said, after she had left and Eileen smiled but didn't speak, her hands smoothing and flattening out the blanket.

"So tell me, when did all this come about?" Eileen heaved a deep sigh.

"Does it matter? It did and I'm dying, and nothing can be done about it now." Her response, so cavalier and devoid of all emotion confounded him. He stared at her in disbelief, so calm and dry-eyed, accepting the consequences as inevitable. He had expected something different, anger, weeping, resentment! Even denial seemed a more acceptable reaction. A false comfort admittedly, but surely it offered a modicum of relief from the horror of reality. There was no use trying to make sense of it. It was Eileen's way, a side to her nature he had never understood. The way she could detach herself emotionally from a grave situation and not allow its influence to distort reality.

He had thought it an admirable trait when they first met, but now somehow it seemed out of place. He wondered whether she was putting on an act, and the fear of dying too intense to allow her to express what was really in her heart? For an instant the reality of the situation overwhelmed him. On his way up the stairs he had been thinking of things he might say to her, words to help cheer her up, to help lessen the gravity of her situation. Maybe even eradicate to some extent the bitter vine that had taken root between them.

But now that he was here he had no idea what or even where to start. He felt helpless and uncertain, reluctant to talk about their marriage or the rift that had come between them. Yet what else was there to talk about? He tried not to think about the last time he had seen her, how she had looked then, so young and vibrant and full of life. Eileen, in the meantime had begun to talk in that mindless way she had, telling him things that had happened in his absence. About her brother Tom's engagement, the weeks she had spent in Galway with her mother, and the wonderful time they all had at Mona's wedding. It was as though they had never parted and the last eight years had never happened.

He listened without really hearing a word she said, wondering as she talked if she realized herself what she was saying? His head felt as though it were about to split apart but he endured, nodding whenever there was a pause or when he thought the conversation called for it. All he really heard was the sound of her voice, a sound interrupted only by the hissing and spitting of wet logs in the grate. The air in the room was becoming dense and he wished he could open a window.

Finally, Eileen stopped talking and lay quiet, her hand once again descending on the blanket, smoothing out wrinkles that did not exist. Bill took the opportunity to apprise her of his own activities. At one point she opened her mouth to speak, but then closed it again, a strange sound, half laugh, half sob escaping her. A nervous twitch had started at the corner of her mouth and tears pooled in the corners of her eyes. She dabbed at them with the back of her hand, muttering something he didn't understand. All at once he was filled with an ineffable compassion, and a cloudburst of memories assailed his mind as he recalled the look on his mother's face in the days before she died. Night after night he had sat all alone beside her bed, knowing in his heart that she was dying, yet believing she'd get well. He was just a lad then, unable to come to terms with the fact that somebody so young could be taken from the world so quickly.

Eileen's voice cut through his thoughts as slowly, but fitfully she began to talk again. "Listen Bill. I want to say this while there's still time. You're all I've been thinking about lately. The rotten way I treated you. The baby, the ...." Bill interrupted.

"We don't need to talk about all that now. Talking isn't going to change what happened."

"I know, but I want to. You see I hated you for running off like that but I never held it against you. I deserved what I got, you didn't. I know now that betrayal is a hurtful thing and not easy to forgive." She shifted on her pillow. "What I did was unforgivable. I should have told you the truth. I wanted to, but I was so....ashamed." She turned her face away. It was as near to asking for forgiveness as she could come and the knowledge plunged Bill into an agony of guilt.

Only seconds earlier, his emotions had been wavering between sorrow and relief, and he finding comfort in the thought that when she was gone he would be a free man. Free at last to marry and not have to live alone. It was only a thought, of course. No, not even that. Not definite and clear like a thought usually is, but fleeting and subconscious. Yet, it shamed him nonetheless. It wasn't as if he had lost all feeling for his wife, but when it came to Eileen he hardly knew how to feel anymore. She had lied, cheated and deceived him, and robbed him of eight years of life. Yet here he was beside her bed like a faithful little dog. He didn't have the heart to admit that he had come because he thought it the decent thing to do? Hurriedly he said.

"You mustn't think about all that now. What's past is past and probably best forgotten." She gave a little nod, whether to express agreement or disagreement he couldn't say. Then she said.

"Maybe so, but you deserved better. You ought to think about remarrying when I'm gone." A lump momentarily filled his throat as he forced a smile to his gloomy face.

"Is it codding me you are? Sure who's going to have an auld fellow like me?" He pulled an ugly face, managing to make her laugh.

"Brede, for one," she replied with an alacrity that surprised him. "I know she likes you, she always has." She had put on a saucy face when she made that declaration. Yet behind the mischief in her eyes he saw the latent panic. He shook his head dismissively.

"Has she now? Well....," was all he managed before the tears welled up in her eyes again. Bill wiped them clean with his handkerchief, and with a sudden surge of emotion, leaned over and kissed her face. "Hush now. Don't talk like that. You're the only wife I've ever wanted. I was mad to leave. I should have had more sense, if I hadn't been so stubborn." She gave him a rueful smile, saying nothing, but he could tell she was happy he had said it. He released the grip he had on her hand, kissed her once again and rose.

"You're not leaving already?"

"You need your rest," he said, returning the chair to the bottom of the bed. "I'll come again, I promise."

"When? When will you come?"

"Tomorrow night, the next night and the night after, if that will make you happy."

"It will indeed. But mind you don't regret it? Maybe I'll get well and you'll be stuck with me."

"I'm willing to chance it if you are." From the evidence he saw in front of him he knew it would never happen. Exhausted finally, Eileen closed her eyes and sank back on her pillow, her breathing coming in rapid waves, each one pulling her a little closer to the end of her existence. Bill pulled the covers up around her shoulders. His heart ached as he looked at her, remembering the first time he saw her so lovely and full of life. He waited by the bed until he was sure she was asleep and then quietly left the room. Brede was waiting at the bottom of the stairs.

"Stay and have a cup of tea before you go," she said. "Mam wants to have a word with you." She saw him stiffen, a defensive expression on his face, as he followed her into the kitchen. The room was empty, no sign of Tom, except for the old woman still seated in her chair. She rose when he came in and the sight of her rail-thin body, shriveled to the bone with anxiety, filled him with remorse. She looked as though she hadn't slept for weeks.

"Bill," she said, reaching for his hand, her face grave. "I'm so sorry. Brede just told me everything." Her voice faltered as she spoke. "In the name of God, what have we done to you? I had no idea." She cleared her throat as tears sprang quickly to her eyes. Bill moved to comfort her.

"Don't be sorry Mrs. F." He emphasized the name, for he knew she liked it when he called her that. "There's no need for apologies." She nodded her head sadly and sat back in her chair weeping silently. Bill was overwhelmed and couldn't imagine what it must have been like for her learning the truth after all this time. It was all too much for him, in any case. Weary from the strain of seeing Eileen and exhausted from the ride, he gladly removed his overcoat and took a chair beside the table. Brede poured the tea and placed a thick slice of currant bread on a plate in front of him, and then went to serve her mother. Only when she returned to the table and took the chair opposite did he lift the cup up to his lips and take a mouthful of the tea.

"Aw! That's grand, just what I needed." They fell into conversation.

"Isn't it amazing how he arrived at the front door just as we were talking about him?" Brede remarked.

"'Tis indeed," the mother agreed, wiping her eyes with the hem of her skirt. Bill grinned.

"Well you know what they say about the bad penny?" Brede laughed and put her cup down on its saucer.

"Did you know Denny Hayse's father died?" she asked, and Bill said he did, that he worked alongside Denny at the mill. He had lost his own father around the same time, he said.

"Sorry to hear that," they both exclaimed, asking how it happened.

"Cardiac failure apparently," he said, not wanting them to know the truth. That his father had died in an alleyway too drunk to make it home. According to the medical diagnosis, he had choked on his own vomit.

"You must find it lonely without him so," Brede said and Bill nodded.

"To tell the truth, I've been thinking about moving to the city," and in answer to their questioning looks. "Well, there's talk about the mill closing and there's not much work to be had in the village."

"Well, I'm sure you could find a job here," the mother said. "There are plenty of mills around."

"But where will you live?" Brede asked.

"I don't know. I'll find a place."

"Your place is here with us," the mother said, "This is your home for as long as you want it. Isn't that so love?" she said to Brede.

"'Tis indeed," Brede said blushing, and fearing her mother might say something more embarrassing, got up from the table and went to stoke the fire, making small stabs at the grate with the poker. It felt strange to Bill, sitting by the table watching her and remembering how Eileen used to do the same thing. He leaned back in his chair and looked at her, slim with blond wavy hair and a slightly tilted nose. The thinness of her face and round solemn eyes gave her face a haunted look. She was not a pretty girl, not like Eileen, at least he had never thought so, but she had an inner beauty that only people close to her could see.

A particular incident came back to him, of an evening long ago when he and Eileen had come in from the pictures and found her sitting by the fire alone. When he asked what she was doing there and not out with a boyfriend, Eileen had answered.

"Brede doesn't like men, do you pet?"

"It's them that don't like me," Brede corrected hurriedly, her shy anxious face turning crimson red, and her whole demeanor shrinking in a mirror image of himself. He was trying now to think about other things, but all that came to mind was Eileen's remark – 'Brede for one'. Emotions swirled around him as he watched her now. Lost in his own private misery he hadn't given much thought to what she might be feeling. He had an overwhelming feeling of tenderness, of wanting to protect her from the world. Half a minute later she returned to the table and sat opposite, pouring herself a second cup of tea.

"Mam's right Bill. This is your home whenever you decide, and I...." She checked herself, the colour in her face deepening. Bill didn't know what to say, his heart appeared to be missing beats, and his throat so tight he could barely speak. He knew that Brede loved her sister and always had, but had never suspected she might feel anything for him. He caught her watching him.

"You look tired," she said suddenly, as though to justify her scrutiny. Bill nodded.

"I am a little?" he responded, though surprisingly he didn't feel that tired.

"You're not sick or anything?"

"No, just feeling the affects of the long ride in."

"Well you don't have to do that again tonight?" the mother interjected. "Why don't you stay? Tom doesn't live here anymore and there's a bed in the spare room across the hall where you can have a restful night."

Bill shook his head, his eyes going immediately to the clock, the hands nearing ten. He wasn't looking forward to the long ride home, and though the invitation to remain in the warm comfort of the house was tempting, he knew he couldn't stay. The idea of sleeping in a bed downstairs with a dying wife upstairs was not his idea of a restful night.

"Thanks for the offer, but I've got to go. I have to be somewhere in the morning," he added with a liar's tongue, and waited for a bolt from heaven to strike him dead. "Besides," he added truthfully, "I don't want to put you out."

"Suit yourself so," the mother said. "But it's no hardship on us, is it Brede?"

Brede looked away. How could she tell him it was what she wanted, that his very presence in the house made her heart race. Her stomach knotted with the effort to keep silent. Bill toyed with his cup and saucer, trying to remember the last time anyone had shown him so much kindness. For the first time in years tears threatened him, but he held them back for he knew if he allowed them to fall, they might never stop.

The aroma from the apple pie, still baking in the oven, filled the kitchen, as Brede bent to remove it from the oven. It was the opportunity he needed to get up from the table.

"Must you go?" she inquired tactfully, glancing at the clock and laying the dish down on the table before helping him on with his overcoat.

"I'll be back tomorrow," he assured her, and with a last few words to the mother, headed out the door. Brede walked silently behind him. Part way along the hall he turned.

"Thanks for everything," he said, his arm outstretched, and Brede squeezed his hand.

"Thank you for coming," she replied, as he stepped out into the night. He looked back once more when he reached the gate, but she had gone inside. He threw his leg across the saddle of his bike, looking up at the troubled sky, the moon competing with the ominous clouds. More rain was on the way, he was sure of it, and hoped he would make it home before it set in.

MALACHI

The early morning sun shone through the tiny bedroom window, and the Old Man felt its warmth when he opened up the door to put the milk bottle out, yet his bones told him the early frosts were coming. He went to the back door to let Meggie, his pet goat, out. She lingered by the door awhile, as though to confirm his belief about the weather, before moving off. He watched her stroll along the garden path and then went back inside and slowly gathered up the dishes from the table and took them to the sink. He poured hot water from the kettle over them, and then refilled the kettle and put it back beside the fire, seating himself in his chair alongside it. There would be plenty of time to wash the dishes after he had smoked his pipe. It was the one pipe of the day he truly enjoyed. Never in all his working years had he had time for that luxury of a morning. Now he had nothing else but time.

Settling down into his soft armchair, his pipe lit, he looked contentedly around. It was a small room by any measure, with no ostentatious furniture. Almost every item in it had been bought second-hand. The only store-bought item was the chair he was sitting in and the small bookcase in the corner. Everything looked as it always did, neat and well cared for. It was how he liked it. He could never stand untidiness. Except for the fresh vase of flowers on the windowsill, there was nothing different. Nothing to show that the day was special, that he had reached his eightieth birthday. Somehow, that idea bothered him and he wondered why, since birthdays had never held importance for him. Not for many years in any case.

A heavy sigh escaped his lips at the memory of his first birthday, or at least the first one he could remember. Four or five he thought he must have been but wasn't sure. All he could be sure about were the images, and it had always amazed him how clearly he could remember them, and with such feeling. He had never seen such a grand iced cake and had not wanted to blow out the candles. The sounds of laughter and raised voices came back to him as he recalled his mother's laughter, his sweet, gentle mother, standing by the table watching. Little did he know it would be the last birthday she would ever celebrate?

His throat knotted at the memory of her frail, wasted body and the horror and gravity of the illness leading to her death. The whole episode had shattered him, and though the years had washed away the fine contours of her face, her memory would remain fresh for as long as his heart kept beating. Four years later his father died and it fell to his brothers Paudie and Peadar to bring him up. Not a day went by when he didn't think of them, as he did their close friends Barry and Kevin Sullivan. How great had been their friendship, how valiant their deeds! Even as a young lad he had wanted to emulate them and later, when he became a man, he had joined them in their struggle for *the cause.*

Then one day Peadar, the youngest brother, crossed the ocean to America and after one or two letters from various corners of the continent, he never wrote again. It was a bitter night in January when Paudie died, his patriotic blood washing through the cobbled streets of Dublin. After that he wanted no more part in *the struggle*, had tried for a while to drink himself to death, and when that failed he had left home forever. Of course there had been other birthdays, but none like the first, none that he had wanted to share with anyone.

He pushed the images from his mind, and tried to concentrate on the few happy years he had had with Ellie, his wife of seven years. For a time her love had filled the empty spaces in his heart, until the day she tired of him. He was trying hard not to think about that, though his mind kept coming back to it. So many years ago, so many heartaches, yet it seemed like only yesterday. A memorable summer day, glorious in its warmth and color, and he helping with the hay in Matty Mulligan's field, when he caught first glimpse of her. She had appeared from nowhere in the narrow lane that ran between the meadows, and was standing by the low stone wall looking in at him. Her hair sparkled like a golden sun. Her eyes were big and beautiful. He had never looked upon a girl so lovely. He couldn't believe she had called his name, as though she had known him all her life. She was beckoning him across, but for a moment he didn't move. Then with laughter she called a second time, and finally he dropped his pitchfork and walked across to her.

"You're a shy one, aren't you," she teased, as he pushed through the gap in the wall and followed her along the lane. The door to the tool shed was open and he could see Matty there, sitting on a plank just inside the door, out of the sun's hot rays. She had brought them tea and sandwiches from the house, and he had noticed Matty grinning, his mouth crammed with the homemade bread.

"You don't recognize her, do you?" he asked, after he had swallowed, and he had stared at him not understanding. "Sammy's girl, Elizabeth!" Only then had he realized who she was. Elizabeth, the daughter of Matty's brother, a man of some prosperity, who owned a grain store in the city and lived in a grand house some miles outside of town. Elizabeth taught school in a village close by.

He couldn't believe it was the same girl he had met some years before. A slip of a thing back then she was, with gangly legs and auburn hair. How had she grown into such a radiant, woman? He couldn't take his eyes from her.

"You can all me Ellie if you want," she laughed, "I'm going to be here for the summer, so I expect we'll be seeing something of each other." She had a lively way about her, laughing all the time and teasing him about the way he spoke. A yokel he had told her jokingly was all he ever was, and they had laughed together over that. Then one day she had turned to him with a serious face and said. "You ought to learn to think more highly of yourself, and not allow people to make fun of you."

Shortly after, they began walking out and he remembered well the moonlit nights when they had danced together at the village fair, or strolled arm-in-arm through the country lanes. She had told him she was twenty-four, five years younger than he, and he had thought that proper. He had loved her more than the mountain air, and one evening on impulse had asked her to marry him.

She had laughed at first, saying they weren't suited and that people would talk, but in the end she had agreed. Though the weeks before the wedding were a blur to him now, he could not forget her parent's opposition, or their glum faces at the wedding. They did not approve of him or his occupation and were quick to let him know with surly looks and snide remarks. Their silly snobbery angered him, looking down their noses, and putting themselves above everybody else. Yet, he had no grudge against them, for he had always admired people who got on, and hoped one day he could do the same. Nevertheless, he disliked their condescending attitude, their formal teas and grand affairs, designed in a way to intimidate, and sure to make any man feel out of place.

A simple man is what he was, who liked simple folk, and with a nature that would not allow him to be otherwise. Admittedly he had never had much schooling and felt more comfortable working with his hands. In the building trade he had found his niche and had hoped one day to use his skills to work exclusively in glass and stone. Maybe create some elegant stained-glass windows. In his father it had been a major talent, one he could never hope to copy, but at which he felt he could make a decent living. Ellie had never quite accepted the idea, and sought to make him something better.

"Why can't you learn to do something more rewarding? Something with a little more prestige?"

"Like what?"

"A publican or businessman, something like that. I'm sure my father would be glad to help you." There it was again, *a businessman like her father.* He was sick and tired of hearing about her father, the solid and substantial citizen who knew this man and that man with pull, and could fix him up with any job he wanted.

In the early months of marriage she had rarely mentioned it but as the years passed she became more and more insistent. His pride had been in his workmanship and in building a home they could easily afford. Hers had been in putting on a show, spending more than he could earn and accepting favors from her mother. It wasn't that he minded her having nice things. He would have bought them himself had he had the means, but anything he could manage was never good enough. Now his work had become an insult in her eyes, as had the house they lived in. The thought of one day owning it and bringing up a family there had meant everything to him, but in that pursuit too he had let her down. For despite their prayers and genuine desire, no children resulted from the union.

Exactly when she stopped loving him, he didn't know. He knew only that she had, and the hating had begun. For months and months he had endured it, believing things would change. Then one day he knew they wouldn't. He had come home from work excited, eager to talk about the day's events, the reality of a possible promotion and their prospects for the future. Ellie had not allowed him to finish. Just looked at him with pure contempt, her anger boiling over, her eyes glued to his mud-stained footprints on the floor. Wild angry words she had flung at him. Words he had never heard her use before and didn't even know she knew. He hated to think about her tear-stained face and the ugly names she had called him. In his heart he knew she was saying only what all along needed to be said, that he had never been good enough for her, never respected by her parents. But *a tramp* he had never imagined her as seeing him, and in a moment of clarity he had realized that in her mind he would never be anything different.

'The clod from Clonakilty,' she had teased when they first met and he had not minded for it was a fact. Now she had made it something to be ashamed about. The insult nibbled at his gut and he could feel the tightness rising in his chest as he tried to will away the anger. Despite the constant arguments and often cruel remarks, he had managed always to keep calm and not lose his temper, but now his patience had reached the limit of his endurance. A fleeting grimace passed across his face as without a word he had gathered up his things and left the house forever.

The recollections became too much for him, and when at last he could no longer bear it, he got up from the table and walked around the room trying to shake the bitter memories. He tried to conjure up images of better times, pleasant times when Ellie had meant so much to him. Once again her face rose up before him as a sudden yearning for the past came over him, and a feeling of deep loneliness settled in his heart. Unconsciously, he sat back down again and began to clean his pipe, thumping the bowl against his knee.

The man from Clonakilty, the traveling man, that's what people called him after that, and indeed in a way that's what he had become. He had labored in the shipyards of Glasgow, on the docks in Amsterdam, and on the sidewalks of New York.

Life had not been easy, but he had enjoyed the work and made his living honestly, and never as a tramp.

His reminiscing took him back again to the old tool shed where he and Ellie had first been introduced. How cold and empty it had looked that first night he had returned to it, the walls no longer ringing with her laughter, the floor covered with old grass and straw, and the planks that he and Matty had sat on lying idly against the wall. He had pulled one down and made a seat of it, then filled his pipe. Later, he had made a bed of straw beside the wall and lay down on it. He had not known when he stood outside the house again that she was dead, and had wondered why it looked so deserted. The paint around the windows peeling, the weeds knee deep in the garden and the cute little window boxes he had made himself one summer, empty and decayed. He couldn't imagine where she might have gone, and thought about going to the nearest pub to see what he could learn.

"Would you happen to know the woman who lived in that house," he had asked of a passerby, and the lad had said yes, that it was a woman by the name of Dempsey. "Did she move away or what?" and the boy had answered not unkindly.

"You might say that sir. She passed away this summer." He could feel his heart begin to race, as he looked about him giddily, aware that the boy was watching. "Nobody lives there now," he heard him offer, but didn't dare reply. All he could think about was what the boy had said, *a woman by the name of Dempsey.* So she had kept his name! He had thanked the boy and hurried off, instinctively turning left and heading up the hill to the Mulligan farm. It had not been his intention to call on Ellie, just hoped he might catch a glimpse of her. Maybe hang around town for a little while and find out how she was.

Now he didn't know what to do. Didn't even know where she was buried. He had taken too much for granted expecting to find her there after all this time. Almost twenty years had passed since he last laid eyes on her. He wished now he had come back sooner and maybe had a chance to make things right with her. Now she was lost to him forever. Wearily he had trudged along the old boreen, past the field where they had met, just walking aimlessly. It was getting dark by now and he was tired, and needed a place to sleep. When he reached the farm gate he had passed inside, intending to march right up and hammer on the door. But now that seemed like a bad idea. Old Matty had long ago been buried and Mickey, his only son, might no longer welcome him. He heard a dog barking inside the house and hurried toward the shed. Luckily the door was open, the same lock he had helped Matty install dangling from the rotted wood. For a while he feared that someone might discover him, but no one came.

In the morning, he told himself, he could steal away but had awakened late to find young Mickey standing over him. There was no escaping after that. From Mickey he learned what he needed to know about Ellie. How she had gone back to teaching after he had left but had chosen to remain in the house alone.

"She often spoke about you," Mickey said. "Told us she had wronged you and wished that you'd come back."

"She used to come up here every chance she got asking questions about you," Mickey's wife put in.

"What kind of questions?"

"Oh, you know, the usual. Wanting to know if we had heard from you and whether we thought you would ever come back, things like that. It was sad really."

"She must have been lonely living in that house all by herself," Mickey said.

"How did she die? What happened to her?"

"Well, she seemed well enough until a year ago when she came down with a cold. It was discovered then that she had consumption and had had it for some time. I would have let you know but I didn't know where you were. You had stopped writing by then." The Old Man nodded silently. *So, she had paid dearly for her foolishness, as he had paid for his pride.* For the longest time he had mourned her passing, and visited her grave every chance he got. He made few friends around that time and as the years went by he too had found himself alone.

An outspoken man with his own ideas about everything, people didn't always take to him, were suspicious of his actions and critical of his views. Well, he couldn't change that any more than he could change his nature. With Mickey, however, it had been different they had hit it off at once. Sadly, though, a few years after his return, Mickey had suffered a minor stroke, which had left him weak on one side and with a lack of hearing on the other. As a consequence he had given up his job in the city and retired to his father's farm where, with a little help from Malachi, he raised Black Angus cattle and a few pigs and hens.

A jolly little man with a generous heart, he loved a joke and refused to allow life's miseries to defeat him. In fact his eternal optimism in the face of any situation be it tragic or otherwise, was often a bone of contention between the two. Yet, in spite of the different temperaments and a marked difference in ages, they had become fast friends. It had gotten so that the Old Man spent more waking hours at Mickey's house than at his own.

He had laid down his pipe and had started to get up, when a fit of coughing overwhelmed him, the pain across his chest almost crippling. Quickly he sat down again. '*Damn Pleurisy*' he thought, remembering the bout he had earlier in the year. He sat still and waited until the pain was gone, then he got up slowly and with more care. When he had finished washing up the dishes, he made his bed and tidied up the room. Then he rinsed the shirt he had worn yesterday and hung it out to dry. He checked to see that Meggie was safe behind the wooden fence before going to the front door to look outside.

There was no sign of Mickey, though he had promised faithfully to be on time this morning to meet an old friend at the Market Square. *If only I could teach him to be on time,* the Old Man sighed, remembering Mickey's father, with whom he'd had the same complaint. *The apple surely didn't fall far from the tree in this case,* he chuckled. A few early shoppers were already on the street: Mrs. Brennan with her basket, off to get the first loaves from the bakery and Molly Cunningham behind, hurrying to catch up with her. Quickly he stepped back inside the house and waited until the footsteps passed. He heard a few more people passing. Any minute now Paddy Whelan would appear, on his way to the lumberyard opposite. He stepped back to the door and saw him coming, recalling a time when he too had worked at the lumber yard and could split a log with the best of them.

Nowadays the firewood came already chopped and bundled and you could buy it in any shop. Progress they called it. "You had better get used to it, it's the way of life." Well, it wasn't the way of life he had known, nor had he wanted to get used to it, had in fact fought to keep the old way alive. He was younger then, of course, edifying blood coursing through his veins. The only thing he could fight against now was loneliness. The street was empty once again, so he went back inside. The clock on the mantel said nine-thirty. He expected Mickey to be late, but not this late. *Oh well I suppose I had better go and see what's keeping him.* He put on his coat and scarf and started up the hill to Mickey's house.

It was a route he avoided whenever he could, but there was a good footpath all the way and he knew that Mickey used it. Once or twice on the journey up he halted, expecting to catch sight of him coming down the hill. By the time he had reached the top, he was out of breath. He stopped to get it back, leaning heavily on his stick as he gazed around. A few more yards and he would be at the gate. He could see the house beyond it, and the short walk along the lane wouldn't be so bad. The ground there was level and the tall elm trees would give him shelter. At last he reached it and stopped.

The long struggle up had weakened him, and beads of perspiration stood out on his forehead. He rummaged in his pocket for his handkerchief. Above him the stately elms watched silently, their sturdy branches reaching out to touch each other and making a cool arcade above his head. He spent a moment looking up at them, recalling the pride Mickey's mother had felt helping Matty plant them. Too bad she never lived to witness their growth. It was hard to believe that they were both gone. *How long before I go,* he wondered? That pain across his chest had startled him, and the trek uphill depleted him. He had never felt his age so keenly. He cursed Mickey for his tardiness. Had it not been for the fact that they had made a promise, he would have stayed home. How easy it would have been to do just that, to have stayed in the comfort of his soft armchair.

When he reached the house, he found the front door open and with familiar habit he stepped inside. Mickey's wife met him in the hall, her coat already on. She rushed up to him.

"Oh Malachi! Malachi! Weren't you great to come, I was just coming down to get you." Her voice was fraught with urgency as she ushered him inside where he heard the sound of voices and caught the faint smell of alcohol. He stepped into the room and saw Mickey stretched out on the daybed beside the window, his feet jutting over one end of it. Apart from his missing shoes, he was fully dressed. His face, what little he could see of it from behind the priest, was deathly pale, and a bloodstained bandage was wrapped around his head. His eyes were closed and his hands folded on his chest in the manner of a corpse.

"What happened? How bad is he?" he inquired of Dr. Fennessy, but the doctor didn't hear, his eyes looking past him to Mrs. Mulligan. The Old Man glanced around him helplessly and for the first time noticed Mrs. Kennedy standing silent in the corner. So, it was she who had been to fetch the doctor. A picture flashed across his mind of the black car in the yard outside. They must have stopped along the way to pick up the priest. So why couldn't they have stopped for him? After all he was Mickey's closest friend. A sense of injury passed over him as he pushed himself between the doctor and the priest. The fear he had felt when he first came in turned quickly to alarm as he knelt on one knee looking down at him.

Below the level of consciousness Mickey stirred. He had heard the Old Man's voice and was struggling to connect. A tiny corner of his brain told him he was lying in the family room, but he had no memory of getting there. Images kept floating aimlessly inside his head, but he could make no sense of them. From a long way off he heard a dog barking and the sound stirred a memory. Grimly he held on to it. Yes that was it! He remembered now. He had gotten up early to go somewhere and had come downstairs. He clung to that memory and nurtured it until another surfaced, and he recalled the milk churn in the corner. He had walked across the yard to empty it. Now it was coming back!

He had picked it up and began pouring out the residue when suddenly his vision blurred and the yard began to swim in front of him. He had fallen forward on the cobbles. He must have cried out or made some noise because suddenly his wife was bending over him. He felt her hands beneath his head and tried to speak but couldn't. Then everything went black. When he woke again he was inside the house with someone standing over him. He heard someone mention the word stroke, and terror flooded over him. He tried to speak, but couldn't. There were other people in the room, he could hear their conversation and realized they thought he could not hear.

Frantically he had tried to signal, to let them know he could, but he couldn't move a limb. Even the effort to raise his lids exhausted him. Frustrated and afraid he had lain still and listened. *Oh! God in heaven, not another stroke. I would rather die than be left a cripple.* Again his mind sought refuge below conscious thought. He came awake the second time when he heard the Old Man's voice. This time he forced his lids to open and very soon a face appeared, fuzzily at first but gradually coming into focus. There was a second face but it was turned away from him. He tried again to speak, but the words would not coagulate. No matter, if anyone could see into his mind and know that it was active, it was Malachi. He fixed his eyes on him, willing him to see.

At first the Old Man had assumed, as did the others, that Mickey was indeed comatose, but now he felt certain they were wrong. This fact he tried to convey to them, as they stopped mid conversation to take a closer look. The priest, unwilling to concede, waved his hand derisively.

"Nonsense," he declared in a cold pedantic tone, "the man is not coherent. He has no communication with his senses."

Anger rose in the Old Man's chest as he strove to restrain his temper. He had noticed the sour look on the priest's face when he first came in and guessed he was still rankled by their confrontation of a few days earlier. It was common knowledge how he felt about religion. He made no secret of the fact. All his life he had lived with the stern belief that people should be free to make their own decisions about God and not be fettered by tradition, or coerced into it. He was only saying what he thought was true, but the priest had walked away disgusted. In no way did he want to make matters worse, yet neither could he allow the priest to dismiss the possibility that Mickey might be cognizant.

He tried to think of a nice way to phrase his disagreement but before he could, the animus spilled over and the words slid off his tongue. "For the love of God man, how can ye make that statement, when any fool can see the man is conscious?"

"Is he indeed," the priest replied, "and from what institution of learning did you acquire that knowledge?" He glanced smugly at Dr. Fennessy, thereby drawing him into it. The doctor coughed uneasily, a flicker of annoyance passing over his face. The fact was, he agreed with the Old Man but not wanting to offend the priest by contradicting him, had suppressed the urge to disclose that fact. Furthermore, he had no desire to see a casual conversation turn into a highly emotional argument. An awkward silence followed, with the Old Man glaring at the priest. *To hear him speak anyone would think he had a monopoly on mortality.* He had listened to him preach about God's will and the fact that death was merely a milestone on the way to eternity, and it maddened him to think that Mickey might be listening. The minutes passed; the only sound that of a crackling fire and the tick-tock of the clock. Finally the doctor spoke.

"Well now," he said, peering through his half-moon glasses while jotting down something in his little black book. "I think I've done all I can for now." He shrugged and glanced around. "Still, who are any of us to say...."

Who indeed thought the Old Man sourly, reflecting on the merits of modern medicine, too often wrong in cases of this nature. What extraordinary remedies were there that could stop a mind from thinking, or setting up its own machinery of destruction? Too well he remembered poor Johnny Hayes, a victim of several strokes, telling him that the most terrifying part for him was the awful feeling of helplessness, being cut off from the world, unable to speak or communicate. Without waiting to consult with anyone, except for a quick glance at the doctor, he took hold of Mickey's hand and in a clear but gentle voice said.

"Listen to me lad. I know what ye must be thinking, but ye can't let anything ye might have heard here bother ye. You'll be

133

up and about in no time. Sure all ye have is a bump on your head. D'ye hear me now. There's nothing wrong with ye that a good pint won't cure." Aware of Mickey's penchant for the comical, and despite the priest's objections, he continued. "If ye want the truth, 'tis I'm the one who should be lying there, walking up that blooming hill at my age! Sure that's enough to kill anyone. For two pins I'd jump in there beside ye." His common sense told him not to expect an immediate reaction, but as the minutes stretched to what seemed like hours, with no change in Mickey, he began to feel the misery of defeat and let go of Mickey's hand.

Mickey in the meantime, aware of his old friend's efforts, was trying desperately to respond. But try as he might he could not get his words to coagulate, or force his limbs to move. Frustrated, he lay still, his breath loud and labored. The Old Man patted him on the shoulder and started to get up, aware he had done everything he could. But no sooner had he laid his elbow on the bed than Mickey made a sound and a tiny curve, like the makings of a smile, creased the corners of his mouth. Within seconds that grim look of terror seemed to vanish from his eyes as he raised himself slightly on his pillow. *"No need to shout, I can hear you fine,"* he sank back on his pillow. The Old Man was jubilant.

"There! Ye see! Ye see! What did I tell ye!" his face contorted with emotion. The doctor, who at that moment was consulting with the wife, looked up and smiled. He admired the Old Man's tenacity and reveled in his success. For the past half hour he himself had been undecided. Should he send for an ambulance or should he wait? Experience had taught him that in cases like this, waiting and patience was sometimes the better choice. On top of that, he had been moved by the intensity on the Old Man's face and the nostalgic memory of his own first efforts to prolong a life - so many years ago he had almost forgotten.

"It's a miracle! A miracle!" cried Mrs. Kennedy, crossing herself repeatedly and gazing at the priest. Tears had filled Mrs. Mulligan's eyes, eyes that rested lovingly on her husband. Nobody had to tell her that something other than a miracle had taken place. Too well she understood the depth of the friendship between these men. Had she not been present when Mickey's mother died and heard the Old Man promise to always be there for her son. Over the years he had fulfilled that pledge, cementing a friendship that was made to last until one of them died.

Mickey sighed contentedly. Only minutes before he had wanted to die. Now he felt grateful to be alive. He looked at the anxious faces bending over him before closing his eyes and drifting quietly back to sleep. It was more than the Old Man had expected. For a moment, his gaze lingered on the stricken face, more relaxed and peaceful now. Then quietly he rose, wiping as he did the solitary tear making its way down Mickey's face.

There was happiness all about him now, expressions of joy and disbelief. Yet all he could think about was getting outside, away from the hypocrisy, from people calling it *a miracle* and thanking God for his delivery. "Miracle indeed!" he thought bitterly as he walked out of the room.

Outside in the lane again he heard the town clock strike eleven, *an hour late already* he thought remembering their waiting friend. He didn't look forward to that journey now, but felt he should let the man know what happened. With a bit of luck he might make it to the Market Square by twelve. For Mickey's sake he wanted to for he knew how much it would mean to him. He and Meehaul Lannigan had been friends since birth, but at age fifteen Meehaul had gotten into trouble with the law and was sent away to reformatory. By the time he got out, the family had moved and the two boys lost touch. Years later, however, Meehaul returned to the county of his birth and took up farming in a village nearby. Now the two men got together this one day in the year, when Meehaul made the journey into town to sell his produce at the Market Square.

As hoped, the Old Man reached the square by twelve, but only a sprinkling of people were left. Most of the farmers with produce to sell had done so and headed home. A few dairy stalls with plucked poultry hanging from the beams, were still open and some tinkers with their caravans had positioned themselves inside the gate begging alms from passers-by. One old tinker woman, beset by some dementia, was casting insults everywhere. Guard Sinnott, his arms folded across his chest, was standing in a corner keeping watch on her. The Old Man walked by unnoticed, arriving at the spot where they had arranged to meet. It was past noon now and the sun was hot. He wiped more perspiration from his forehead and looked around. His legs felt weak from walking. Nearby, two farmers standing with their backs to him were haggling about a horse and after a while one of them looked over.

"Good day to you sir," he shouted. "Would your name by any chance be Mulligan?" The Old Man shook his head, and then explained his presence. "I've a message for you so." Meehaul, the message said, had waited for as long as possible but with urgent business elsewhere had had to leave. Disappointed, the Old Man thanked the man and walked away. He supposed he could get in touch with Meehaul by mail, but he had wanted to have a drink with him, especially today. Besides, the long walk down had made him thirsty. Wearily he made his way back to the market gate, and then headed to the nearest pub. To his relief, he found it almost empty. He made his way directly to a corner and sat alone. It felt good to be off his feet again. He stretched them out beneath the table and took out his pipe.

The proprietor, a small portly woman of middle age, leaned toward him across the counter. "The usual is it Malachi, a

Jameson?" she asked, remarking on how long it had been since they had last seen him. He nodded absentmindedly, then changed his mind, saying he would have a Guinness instead, if it were all the same to her.

"A Guinness it will be so," she answered, reaching for a glass and beginning to pour. "How have you been anyway?" She approached the table.

"Not bad. Not bad at all," he answered hastily, holding out the money. It was his way of letting her know he didn't want her to sit down. Kitty, as she was known to all her customers, was a friendly talkative woman who would have loved to chat, but knew by the grim expression on his face he didn't want her company.

"Will that be all," she asked more formally, delving into her pocket for the change.

"I'll take a Baby Power to go." He nodded at the change.

"Right so," she answered, "it's as good a drink as any," and returned to the bar. He felt mean, for it wasn't that he didn't like the woman, but she could talk the teeth out of a donkey, and at the moment he couldn't handle that. He picked up his glass and drank thirstily feeling the Guinness soothe his throat. If only it could do the same for his shrieking nerves.

The sound of laughter came to him and he gazed about. The small bar was comfortable but the patron's faces were unknown to him. None of the men he used to know were present. *Surely to God they can't all be dead!* A more careful computation told him that they were, plunging him deeper into depression. Not that he felt sadness at their passing, for he never knew them well enough for that. He had never been what one might call a drinking man, and certainly not a buddy.

But he used to like to sit with them and listen to them talk. The sound of laughter came again, this time reminding him of Mickey - poor foolish Mickey. It was different with him. He had grown to love him like a son. He took another drink from his glass and sighed heavily, the present now becoming dim as thoughts and images of his friend surrounded him. All those nights they had sat up arguing about one thing or another. Yet never had they had a falling out. He had always thought he'd be the one to go first, that seemed only natural. Now he didn't know what to think. If Mickey had another stroke it would finish him. He didn't want to contemplate a life without him, the emptiness and silence slowly killing him.

The tears wet his whiskers and he rummaged in his pockets for his handkerchief, looking furtively around before bringing it to his face. He stuffed it back inside his pocket and finished off his drink. Then he sat and smoked the remainder of his pipe. *A fine birthday this turned out to be!*

A few more people drifted in and the empty table next to him became occupied. Out of decency he lingered a few minutes more, then dragged himself to his feet, wincing as a pain shot up his back. He made his way up to the counter.

"I'll say goodbye so Mrs. Henderson," he called. Then added guiltily. "T'was good to see ye looking well." Her face softened.

"You're off then Malachi?" She moved to clear his table. He raised his hand in parting. "Don't be such a stranger now," he heard her call after him as he passed out through the door.

Slowly, he made his way along the path and was about to cross the road to take a short cut home when he noticed Barney Callaghan, leaning on the handlebars of his bicycle and chatting with father Commerford outside the rectory gate. Barney had his back to him but the priest saw him coming.

"Don't listen to a word he's telling ye father," the Old Man called out as he got closer and Barney spun around. "Have ye nothing better to do Callaghan than to stand here wasting this good man's time?" The priest grinned knowingly, the stories of rancor between the two men well known to him.

138

"And what has it to do with you if I stand here all day?" Barney asked.

"Nothing I suppose. But if inspector Rabbit chances by an claps an eye on ye, 'tis your walking papers you'll be getting."

"A lot I care about inspector Rabbit," Barney scoffed.

"Oh! 'Tis like that is it! And I suppose ye think that uniform entitles ye to special treatment?" Barney sighed and rolled his eyes as though nobly enduring the ill deserved treatment of the world. The priest smiled indulgently.

"Isn't it time the two of you gave over your shenanigans, and declared a truce?"

"The divil take me," the Old Man cackled and Barney sighed, while launching into a lofty speech bewailing the profundity of his woes and the general lack of sensitivity to erudite men like him compelled to associate with inferiors. His rhetoric was an allusion to his promotion to chief constable, a plum delivered toward the end of a long career. It was said by some that following the promotion Barney had begun to change, determined to make a favorable impression and ingratiate himself with what he called *'the right sort of people'* by insisting on the use of his proper name.

Of course that was all the ammunition the Old Man needed. Undaunted by the limitations to his own oratorical skills, he gave a loud snort. "Will ye listen to the man putting on the airs, anyone would think he knew what he was saying. 'Tis a mystery to me how the other guards put up with him." To the priest he said. "I'll tell you this father, if anyone up and ordered me to call him Barnabus when I knew full well his name was plain auld Barney, I'd do six months for him, I would faith." The priest exploded in a fit of laughter and Barney shook his head.

"Arragh what's the use. That man won't rest until I'm under. I'm beginning to think the good Lord put him on this earth just to torment me."

139

"And so he might. So he might," the Old Man cackled.

The introduction of the Lord provided the priest with the catalyst he needed to change the topic. "You look a little flushed Malachi, what have you been doing, and what brings you down around these parts?" The Old Man sighed and explained his trip to the Market Square.

"Aw whisht! Sure I'd hate to tell ye of the trials I've come up against this morning. Little I thought when I got out of bed to find such misery awaiting me."

"Ah yes. Poor Mr. Mulligan. I heard about that," the priest replied, commenting on the situation." Barney gave them both a puzzled look.

"Hold on a minute now. Mickey is it you're talking about? What's wrong with him?" Both men regarded him with genuine surprise.

"Ye haven't heard then?" the Old Man asked.

"Of course I haven't heard. Would I be asking if I had?" Reluctantly, the priest informed him, adding that he had heard the news himself only moments before bumping into him. Barney, usually never at a loss for words, was uncharacteristically silent, while the priest struggled to hide his embarrassment.

Remembering his own hurt feelings earlier the Old Man had started to explain, when a young lad he did not know walked up and interrupted. "Excuse me sir," the lad said, nodding at them, and taking Barney to one side. They talked in whispers for a second or so and a moment later Barney threw his leg across the saddle of his bike and with a few hasty words of departure, pedaled off.

"Pity he had to hear it like that," the priest remarked, looking after him. "I'm told he's very fond of the Mulligans." The Old Man wagged his head in silence, a strained look on his wrinkled face. He was thinking about the affect the news would have on Barney, and the fact that he hadn't been notified. Why, the very idea of someone else possessing information that he was not privy to was usually enough to cause him grief, much less a thing like that. The thought stayed with him as he chatted with the priest. There was no reason he should feel guilty about the whole affair for there was nothing he could do, but for some disquieting reason he did. He remained a few minutes longer with the priest before glancing at the sky. The morning sun had disappeared and dark rain clouds had gathered overhead. In fact, in the east where the sky was already dark, lightening flashed and thunder rumbled in the distance.

"I should be off myself, father. Like as not we're in for a downpour." He shook the priest's hand. "'Twas grand to see ye at any rate." The priest agreed and lifting the latch on the rectory gate passed into the yard. As the first large drops began to spatter on the street the Old Man reached the shelter of his own front door. He felt one large drop strike his forehead, then another strike his face before he managed to insert the key into the lock. The room was warm and cozy, heavy with the smell of rabbit stew simmering on the hob since morning. It was a pleasure to come in from the cold and find the fire still burning. He had banked it down before he left that morning and was looking forward to a quiet evening with his feet in front of it.

He removed his coat and hung it in its place on the peg behind the door, then went to the back door to let Meggie in. She went immediately to her corner, making little mewling sounds as he raised the lid on the simmering pot. He poured some stew into her dish and laid it down for her. Then he set his own dishes on the table, and cutting off a chunk of fresh soda bread, filled his bowl with the rabbit stew. It tasted scrumptious, the meat soft and tender, just the way he liked it. A mug of tea and slice of marble cake would finish off the meal.

Leaning backward to the wooden shelf behind him, he turned the knob on the wireless to listen to the news, but with nothing interesting to hear he turned it off again. By the time he finished eating, it was getting on for six and becoming dark outside. The rain beat steadily on the window, and leaving the dishes in the sink, he rekindled his pipe and sat himself down in his soft armchair.

On the table beside his chair sat his birthday bottle of whiskey and a book he was still reading. Had it not been for the rain he might have tackled the trip to Mickey's house. Now it would have to wait 'til morning. For some strange reason he began to think about Barney and the hurt look on his face when he learned the news about Mickey. It was hard to believe that a man in his position could be so put out over little things. Yet, he knew that Barney had a tender spot for Mickey, even if he never had one for him, and had often heard Mickey mention Barney's name in connection with some family event. He wondered why he had never married, and whether he ever felt lonely. From the little he knew of him, he had no living relatives and lived a fairly circumscribed life. Yet he was a handsome enough man for any woman, with his fine physique, striking green eyes and mop of slightly graying hair. Though he could never admit to liking him he had to acknowledge that over the years he had developed a sort of grudging respect for him.

As it turned out, the encounter had a pleasant sequel when Barney turned up at the front door several minutes later. The Old Man couldn't believe his eyes. "Well! Well! And to what do I owe this pleasure?" He invited him inside. Barney nodded silently and stepped inside. The Old Man didn't know what to say, or whether he should say anything. "I'm glad ye came," he finally managed. "I wanted to talk to ye, to explain..."

"What's there to talk about? I know what happened. Anyhow I didn't come for that. I came to give you this." He drew from his pocket a brown paper bag containing a bottle of Jameson whiskey. "Compliments of the Mulligans. Is it your birthday or what?" and before the Old Man could answer, "a nice comfortable little place you've got here," he said, looking all around, and catching sight of the whiskey on the table. "I see you've already got yourself a drop," he nodded to the Baby Power.

"I can put that away now," the Old Man cackled, reaching for the larger bottle. "Ye'll have one with me won't ye?" He handed Barney a glass.

"Be gor and I won't say no. 'Tis a luxury I don't often have," Barney replied good naturedly, removing his wet coat and draping it over the back of a chair. He took the glass the Old Man offered and seated himself beside the table while the Old Man poured the drink. It was dark outside now, the rain still coming down, barely a drizzle one minute, a steady torrent the next. The goat snored loudly in the corner and Barney grinned.

"You still have her I see." The Old Man didn't answer. He was busy lighting the lamp and placing it on the mantel, its flame casting an eerie shadow across the walls and ceiling. "I take it you went by the farm?" he said, when he finally sat down.

"I did indeed and Mickey is fine. He's not talking much but he's improving." He sipped his drink thoughtfully before continuing. "I heard about your run-in with the priest."

"Aye, I thought ye would."

"Well, you don't want to let it worry you, you're too old to lose sleep over a thing like that. How old are you anyway?"

"Older than I want to be. As of today I'm an octo-gen-arian." He stressed the final syllables.

"Really! I didn't realize you were that old. You don't look it." He held up his glass. "Here's to you so, congratulations, and may you have many more years of hardship." They both laughed simultaneously and after a couple of deep slugs of whiskey, Barney lit a cigarette and said. "Tell me Malachi, where have all the years gone? I was only this morning thinking about poor Tommy Darcy, God rest his soul. Do you remember

143

him?" The very mention of the name caused the Old Man to flinch.

"Of course I remember, why wouldn't I? Wasn't I there when they evicted him." Barney leaned across the table.

"The way I heard it, you were not only there but drunk and disorderly."

"Well, I'll admit to being disorderly."

"Tell me about it," Barney urged, and the Old Man settled deeper in his chair.

"Well as I remember, it was a man by the name of Monaghan, overzealous in his duty as an agent of The Crown. He arrived up at Tommy's house brandishing a club and ordered him outside. Wouldn't give the man a chance to pull his boots on. Just threw him out on the road like a piece of turf, and he with a wife and child. Put me in mind of the famine days it did. Aye, and there was another fellow with him, eager to pin the eviction notice to the door, but I'm damned if I can remember his name."

"Hogan," Barney offered, "a fierce bully of a man. Did a stretch in jail for robbery before going to Australia."

"Is that a fact? I didn't know that! Well, I wouldn't say he was missed." Then with a glint of mischief in his eyes, "of course, I didn't know Monaghan at the time and he didn't know me, but I promptly introduced myself by landing him back of the head with a boulder." Barney laughed.

"I'd say he didn't know you for a long time after, either. Yet, from what I heard, you took a good belt around the head yourself?" The Old Man frowned.

"I don't remember that part of it. The only clear memory I have is of sitting in a chair with a doctor standing over me. Hardly more than a scratch, he said it was, and put a few stitches there." He touched the hairline on his forehead, where a tiny scar bore testimony to his story. He straightened up. "Well that's enough about me, tell us something about yourself." Barney shrugged.

"There's nothing much to tell. I hardly remember anything about my parents. In fact I didn't know my father, never even knew his name. I was eight when my mother died and I was sent to a welfare home. When I came out of there I was in my teens and that's when I joined the Force."

"But did you never marry?"

Barney stared into the fire as though deciding what to answer or whether to answer at all. Finally he said.

"Arragh sure what's the use of talking. What's past is past." He took a few gulps from his glass. "I did come very close once, but it wasn't to be. Something unexpected happened and she had a change of heart. I never bothered after that." It was obviously a subject he didn't want to talk about and so the Old Man didn't pry.

Both men now in a reminiscent mood began calling up old friends and recollecting scraps from the margins of their minds.

"I know we were on different sides back then and not always on good terms, but do you ever think about those years at all?" Barney asked.

"I try not to. Sure a man could drive himself to drink thinking about the things that went on in this Country back then, things that no human being should have to witness. Millions driven from their homes and forced to live like animals in the fields, and them that survived packed like cattle in the coffin boats to America. Who could forget such a desperate chapter in their history?" He paused a moment to reflect. "I didn't witness the Famine days myself mind, but my own father did and could never forget it happened. There were times, he told me, when he would hear the poor, sad voices of the children crying out for food long after the event." Barney took a drag on his cigarette.

145

"I know what you mean. I feel that way myself at times." There was a note of sadness in his voice that surprised the Old Man, and he wondered whether Barney actually felt remorse or was just haunted by old memories. "We've had a few laughs from time to time in spite of it," he said. "Do you remember the time old Hoppy Hehir was carrying the banner in the St. Patrick's Day parade and stepped into the manhole?" The vacant look on the Old Man's face told him that he didn't.

"You don't remember that? Is it gone entirely your memory is? Sure his curses were heard all over town."

"Wait now. Wait now," the Old Man said, holding up his hand, "'tis coming back to me. I wasn't there, mind, but I do remember someone telling me. Some prankster had removed the cover from the manhole and Hoppy, with his head forever in the clouds, stepped right into it."

"Ye have it now," Barney said, with another burst of laughter. "Ah but wait until I tell you what happened after that. To add insult to injury, as soon as he disappeared inside the hole, Jimmy Hickey, his old nemesis, kicked the lid back on and marched off with the banner."

"Ye don't say?"

"I do indeed, and to make matters worse Hoppy had to stay down in the hole while the parade continued over him. You should have seen the state of him when we pulled him out, covered with slime and excrement, and he bawling for his banner."

"The silly old fool," the Old Man chuckled.

"The sad thing is, he died of an aneurysm a few days later and I often wondered if he hadn't hit his head that day, but was too proud to let on."

"Oh well! We'll never know now in any case," the Old Man sighed. They were silent for a moment then, both thinking their separate thoughts while the rain beat against the windowpanes.

"'Tis funny, all the same," said the Old Man, "how some things slip your mind and others don't."

"It is indeed, though there are a lot of things I'd like to forget and can't," Barney said, staring at the fire. "It might be hard for you to understand, but being a policeman in this country wasn't always easy, with the political climate being what it was and people reacting to a policeman as they would a murderer in their midst. At times it became insufferable with the name calling and lack of respect."

The Old Man looked at him amused, the wheels of remembrance churning in his head. *Respect indeed! And they to blame for the lack of it, with their misguided loyalty to The Crown. Surely he realized they had lost all right to it with their constant vigilance and needless raids on people's homes. Turncoats and informers is what they were, and in a Country already demoralized by fear. No stouter body of men had ever marched beneath the royal banner, content with a decree of prejudicial legislation allowing that the killing of an Irishman be not considered murder. Was it any wonder they found themselves despised?*

Barney's kind of military reasoning was anathema to the Old Man's mind, as it was to most Irish people of the time who could not come to terms with the policies of any established order designed to intimidate the minds of simple folk. Still, hearts could not remain fixed forever in the past and a certain cordiality had found its way into contemporary feeling, whereby the motives of the constabulary were not all the time suspect. He knew he should say something in reply, if only to remind Barney of all the needless suffering they had caused, but he couldn't think of a single thing to say. Besides he had given up fighting for *the cause* a long time ago. *Better to let sleeping dogs lie,* he told himself, rattling the poker against the grate.

Barney, in the meantime had gone quiet, gazing thoughtfully into the fire, but the Old Man had the feeling he had something else to say. He watched him light another cigarette.

"In retrospect I suppose you couldn't blame them," he said. "We must have seemed like traitors to many, and who knows but they weren't wrong." He grinned apologetically. "If you want to know the truth, there are times when I wish we could turn back the clock." The Old Man waved derisively, and a cynical look flashed across Barney's face. "You don't believe me, do you?"

"I didn't say that."

"You didn't have to. Your look said it all. But I understand. We could have done things differently, I suppose, but back then it seemed the right way to go."

"Well, things have changed for the better now, and that time best forgotten, so drink up and don't worry about it." And so the evening passed with both men sitting quietly in the firelight. The wind was howling in the chimney now and Barney, draining the last dregs from his glass, pushed his chair back from the table and hauled himself to his feet.

"I'd better go. That wind is picking up and I'm on my bicycle. Thanks again for the drink. No don't get up, I'll let myself out," he said, as the Old Man began to rise. He pulled on his coat and started for the door. "By the way," he said across his shoulder, "don't worry about Meehaul Lannigan, I'll get a message off to him. I can do that from the station."

The Old Man thanked him and wished him well, then listened to his footsteps going down the path. He had shared Barney's company several times before but usually with others present, and none of those times had been particularly memorable. This evening had been different. The unexpected visit and painful attempt at atonement for the past had made his day, and maybe even his life, a little brighter. Alone now with his solitude he sipped his drink and stared into the fire. The day had turned out special after all. In the space of several hours, he had walked up the hill to Mickey's house, then all the way down to the Market Square, a trip of several miles. If his back didn't hurt tomorrow it would never hurt again. Taking a last gulp from his glass, he laid it empty on the table, stretched his toes out to the fire and sank back in his chair. *All's well that ends well,* he told himself, contented.

A MATTER OF HEART

One fine afternoon as the summer was drawing to a close I stood alone by the scullery sink washing dirty handkerchiefs for the family. Earlier that week my mother had put them to soak in a bucket of soapy water, which by now had turned a slimy green, with globs of nasal excrement floating on the top. It was a job I disliked doing, but had promised my mother I would. I had emptied the bucket into the sink and began the unpleasant task when I heard Timmy, our little wire-haired terrier, wailing and clawing feebly at the back door. I recalled I had let him out earlier and walked to the back door to let him in.

"Come on Tim," I said, holding the door open. But Timmy didn't move, just stood in the yard looking up at me, his eyes glazed, his little pink tongue, now a black monstrosity protruding from his jaw. I knew right away something terrible had happened. "-Dad! Dad! Come quickly, something's wrong with Timmy."

My father came immediately, but there was nothing he could do. Timmy died right there in front of us, his tiny body trembling, his eyes dull with pain. I could never erase that image from my mind, the tiny body with no life in it, the eyes and mouth frozen in the rigor of a horrible, painful death. He was five years old. It made me wretched, and desperately I tried to bury it in some isolated corner of my mind. A dark shadow passed across my father's face and there was a moment of unbearable silence before he spoke.

"Someone's poisoned him, poor little lad," he said, pacing back and forth across the yard trying to figure out how it had happened. Could it have been deliberate? We both had our suspicions. It seemed an awful thing for anyone to do, and made me positively ill to even think about it. My mother came to join us in the yard, her face grave.

"Is it what I think?" she asked, and my father nodded silently.

"Heartless bastard," she spat, scarcely able to believe the reality of such a rotten crime. My father threw a worried glance in my direction.

"We don't know that for certain Bride. Better not to jump to conclusions." Mother gave him an impatient look.

"You know as well as I do who's responsible. It tears the heart right out of me to see the poor creature lying there like that, such a good little dog" Her voice rose in anguished retrospect. "That bugger better not let me catch him anywhere near this house," she said, muttering to herself and going back inside, barely able to contain her anger.

Shocked beyond belief, my father sat on the coal bin near the door and buried his face in his hands, as if doing so might obliterate some of the misery he was feeling. My heart ached for him, for I knew what he was feeling, my own grief so intense as to render me incapable of expressing an emotion. I stood silently and waited.

After a few minutes, a corner of his mind began to work again and he got up from the coal bin and looked around. He found some empty sacking in a corner by the door, and lifted Timmy's body onto it. He wrapped it tightly around him and tied it with a piece of string. Then he went to get his shovel. As I walked behind him down the garden path, my eyes glued to the limp little bundle in his arms, a terrible hate came over me. I cursed the man I believed responsible. No animal deserved to die such a horrible, painful death, no matter how many times he dug up your potatoes.

With eyes blinded by tears of anger and despair, my mind raced back in time to a solitary day in the first year of Timmy's life, a cool moist day in August. Timmy is standing on the kitchen floor; both ears erect, his little head cocked saucily listening to Sheilagh explain what he had to do when the cage door was opened. "Now listen Timmy. You mustn't be afraid," she was saying, trying to hold eye contact as Paddy Brennan had instructed. Timmy barked excitedly and ran around her legs.

"Aw, I don't think he understands," she wailed, throwing up her arms.

"Don't worry, he'll do fine," the rest of the family encouraged, for we too wanted him to pass the test.

"But he's so tiny, he'll never be able to do it."

"Yes he will," Jane, whose belief in the benevolence of the Almighty was unshakeable, assured her. "We'll all pray for him, won't we lads," and we all agreed enthusiastically. The thing was, Timmy was just a puppy, not even a year old as far as we could tell. A week or so before, Sheilagh had found him lost and wandering in the street, a heavy rope tied around his neck. At first he was frightened of her and tried to run away, but was hampered by the rope. She bent down and picked him up. His fur was wet and slimy as though he had been dragged through mud and he shivered uncontrollably. Sheilagh knew immediately that someone had tried to drown him. Poor little lad, she thought, ridding him of his heavy rope and wrapping her scarf around him. He had relaxed then and licked her face, but when she tried to put him on the ground again he clung to her. So, despite my father's probable disapproval, she had brought him home.

At first my father was annoyed and told her to get rid of him. But later he yielded to our begging and said he could stay on one condition. He must prove himself worthy of his keep in the only sure way he knew of, by hunting down a rat and killing it.

"But he's too young to hunt a rat down by himself," my mother interceded, "he's only a pup for heaven's sake." She had taken a liking to the little terrier when Sheilagh brought him home and, like the rest of us, didn't want to lose him. We knew this, not by any admission on her part, but by her odd behavior in the minutes leading up to the event, when she betrayed her anxiety several times by throwing up her hands and looking at the clock. Though she didn't say so at the time it was her belief that the whole business of dogs having to prove themselves in such an odious way was inhuman. Not that she was opposed in principle to the discipline involved, for as a mother of many children she knew well the benefit of that, but the emphasis on the dog's performance sickened her. For what became of all the dogs that failed, or got bitten by the rat and had to be destroyed? Not wanting to defy my father, she had suggested.

"Why not get Paddy Brennan to bring home a rat. You can let it loose in the Fair Green and see how the dog handles it." And so it was decided. Paddy had trapped and caged the rat, and was to bring it to our house that evening. Now the hour had come and the decision as to whether Timmy would stay or not would be decided shortly. I felt an ache around my heart as I looked at him so tiny and inexperienced, prancing and yelping excitedly not knowing what was coming. We had been to see the rat that morning and thought it much too large.

"He'll never be able to kill that; that thing will eat him," Sheilagh cried, wondering why Paddy had brought such a large one, when a smaller one would do. Paddy, his faith in Timmy's valor more confirmed than ours, assured us of his fighting spirit. He had seen it in little dogs before, he said, and was willing to bet on Timmy.

"This fella may look big," he said, looking at the rat, "but never you fear, he'll meet his match today." I had my doubts, for I remembered Molly Hogan telling me about their dog, and how the rat had sunk his teeth into his muzzle and tore the lips right off of him. We waited anxiously for my father to come home, and when he eventually did we followed him to the garden wall where Paddy waited in the Green beyond.

We children were told to stay behind the wall, for they needed no distractions. So Mother, who had delayed coming until the last minute, lined us up beside her – Peg and Tom on one side and Sheilagh, Jane and me on the other. Anxiously, we leaned out over the wall to watch. Paddy was standing in the Green, his arms folded across his chest, the cage resting by his feet. Father stood for a moment looking out at him and it was difficult to tell what emotion he was feeling, or if in fact he was feeling any.

"Give him here pet," he said, taking Timmy from Sheilagh's arms, and climbing over the garden wall he walked across to Paddy.

"Oh God!" Sheilagh moaned, clinging to my mother's arm and trying unsuccessfully not to panic. Mother told her to stop her whinging that Timmy would be fine, but that once they opened the cage door there would be no turning back, so if we had any prayers to say we had better say them now. We watched as my father knelt beside the cage allowing Timmy a glimpse of his opponent, who looked mean and menacing inside the bars, his red eyes fixed on Timmy's nose.

Timmy's senses flared and trembling with excitement, he almost leaped from my father's hands.

"Watch out lads," Paddy called to us, and I forced myself to look, my heart pounding in my chest as all at once the cage door flew open and the rat spilled out onto the grass. For a moment nothing happened as he recoiled around the cage in a frantic search for cover. But Paddy kicked the cage away forcing him to run and he dashed across the Green in our direction. Without a moment's hesitation Timmy took the scent, his instinct now in harness. Like a bullet from a gun, he shot across the Green, his eyes focused on his quarry.

Ahead of him the rat had reached the high stone wall, and a failed attempt to scale it had him scurrying about, first in one direction then the other. He turned, and turned again, frantic for that one last chance to live, but there was no escape. With a frightened squeal he rose up on his two hind legs, his back against the wall, and faced his executioner. Timmy barked and growled at him, wanting him to run so he could tackle him with safety. Aware that he was trapped, the rat seemed rooted to the spot, but finally dropped to the ground again to make a final dash for freedom. Faster than a rattlesnake, Timmy was upon him, sinking in his teeth and holding fast.

At this point I turned my head away not wanting to see the kill, for the rat's fatal squeal had awakened a forgotten memory of two boys flushing a hare from the briar and their dogs bringing it to ground. The sound of that poor creature's cries as the dogs bore down on it had turned my guts to jelly, so like a child's cry it was. When I looked up again, the rat was a mangled heap of fur hanging limply from Timmy's jaws.

"He did it. He did it," the cry went up and everyone rejoiced. Jane turned to me.

"You can stop crying now," she said, jumping up and down.

"I wasn't crying," I told her, ashamed of the emotion. She wrapped her arms around my neck.

"You can pretend you weren't if you like, but I know you were. You really are a softie, aren't you?" I made no reply, but wished she hadn't said it in front of everyone, and though I was delighted that Timmy had succeeded, my elation was tainted with the memory of the rat, its back against the wall in its own frantic effort to succeed. What chance had it really had, when all was said and done? Paddy was right, in any case, the rat had met its match and Timmy hailed triumphant.

Theresa Lennon Blunt

All that had happened about four years earlier. Now Timmy himself was dead, ironically killed by the very device designed to eradicate his enemy, for we found out soon enough that our suspicions were correct. A certain disgruntled neighbour had murdered him. Fed him meat laced with rat poison. As long as I lived I knew I would never forgive that man. I used to watch him stride along the street each day, a satisfied look on his surly face, and I hoped with all my heart he would meet with some terrible accident. My wish was granted, when some months later I learned he had been kicked in the head by a large Dray horse and died of a blood clot in his brain. I thought it a fitting punishment.

A CHANCE ENCOUNTER

A fine fresh morning it was after a night of rain, as Molly Flaherty wandered about the back yard of their house wondering whether to go right away to her friend Nora's house or wait. The sun, but a shimmering arc on the horizon earlier, was now full in the sky and the sky itself awash in a blaze of colour. Even the heavy mist she had noticed earlier had evaporated. It was going to be a glorious day, she told herself, and was glad that she had risen early.

It was Sunday and except for her brother Dominick, who was still asleep in bed, Molly was alone. Her mother had gone to the ten o'clock Mass along with Mrs. White. Molly had opted for an earlier Mass so she wouldn't have to listen to Father Heany preach about doom and damnation. She couldn't stand the man. If only he would say what he had to say and get down from the pulpit. But no, he had to go on and on, putting everyone to sleep, or sitting there like dummies, heads nodding and wishing he'd shut up. It was just not good enough. Sunday was the only day of the week people had to relax, and how could anyone relax cooped up in the church listening to all that. She began to get angry thinking about it.

It was then she remembered the cigarette she had hidden in her pocket. She took it out and began smoking it. Her mother would kill her if she found out. She had smoked it down to a butt when she heard her coming, so she threw it away and went back inside. The church bell was already ringing for the eleven o'clock Mass.

"You were right about Father Heany," her mother said. "He's a nice man, but he does go on."

"Aye, and I wouldn't mind if he had anything good to say about people," Molly said. "So, what was he on about today?"

"He thinks there's too much drinking in the parish and wants everyone to take the pledge."

That's a good one for you, I must say. Though she didn't hold with excessive drinking, and knew in her heart the priest was right, she found it hard to agree with him. *What right does he have to criticize when he's guilty of the same thing? Had she not seen him herself in the Metropole Hotel in the company of Matty Ryan, a man known for his ability to down any amount of liquor. If the truth were told, the clergy do their own share of drinking. Yet, people have the good manners not to mention it, not even when they see it every day. One only has to look at Father O'Neil, a quiet saint of a man, sensitive to any kind of discourtesy and given to blessing people in the street, yet with a yen for Satan's Syrup the likes of which she had never seen. Transubstantiating his way through one Mass after another every morning of the week. Sure it was a miracle there was any wine at all left in the city. Somebody ought to have a chat with God about it.*

She came alert to her mother's voice. "Is Dominick not up yet? I thought he'd be well up before I got back. I don't know what's gotten into him, lying in bed 'til all hours. It wouldn't kill him to get up early for once." Molly pretended she didn't hear as her mother continued in the same vein. "Is he not going to Mass at all today? He'll have the priest down on us. Since he got that job at the factory there's no talking to him at all. It's times like this I wish I had your father back." Molly remained silent. She had heard it all before and didn't want to agree and get Dominick into trouble. Nor did she want to hear about the no-good father who had slunk away to England and left his innocent wife to raise two kids. She moved across the floor to the kitchen door.

"I expect he'll be up in time for the last Mass," she said, across her shoulder, "or you could go in and wake him."

She found Nora at the kitchen table polishing her nails, her hair still up in curlers, magazines scattered on every chair and dirty dishes in the sink. A pretty girl of seventeen, one year younger than Molly, she had auburn hair, fair skin and a spray of freckles on her nose. Molly really liked her, despite the fact she was sometimes crass and displayed a propensity for idleness. She gave her an impatient look, and Nora shrugged.

"Well how was I supposed to know you were coming early? You might have let me know."

"And how should I have done that, by wireless? I'm lucky I suppose to find you up, or even in for that matter."

"Where else would you expect to find me?" Molly shrugged.

"Do you have any money," she asked.

"A bob or two, why?"

"Because I don't have a penny, I spent it all on me mam's birthday gift, but I thought we might go to the carnival before it leaves."

"Oh great! Now I work for nothing."

"I'll pay you back."

The door opened and Nora's mother came in. She was a short, squat woman of about fifty and Molly liked her. She had lost her only son when he was three and she had never gotten over it. Her face always had a sad look to it and whenever she saw a little boy playing in the street, her eyes would become all watery and a lone, silent tear sometimes slither down her face as once again she is in the scullery. *Tommy is playing outside in the street with his new fire engine. She hears the familiar sound of Dickey Doran's lorry coming around the corner. Then someone shouting a warning before the screeching of brakes brings her to the door. With her heart pounding in her chest she looks out and sees the red fire engine, still in one piece, on the path. Relief floods over her until she steps into the street and sees Tommy, sprawled across the ground, his head twisted unnaturally to the side, his hair matted with a dark slime of blood. "Tommy," she screams, "Tommy," and runs to him, her mind unwilling to accept the full meaning of what she sees. She bends down over him her eyes fixed on his, and for a second she thinks that he's alive. Her mind grasps at the ray of hope, until all at once she realizes that what she sees in Tommy's eyes is not life, but an unblinking gaze of death. In a moment, the truth washes over her and finally she lifts him up and hugs him to her, his little head rolling to one side, his arms and legs hanging limp.*

Try as she might, she could never wash that image from her mind, and as the years went by she had stopped trying. With her usual pleasant manner she acknowledged Molly's presence.

"I thought I saw you at the eight o'clock Mass if I'm not mistaken."

"You did indeed," Molly said, not bothering to explain what she had told her mother earlier.

"I was surprised to see you there so early. Might it have anything to do with that nice young Michael Brannigan? I noticed he had an eye on you while passing the collection plate." Molly blushed.

"Not at all," she lied, "sure I hardly know the lad, but isn't it awful weather we've been having lately?" she injected, in an effort to change the subject.

"'Tis indeed, but sure it's grand today," the mother replied, giving Nora a despairing look. "That's a nice way to receive a friend I must say," she snorted. "You might at least ask the girl to take the weight off her legs." She began snatching up magazines from around the room.

"Receive!" Nora grinned at Molly. "I think she knows me well enough by now."

"I do indeed," Molly responded amicably, sitting on the now empty chair in front of her.

"You could show a little decency all the same," her mother grumbled. Nora didn't answer and her mother, having failed to achieve the intended result, covered her defeat by turning again to Molly. "And how is your poor mother keeping? Has she got over that flu yet?"

"She has indeed. She's grand now, thanks. You'd never even know she had it."

"Well she's a lucky woman to have two such caring children. You're both a credit to her." Her tone was tinged with sarcasm again and Nora knew the remark was meant for her. She put down the nail polish and folded her arms across her chest.

"Now don't start on about that again, please Ma." Her mother grunted and after a few minutes Nora stood up, removed the curlers from her hair and ran a comb through it. Then she went to the mirror in the hall and studied her face in it.

"Okay, I'm ready, let's go," she said, looking decisively at Molly before heading for the door. Her mother, hands deep in soapy water by the sink, swung around.

"Surely you're not going out like that, without a coat or cardigan. It's damp outside, do you want to catch your death?" Nora ignored her and stormed out the door and Molly, feeling awkward and embarrassed said a quick goodbye and followed.

Outside on the street they saw Bridie Morris with her head stuck out the window. "Where are you lads off to?" Bridie asked, and Molly told her. "Sure 'tis well for some people isn't it? You'd want to watch yourself now with them carnival lads."

"Maybe we'll bring one back for you," Nora teased, and Bridie laughed.

"That'll do ye now. Just mind yourselves with them lads and don't get into trouble." She pulled her head back in.

The carnival was almost empty and that was not surprising after all the rain they'd had. Most of the rides had already been dismantled, but one or two stalls were still open. They walked around a bit, and Nora tried her hand at the shooting range where she actually won a prize.

"If you ask me that fellow just gave it to you," Molly teased, "because from what I could see you didn't hit one target. What is it anyway?"

"Some sort of mug. Plastic wouldn't you know, and with a great big scratch down one side of it. Sure who would want to drink from a thing like that?"

"You're not supposed to drink from it. You're supposed to keep it as a souvenir."

"Right." Nora said, giving it a sour look and tossing it into a dustbin. "Do you fancy a ride on the chair-o-planes?"

"Not really. The seats are still wet, and besides there's nobody here to run the thing. I doubt if they would even let us up with just the two of us."

"You're probably right. They're a funny lot these carnival folk, living in caravans all year round and depending on fine weather for a living. In a way I pity them, especially the children, never knowing what it's like to live in a house."

"I pity them too, but think of all the fun they must have on the rides." Molly stopped a moment to reflect. "Come to think of it, I don't remember ever seeing any children with a carnival."

"Me neither. But that's because their parents sell them."

"I don't believe that. That's just an old wives tale. But they sure are a queer lot all the same." Nora agreed.

"Did I ever tell you about the time Nuala Flynn and myself were in the Fair Green and this fellow from the carnival came up to us. He had a little dog with him, a Kerry Blue I think, and said that we could pat it."

"I don't think so."

"Well, I was only about twelve at the time and Nuala was eleven. He began to talk to us, saying what a lovely town Kilkenny was and how he always liked coming here. He used to be a boxer, he said, and had won a lot of medals in the ring, but had to give it up when he hurt his back. That was when he joined the carnival. He walked around with us for a while chatting about himself and his little dog. Its name, he told us, was Towser and he had rescued him from a burning house. It never occurred to us that he might be lying. But after a while the dog wandered off and wouldn't come back when he called to it.

'Ah, let him go then,' was all he said, not even bothering to go after it. Then he asked if we liked Rainbow toffees. We said we did and he gave a laugh, saying what a coincidence for didn't he happen to have some in his trousers pocket.

He told Nuala to put her hand in and take one and she did. But of course there were no sweets and no pockets either. All Nuala could feel was a big hot lump of flesh. It took her a minute to tumble, and when she went to pull her hand out he wouldn't let her. He clamped his own hand down and kept it there. He seemed such a nice man too. Yet we should have guessed he was up to something the way he kept looking around as though making sure no one else was watching."

"Did you ever tell anyone about it?" Molly asked.

"Not then we didn't. Nuala was too embarrassed, for what did she know about sex poor thing?"

"What did any of us know back then, or know now for that matter. It's all a mystery to me."

"Maura Hogan told me you can get a baby just by lying close to a man and praying."

"And you believed her."

163

"Of course I didn't, but that's what she believes." Nora looked around her absent-mindedly. "I don't know what we'll do when the carnival is gone."

"The same as we did before I guess. Not that we saw much of it this time around, with all that rain we've had."

"Where to now?" Nora asked when they had finally left the grounds.

"I don't know, let's just walk and see what happens."

"Why don't we walk to the Ball Alley and see if any of the lads are there?"

"Way out on the Freshford Road! It's a long hike, Nora. Still, I suppose we have nothing better to do. I have to be home by six, though, I promised Mam"

The Ball Alley, cold, damp and little used, was built entirely of concrete with only one door and absolutely no adornment. It was no place for girls and used mainly by boys, though one or two girls did at times frequent it. The girls were standing outside the door debating whether or not to enter when a male voice called out to them.

"Are you planning on going inside, or what?" Eamon Devlin came up behind them. Nora recognized the voice and swung around excited.

"We didn't hear you coming, did we Molly?" she exclaimed, her face alight with a dazzling smile. Everyone knew she had a crush on Eamon, despite the fact he was a proper scamp and had no respect for girls. A handsome lad with a charming smile who could talk a rattlesnake out of its skin, he honestly believed that God had created the female form solely for his gratification. Nora's interest worried Molly because she'd heard through the grapevine that Eamon had put a young girl in the family way, and she didn't want the same thing to happen to her friend. Eamon had taken her to the pictures once, said all the silly things boys say to girls, and Nora believed every word of it.

"Is there anyone in there? Have you been inside?" Nora asked, merely to keep his attention focused.

"Well, there's no game going on, if that's what you mean. I think the place is empty." Molly felt like asking what he was doing there then.

"We could have saved ourselves a trip," she said beneath her breath, as Nora suggested they go inside. "For what?" Molly asked, "if there's nobody in there."

Eamon sighed. "Wait here and I'll have a look." He touched Nora's arm before pulling open the door and then disappeared inside." After a minute he came back out. "All clear, you can come in if you like."

The girls moved warily inside the door and looked around. The whole place was filthy, with spent matches, cigarettes butts and paper cartons strewn about the floor. The stench of urine was overpowering. "Looks like this place hasn't been used in ages," Molly said. "I'm not going to hang around in here, I'm going outside. Maybe we should think about going home."

"I don't fancy that long walk back again, with no shade or anything, do you?" Molly knew Nora was only saying that because she didn't want to miss her chance with Eamon.

"I know a short-cut to the river," he offered then, "it's a nicer walk home, if you're interested."

He led them across the road to the other side and over a low stone wall. "It's only a narrow footpath mind, a bit rough in places, but I think it will get us there."

The short cut proved a nightmare of obstruction with knee-high weeds and fallen trees, and hordes of overgrown nettles wrestling for position on a few inches of soil. When at last they scrambled through the bushes and out the other side, Molly couldn't believe the ladders in her stockings and the scratches on her legs.

"Trust you Eamon Devlin," she growled, "only a total imbecile would take a girl through that." Eamon shrugged. They found a dry spot beside the river and sat down. Eamon had taken off his shoes and socks and went paddling in the water. Molly made a pillow of her cardigan and the girls lay back on it looking up at the sky. It was a glorious day indeed, the sky blue and fathomless, and except for the rippling of the river and the twittering of birds in the trees nearby, there was not another sound. A great and blessed silence surrounded them.

Molly had almost fallen to sleep when she heard Nora yelp. She came awake immediately and sat upright. A small dog had wandered over and was sniffing at their legs. Nora, who disliked dogs immensely, grabbed a stick from a nearby bush and began to shoo it off.

"Leave it alone Nora, can't you see it's friendly, it won't harm you."

No sooner had she said it than they saw the bushes parting and there stood Michael Brannigan. His face beamed when he saw her and she felt her heart begin to race. "Well, hello again," he said, with a pleasant smile, his eyes washing over her, taking in her face, her huge brown eyes, dark shoulder-length hair and smashing figure, much prettier than he had remembered.

"Is this your dog?" Nora demanded curtly unaware of who he was. He nodded that it was. "Well you ought to take better care of it." Molly could feel herself getting red for she hadn't told Nora they had already met. One evening on her way home from work she had run into him and he had walked with her to their front door. She had liked him right away and knew instinctively that he liked her.

"Do you mind if I sit down?" Michael asked.

"No, not at all," Molly said, making room for him and glad that he had asked. It was at that moment Eamon chose to return from the river. He said hello to Michael, played a moment with the dog and then pulled on his shoes and socks. Nora moved beside him.

"Are you up for a bit of exploring?" Eamon asked. "I'll show you where I used to live? It isn't far, just over there beyond the fields." Nora stared at him. The only houses she knew of around these parts were those in Talbot's Inch.

"I didn't know you came from there," she said. "Did you hear that Molly? He's from Talbot's Inch." Molly gave her a *couldn't care less* look, not wanting to be involved.

"Well, I've never been there and I'd like to go," Nora said, rising and brushing down her skirt. "Why don't you come Molly," she suggested lamely, knowing full well that Molly would say no.

"I'd rather stay here and talk awhile, if that's all right with you?"

"Suit yourself," Nora shrugged, glad at the chance of being alone with Eamon. They started off across the field.

"We'll cut through over there," Eamon said, pointing to an opening in the hedge. "We'll take this path," he said, when they got there, and pointed to a trodden-down track of vegetation leading off to a wide expanse of grassy land. "Just follow me and stay close behind." Nora had heard about this stretch of ground and knew that beyond a certain point the open fields would disappear, giving way to tall reeds and patches of boggy ground. It was considered a dangerous trek to anyone not familiar with the area and many accidents had been attributed to the swamp.

She thought she better mention this to Eamon, expressing her anxiety, but he just laughed. "Just follow me, don't worry. I've been there before. Look, we'll stay on this path, and when we reach the middle, we'll cut across to another track that will take us to dry land." She was to stay behind him on the path, and watch her step. She nodded that she understood and moved along behind him, feeling for the ground with every step. When they reached the middle, Eamon waited for her to catch up and without speaking, pointed to another path branching to the right, then hurried off along it.

All at once, green walls of rushes began closing in around her and the soil became damp and squashy, with black gaping holes of water glistening in the sun. Looking at the water, Nora began to feel afraid. She could see no sign of Eamon and knew they were heading into even taller reeds. Slowly and cautiously she moved along, trying to keep up. At times, one could scarcely tell where the path was, and once or twice her feet sank into water. Around her the air was filled with the buzzing sound of insects and here and there, through an opening in the reeds, an animal form went scurrying. She kept calling out for Eamon, terrified of continuing, yet frightened to turn back. In an effort to avoid the water, she put one foot forward in a giant step, and the ground in front of her moved away. She screamed and called again for Eamon. Nothing could induce her to move another step. In the loudest voice she could muster, she called his name again, and just when she thought he had left her there to drown, she saw him coming through the reeds. He looked angry.

"Why are you screaming? Why can't you just follow me?" Then seeing the panic on her face, his voice softened. "What's the matter? You're not afraid are you, because if you are you needn't be? Here give me your hand." Nora extended hers, the anger she had felt a moment earlier melting with the romance of his touch. They plunged onward through the reeds, this time with Eamon marking every step. At one point he stopped and pointed up ahead.

"Do you see that big house over there?" he asked, and she looked and saw the red-roofed house way up on the hill. "That's where we're going. The village is just beyond, but we can't stay on this path, we'll have to sneak through there." Nora nodded eagerly, the spell of her dread already broken. It wasn't long before their feet found terra firma and, leaving the marsh to its denizens, they scampered up the slope to the grounds above.

An ancient Elm tree inside the fence told them in bold black lettering that there was *NO TRESPASSING* and with venerable respect they made their way a little further down to a less forbidding spot. Here the ground elevated to a steep mound and they could see over the wall to the grounds beyond. They climbed up and looked out over the land they were about to cross. It was not just another field, however, it was the well-cared for grounds of the big house on the hill and Nora was apprehensive.

"I don't know, Eamon. Are you sure it's okay?"

"Of course it is," Eamon lied, knowing full well that the grounds were frequently patrolled. "Okay, here we go," he said, scaling the wall and dropping to the earth on the other side, remaining flat against the sloping ground listening. They heard nothing and Eamon gave the signal to proceed. So, they scurried up the slope, while keeping as close to the ground as possible. Nora was very conscious of the big house on top and hoped nobody was looking out the window. All went fine for a little while until half way up the hill Eamon heard a noise.

"What was that?" he whispered, jerking Nora closer to the ground. She raised her head a smidgen, but couldn't see a thing.

"Sounded like some kind of animal, but I can't be sure." They started off again, keeping close to the ground. There was a whisper of a sound somewhere above, and a movement of black against the outline of the sky. Then all at once a large black mare rose up in front of them, her newborn foal rising warily beside. She jerked her head upright, shaking her mane, then stood still with head erect, watching. Nora closed her eyes in terror, expecting to hear a stallion bearing down on them. But there were no galloping hooves, and no other sound, just the mare and her baby watching. Relief flooded over her.

"Over this way," Eamon whispered, heading for the wall that marked the boundary at the far end of the grounds. Within minutes they had reached it, and with the help of cautious footholds in the stones, they pulled themselves up and slithered over.

Below, nestling in the hollow of a bowl-shaped glen, lay the village of Talbot's Inch. Along the upper edges of the bowl, stood the larger, more stately homes of the rich and way down in the dip, but up a distance from the river, lay the red-bricked houses of the villagers. A hand-drawn pump, surrounded by a low concrete wall beside a wooden bench, filled an open space. They trudged across the road to the main street where the line of houses was broken by a tavern and a general store. The street was deserted except for an old man sitting on a chair outside an open door. All the houses looked neat and clean, their small front gardens filled with roses and wild flowers. They rested a moment by a makeshift railing where someone planned to build a church or City Hall, or something. Here they were regarded with suspicion by another old man wearing a large straw hat. He stared at them with inquisitive eyes, but did them the courtesy of raising his hat. Further along, a small brown dog was lifting its leg on a wireless pole, and nearby its owner, a grey-haired woman with a big belly and a baggy dress, stood calling it.

Eamon climbed up on an open tar barrel filled to the top with rainwater and balancing on the rim, looked out over the land to the river where a few men and boys were fishing. Close to where they were standing, lay an old wagon half filled with turnips, and in a field close by a man and boy were digging in the earth while a pretty girl, whom Nora guessed must be the sister, stood by and watched. A few seconds later she looked up and smiled, then started walking in their direction. She was tall and willowy with baby blue eyes, fair skin and curly blond hair. Without a word to Nora, Eamon darted off to speak with her, as he might an old friend, and Nora saw them stop to chat.

She heard the girl giggling. Saw her incline her head modestly, letting her hair spill down around her face, and she knew right away that Eamon was smooth talking her. Her bubbling energy deflated. Not only did he make no effort to include her, but had the gall to walk right past as if she were not there. Embarrassed and insulted, she made her way back up the hill. Her trip to Talbot's Inch had been a disappointment and she had no desire to stay.

She found a spot at the top of the hill beneath a tall oak tree and sat down to wait. She felt confident that Eamon would return shortly, to take her back. In the meantime she decided to relax and try to enjoy the countryside. "It's beautiful here," she told herself looking out across the fields. Far off in the distance the land was carved by low rolling hills and wide welcome valleys, and down in each valley bottom, rivers twisted and glistened in the sun. Here and there, a little stone farmhouse stood silently in an island of cultivated land, and way off in the distance, miles and miles of ever winding low stone walls climbed endlessly into the hills to make a criss-cross pattern over the whole countryside.

A gentle breeze was stirring the air as she listened to the rustle of the murmuring leaves. Looking up through their maze of dappled light to the blue sky beyond and the silent floating clouds, she was glad that she had come. Some minutes passed before she began to feel acute discomfort in a vital center of her body. She looked about her hopefully and saw a house, surrounded by a privet hedge just one field away. Without lingering, she set off. Squeezing through a narrow opening in the hedge, she emerged in a field on the other side. She could see the house quite clearly and made a dash for it. A lady directed her around the back to the facility outdoors. Nora wanted to thank her before she left but the lady had gone back inside the house. So, she made her way across the grounds to the nearest hedge and clambered through the bushes, believing it to be the field she had come through. She raced across to the other side and clambered through the bushes there, expecting to see the big oak tree and the village down below.

But all she saw were wide, open fields and tall swaying grass. Somehow she had gotten it all mixed up, and couldn't remember which way she had come. She ran to the next field and forced her way through the brambles, which grew larger and less penetrable with every step she took. Soon she was running every which way, tripping and falling over everything, until finally she came down heavily on a half-buried log, scraping her leg quite painfully. Up to this point she had been in a daze, not thinking or acting intelligently. The sudden sting had brought her to her senses and she sat down on the rotted wood to examine it.

There was a long red weal down the side of her leg but the wound wasn't deep, though it stung like an angry hornet. Though her heart was beating wildly, she finally managed to find her wits. There was little point in going on, she thought, because she had no idea where she was. The sensible thing to do was to find the house and start again from there. She remembered now that she had come in at the front of the house, but had left from the back. No wonder she got lost. With difficulty, she located the house again and made her way around the front. From there she was able to locate the field she had originally come through.

When she got back she found the hill still empty. There was no sign of Eamon. Where in the name of God could he have gone? Surely he hadn't gone back without her? In desperation, she went back down the hill to look for him. But there was nobody about but an old beggar man with a devious face and lascivious grin, his large discolored teeth jutting over his bottom lip. His ragged coat was tied around the middle with a string, and he had long hair and a dirty beard. Nora, weary and afraid to approach him, had come to the point of weeping. Her only alternative was to knock on someone's door and ask for help.

She had started toward a house when over the crest of the hill came a literal apparition. The tallest man she had ever seen. He was hatless and swinging a great walking stick, his long tweed-clad figure with a yellow buttonhole, matching the sunshine of the day. He came down the hill with ponderous steps, singing loudly, and Nora began to walk in his direction. He stopped when she was in front of him, lowering the brushes above his eyes to scrutinize her. She told him what had happened and asked if there was a safer route back to the river, and if so would he kindly direct her. He broke into laughter, inquiring about her age and where she was from. When she told him he just bellowed.

"Can you beat that now? Sure I know the city well." Many a trip he had taken there, he said, just to visit a girl, or spend an evening listening to the brass band on the Grand Parade. A trip down memory lane soon followed and Nora did her best to listen patiently. When finally he had said enough, he lowered himself to her level, and turning her in the direction of the river pointed with his stick to a barely visible opening in the reeds, in a spot much closer to the bank. It was a longer but safer path he said, and wondered why Eamon hadn't taken it.

"Keep to the solid path now mind and it will take you directly to the river." He had traveled it only yesterday, he said, and found it to be safe. Thanking him profusely, Nora raced away. When she reached the opening, she looked back and found him watching. She waved in gratitude, for she was relieved to find the path, not only wider than it had first appeared but firm and unobstructed. With optimism restored she hurried on, and when at last she heard a voice and saw Molly up ahead, she knew she was safely back.

"Where did you get to?" Molly demanded as soon as she caught sight of her. "I was just about to go home. You had me that worried." She looked about for Eamon. "And where may I ask is Romeo?" Nora told her everything, trying to sound nonchalant, and conceal her disappointment.

"I looked everywhere for him, but couldn't find him anywhere."

"Well, that's what comes of trusting a fairyman like Eamon Devlin. How many times have I warned you about him? Maybe now you'll take my advice and stay away from him." She took Nora's hand in genuine relief.

"Yeah, I know that now, but I had to find out for myself, though, didn't I?" Nora confessed. "I'll tell you this, though. It's the last time I'll be taken in by him, and if he thinks he's going to get away with it, he's out by the side of it."

Molly said nothing, for she knew that Nora was letting off steam, and that the first kind word from Eamon would have her panting at his heels.

"So, where did your man go? And who is he anyway? I don't remember seeing him around."

"Well, I don't suppose would you? He's new in town. He's the one your mother was talking about, Michael Brannigan."

"Oh yeah. Now that you mention it, I think I have seen him coming out of Mass. How come he left you all alone?"

"He stayed for as long as he could, but he had to be back by a certain time. His uncle lives on the Granges Road, and it was his dog he was walking. I almost walked back with him when you didn't come."

"You like him then I take it?"

"I do indeed and I think he likes me. He's a good sort Nora, quiet-like and shy, not like the lads we're used to." She delved into her pocket and drew something out. "Look what he gave me! It's a Claddagh ring. It was too small for his finger, so he gave it to me.

"That sounds promising. He must like you so. Does it mean wedding bells I wonder?" Molly laughed.

"Hold on a minute now and give us a chance."

"Why aren't you wearing it?"

"I don't know. It's stupid I suppose, but I was afraid he might think me eager if I put it on. I'm seeing him tonight in any case."

"Where does he live?"

"Well, he used to live out this way with his uncle, but he now has a room in town. He works at the Brewery don't you see, and wants to be close to the office."

"A white collar worker? Aren't you the lucky one? I believe they make good money in the Brewery."

"On the floor, maybe, but I don't know about the office. It's steady work at any rate." Nora consulted her watch.

"What time is it?" Molly asked.

"It must be after four," Nora tapped the dial of her watch. "It's hard to tell with this thing, it's stopped again."

"I make it four-fifteen, but mine might be slow. It's time to go in any case." They started to walk. "I think we should stay on this path. It's a longer way home but I couldn't face that short cut again."

"Nor I," Nora said, "I've had enough adventures for one day." They walked in silence for a little while, each in their own little world. Molly knew that Nora was thinking about Eamon and wished for Nora's sake they had never met. As though reading her mind, Nora said. "I still can't believe what he did to me. I wish to God I didn't feel the way I do about him, but I can't help it."

"You'll get over it. When the right lad comes along."

"When will that be, when I'm sixty-five?"

Molly fell into a pensive mood, her head bent, her eyes glued to the ground in front of her. Nora, puzzled, took her arm.

175

"A penny for your thoughts Mol," and they fell again into conversation. In under an hour they were back in town. Later that night Molly went to sleep happy, thinking about all that had happened earlier. From a distance, she had seen Michael waiting for her outside the Metropole Hotel and she had hurried her step, wondering how long he'd been waiting.

"I'm sorry. I got held up," she said, when he saw her and came toward her. "Have you been waiting long?"

"Not very long, but I was beginning to think you weren't coming." She apologized again, explaining about her mother and the chores she had to help with. "Well, you're here now and that's all that matters," he said, the fine lines radiating from the corners of his eyes and crinkling when he smiled. "You look nice," he added, "blue suits you."

"Oh, go on with you," she said, blushing at the admiration in his look.

"Where would you like to go?" he asked then, and Molly said she didn't mind, but that she really had enough of walking. "There's a good picture showing at the Regent, Gregory Peck and Anthony Quinn," Michael suggested, and Molly smiled to let him know that she agreed. In the cinema he had put his arm around her, and pulled her close, when he took her home he had kissed her again and again. She felt ashamed about the feelings creeping over her as she snuggled into him. He had been aware of her affect on him for weeks, he admitted, but was too shy to approach her.

"You must have known I was interested, the way I kept looking at you?" Molly pretended she hadn't noticed, but the beating of her heart almost gave her away.

"When can I see you again?" he asked, "would tomorrow be too soon?" Molly laughed and asked if he was serious.

"Of course I'm serious. More serious than I have ever been in my whole life." Molly found she couldn't answer. Here was the man she'd been waiting for, gentle, considerate and nice looking. Someone she could love. Too excited to sleep, she lay awake thinking over every minute she had spent with him and dreaming ahead to their next rendezvous. She felt happy and contented, with good reason at last to hope.

THE COMRADES

It was almost midnight and old Jim Cassidy sat alone in his kitchen watching for signs of water seeping under his back door. It had been raining heavily for more than a week and the river behind his house had been rising steadily all day. Earlier in the evening he had gone to look and saw that the water had burst its banks and broken through a gap in the stone wall at the bottom of his garden. He had watched helplessly as it crept slowly, inch by inch toward his back door. He wished now he had left the house when he still had time and wondered whether he could make it as far as his friend Dan Ryan's house.

All that lifting earlier had weakened him. Everything he could possible lift he had lifted and dragged up to the loft, or stacked on shelves and tables in the room below. Even the bedclothes and the mattress he had managed to drag up and what books he had had no room for, he had moved to higher shelves. Not that he expected things to be that bad, but you could never tell. One thing he knew for certain now, the water would come in. He had been outside to check on it and had never seen the river so demented, or rise with such ferocity. It had taken him by surprise, the roar of it almost deafening. Like a thing alive it was, willful and treacherous, straining at the chance to burst its chains and show itself stronger than man or God.

Yet, the river wasn't all that was on his mind. For months he had been aware of a queerness in his head. A sort of light-headedness which left him at times in a state of shock, when he would have no memory of certain times or actions. There was no warning of its coming. It simply came and went, as though a trigger were pulled in the depths of his subconscious. At times he could sense a numbness gather in his brain, then rise like bubbles to the surface of his mind before dissolving in a wave of dizziness. About ten days ago it had been like that, but he had had no loss of memory, so he had let it pass. Now it had come back again. Only a short while earlier, while standing in the scullery, something had sent a tremor through his head and all the way down to his shoulder, and in the very instant of reaching for a chair, had caught him in the grip of excruciating pain. Some minutes later, he had picked himself up from the scullery floor.

Now he was sitting on the edge of his chair debating whether to take a friend's advice and seek shelter someplace else, or wait it out as he had done before. If only Dan had been home when he called on him earlier. He hated to bother him now at this late hour, but surely he would understand. Jim got up from his chair and looked around for his coat and scarf, found them and put them on. His cane was in the scullery. He flicked on the light and went in search of it, but no sooner had he got it firmly in his hand than the first rush of water crashed against the house. The back door flew open on it hinges, knocking him back against the wall. He could feel the current pulling at his feet as he flattened his body against a beam trying to keep upright. The force of the water frightened him for he could barely keep his balance. *Where in heaven's name is it all coming from?*

It was a question left unanswered for the present, for unknown to Jim the arch under which the water flowed, and located near the bottom of his garden, had become constricted. The dead body of a cow, together with bits and pieces of furniture, had jammed against the opening causing the river to divert its flow directly toward his house.

Like a great tide it rushed along the garden path, through the scullery to the room beyond, and slammed with force against the inside of the front door, before doubling back and flowing in a whirlpool around the room. The heavy table in the middle of the floor, which he had earlier stacked with furniture, began at first to wobble, before sliding backward toward the wall, cramming itself into the narrow hall. Disbelieving, and too dazed to move, he had stood there watching until it occurred to him that he was wasting time. In order to get to the outer door, he would have to move that table. Carefully, he fought against the swirling water, avoiding planks and other objects being swept in through the open door. With all his strength he pushed against the table, finally dislodging it. But try as he might, he could not budge the door. Picking his way around the table, he made his way to the window. Never in a million years could he squeeze through the tiny frame, but maybe he could attract someone's attention.

Drawing back the curtain he looked outside. All he could see was water, all the way down to the corner of the street, with nobody in sight and nothing to be heard but the sound of it lapping and sucking against the walls. My God! He thought with imminent alarm, I'm surrounded. Pulling down the top half of the window, he stuck his head out to get a better view. He wished now he had modernized the windows as he always had intended, made them larger and more in keeping with the times. The house, a small brick bungalow, was located in a lane at the bottom of a steep hill and hidden from view by a stand of trees. It had been the only one left standing after all the others had been demolished to make room for new development. It was an old house, one of those where you came in the front door and walked out the back.

To the right of it, where the river passed underneath the bridge, the water looked deep and treacherous, but to the left, where the lane ended and opened out onto a street it was still shallow. If only he could get the front door open. The only other way out was through the back door, and he couldn't see how he could manage that without the risk of being sucked into the river. The only chance he had now was in the loft. Quickly he made his way back into the scullery, fighting to keep his feet aground. Luckily the trap door was still open and the ladder hanging free. But the water rushing through the open door prevented him from reaching it. Time was running against him now, the water already around his hips. He simply had to get to it. With one great heave, he flung his body forward and grabbed the side of the ladder, holding tight and groping with his foot for the lower rung. He found it and climbed up through the opening. Sitting aloft, he looked down into the water and could not believe the scene below. Never in all his years had he seen a flood so menacing. The rush of water through the door was unbelievable, and he had no way of knowing how deep it would get before rescue came. He had known floodwater to rise up in the morning and recede again before nightfall, but never in such volume. There was nothing he could do in any case, but wait and keep awake if possible.

The cold crept up around him as he removed his boots and sodden socks. The rest would have to wait 'til morning. At least he had the comfort of his overcoat and scarf. He tried to keep himself alert by making check marks on the wall below and counting off the minutes until the water reached each level. After a while, though, he began to tire and wanted desperately to sleep. There was little room inside the loft, or what he called a loft. A crawlspace was really all it was, with little room for standing and the only light from down below. Yet, he managed to locate the mattress and wearily crawled onto it, twisting and turning to find a comfortable spot. He tried sitting up straight but that was no good. So, he went back to lying down again, but couldn't stretch his legs. By midnight they had begun to cramp, the tightening in his calves tormenting him.

Funny, he thought, the way things turn out. When his wife had died ten years before, he too had wanted death. Had thought about it constantly. Only the dishonor of such an action had prevented him from doing it. Instead, he had gone on living, while knowing in his heart that it was he who should have died. How time changes everything, he thought. At least when Mary died she had someone left to mourn her, and died knowing it. But what if he should die alone here in the attic? Who would mourn him? Not many, he thought, for he had few friends left. A few ill-chosen words to an ill-chosen clergyman had taken care of that. Had, set him adrift on a current of derision, when all he had been trying to do was to get his point across. Dispel the notion that the people were to blame for the lack of faith. Jokingly, he had put forth his argument, sure that the priest would understand. Instead, the priest had turned on him, denounced him as a heretic.

"People around here can do without that kind of thinking," he replied. It seemed to him, he said, that it was people like Jim and their Protestant way of thinking that had been what cursed the Irish. Never thinking for a moment he had said anything offensive, he had concealed his astonishment and turned away. But then on impulse he had turned back.

"If there's a curse on Ireland, father, it was not the likes of me, or the Orangeman, who put it there."

For those words alone, he had become a marked man, a dangerous one, one to be preached about from the pulpit. Lord! How he had suffered on account of it. Parishioners asking how he had the gall to speak to a priest like that. Some afraid to speak to him. Avoiding him. Shunning him. Until in the end he had begun despising them. Except for one or two loyal friends he had overnight become outcast. Admittedly, the continuity was largely his own doing, for though the priest had long ago

apologized and they become good friends, he could never find it
in his heart to forgive the so-called-friends who had so readily
forsaken him. Instead, he simply avoided them.

Let them think what they like, he told himself. People are the
same the world over, here today and gone tomorrow. Fragments
of the past began to come alive in the deep caverns of his mind,
as he thought about the summer of his eighteenth birthday when
he had experienced an event he would never forget. He was
alone at the time, lounging outside a jewelry shop in Carlow
pretending to be looking at something in the window, while
waiting for a certain girl to go by. It had been raining and the
streets were almost empty. But looking up, he had seen Paddy
Pearce coming toward him on the path. Paddy, a big strapping
lad a few years older than himself, had been a boxer in his teens.
He had big broad shoulders and football fists. His mop of ginger
hair, so thick you couldn't pull a comb through it, made him
stand out in a crowd. As usual he seemed in a lively mood,
swaggering and grinning.

But it was hard to tell with Paddy, for he was always grinning.
Jim often wondered what on earth he had to grin about, since
everyone knew he had a miserable life with a bully of a father
who drank every penny he earned, too often leaving the family
hungry, forcing them to beg food from the neighbors. Though
Paddy never mentioned it, Jim couldn't help noticing the
constant bruises on his face and arms. Later on, it had occurred
to him that it may have been the reason Paddy took up boxing
in his teens.

The eldest son in a family of five, he had been kicked out of
school when still a lad for lack of a brain to learn with. What
people failed to understand was that he had Dyslexia, and
couldn't read. But he was an honest lad with a big heart and Jim
had always liked him. Slapping him heartily on the back, Paddy
asked how he was keeping and the two fell into easy

conversation. They had been chatting for a while before Paddy said he had some business to transact inside the shop and asked if Jim would accompany him. Curious as to what business Paddy might possibly have in a jewelry shop, Jim followed him in.

The shop was in semi darkness, getting ready to close up, and Paddy stood for a moment looking around, his eyes searching every corner. The only other person in the shop was the woman behind the counter. She had been counting the day's receipts and didn't bother to look up. Without a word of warning, Paddy pulled out a flicker knife and shot the blade open. Then he stepped up to the counter. He had pulled a scarf up around his face but Jim had not noticed until the woman screamed. The knife was at her throat before he knew what had happened. He saw Paddy grabbing up the pound notes from the till and stuffing them in his pocket. Only then did he realize what was happening.

"Paddy, for God Almighty's sake...," he began, but Paddy glared at him and told him to shut up. Jim couldn't believe it was happening and told himself it had to be a prank, because this wasn't the Paddy Pearce he knew. The lad he had grown up with. The one he had played with in the streets, gone to school with, and spent whole weekends sparring in the ring. That Paddy, couldn't possibly pull a knife on anyone. He tried again to talk to him, but every time he opened his mouth Paddy glared menacingly and waved the knife. Jim was hoping that nobody would come in and maybe make things worse, for he didn't like the look on Paddy's face and knew he wasn't thinking straight.

No sooner had the thought passed through his mind than the shop door swung open and a little old lady walked in. The sound of the entry bell caused Paddy to swing around, the scarf slipping from his face. For a split second, the woman stared at him before throwing up her arms and making for the door. Paddy, intending only to detain her, grabbed her by the arm, the knife still open in his hand and accidentally grazing her ear. The woman struggled and began to scream, causing Paddy to panic and look around him wildly. Jim could see the fear in his eyes as he held the knife in front of her, warning her to be quiet. The woman instantly fell silent. Stunned, and unable to absorb what was happening, Jim hadn't moved. Everything was happening too quickly. Apart from an anxious glance at the frightened woman, he remained where he was standing.

"That's better now," Paddy sighed, closing up the knife and returning it to his pocket. Then he turned to Jim.

"See you around Jim boy," he winked, and quickly left the shop. Struck by the audacity, and too dazed to think about what to do, Jim foolishly followed him out. Recovering from her shock, the shop woman raced after him, yelling for a passerby to hold him. He had had no part in the robbery. Not lifted a finger in support of the thief yet, to his astonishment, both women swore an oath before the judge that he had been an accomplice.

Not wanting to incriminate Paddy further, Jim decided to not say a thing, for he knew in his heart that if they got their hands on Paddy, they would lock him up for life. He couldn't be the one to sanction that. Paddy was closer than a brother to him. He had been an orphan with no real family of his own when Paddy had befriended him, and Jim had clung to the outstretched hand, as a drowning man might to a rescuer. He had known Paddy only as a gentle man, and never once saw him do a wicked thing, much less commit a crime. So, how could he willingly betray him?

For that bit of loyalty, he had served seven years. *So where is the luck in that?* he asked himself, remembering what the midwife had told his mother. 'He'll be lucky all his life missus', she supposedly said, when the caul was removed from around his head. *Well I could tell her a thing or two.* When he came out of prison he was twenty-five and couldn't find a job. He decided to move to Kilkenny where people wouldn't know him and wouldn't be ashamed to be seen with him. Two years later he landed a job on the railway line, met Mary at the farmer's market and fell in love. He had seen her standing at one of the stalls, polishing the fruit. A plain looking girl with a friendly smile, she had looked around when she saw him coming. He had walked right up to her and began to talk, mainly about the merchandise and then about the weather. Laughing, she asked his name and where he was from and before he knew it, he was pouring out his story.

Mary had listened carefully to every word he said, and when he finished she had said nothing, just studied him a moment before holding out her hand.

"'Tis a pleasure to meet you Jim Cassidy." Jim took the hand she offered and at that very moment he knew he loved her. The following Saturday morning he asked her for a date and they started walking out. One year later they were married.

Life had been happy with Mary around. She had a jolly disposition and they seldom quarreled. Within six years she had borne him two fine sons and a lovely daughter. Sadly, they had lost little Una when she was only three to the onslaught of Diphtheria. But the boys had grown to manhood, and later had gone their separate ways, one to die on the beaches of Normandy and the other to seek his fortune in Australia. He was sixty-one when Mary died and he hadn't seen them since. But it was Mary he missed the most. She had been the jewel around which his life revolved.

A grand, wholesome woman with a large heart and a jovial manner, she never lost her head in any situation and always knew what to say or do. In their life together she had been his friend and confidante. He hated to think about the day she died. Dropped dead in her own back garden. He remembered the incident clearly. It was nearing sunset that Sunday afternoon when she got up from the kitchen table where she had been writing a letter.

"I think I'll take a walk outside, I could do with a little fresh air."

Those were the last words she ever said to him. It had been in his head to follow her out, but some little task had kept him inside. He had never forgiven himself for that. Yet with the way things were going now he might follow her tonight, drowned like a rat in his own loft. For the first time since she died, tears threatened him and overcome with a sudden grief, he turned his face into the blanket and finally fell asleep.

Later that night, the water had receded and by morning the river was back inside its banks, and shortly after dawn, Jim stiffly descended the ladder and went outside to have a look around. The piles of muck and scattered junk made it difficult to walk and the grass, which had been blowing in the wind just the day before, was either beaten up or flattened. *No matter, it will come back again,* he thought. It was then he saw the dead cow lying in the garden beside the river. He walked over to have a look, and that was when he saw the dog, a black and white cocker spaniel with a large bare patch on its head. Miraculously, it was still alive. With difficulty he lifted it and undoing the buttons on his coat held to his chest, trying to share with it the only heat he had to offer. Then he carried it down the road to Dan Doherty's house where he knew it would be looked after.

It was a while before things got back to normal, and by that time Jim had learned that he was dying. The irony of it! He had discovered the lump a few weeks before the flood, while shaving one morning at the mirror. Behind his ear it was, and jutting up through his hair like a ripe crab apple. It must have come up overnight he had decided when he first saw it, for he hadn't noticed it before. Could it be an insect bite, he wondered, though it looked too big for that? Later the following week he had been to see a doctor.

"It isn't cancer is it doctor? Surely, it isn't that?" Lightly he touched the malevolent lump. "Some sort of cyst I reckon." The doctor shook his head.

"It's hard to say what it is at this point, we'll know more when we've had a look inside. But it's not a cyst, I can tell you that." Jim jerked his head defiantly, the incautious movement sending a jab of pain along his neck and shoulder.

"Couldn't we just wait and see what happens? Who knows, it may be gone again in a day or two."

"It's not going to go away Jim. If anything it will get bigger." Depleting all his arguments, Jim finally agreed and the surgery had been scheduled for the following week. He had walked alone to the County Hospital. Never having been in a hospital before, he was filled with apprehension. Before passing through the door he tilted his head to one side in order to feel the lump, half hoping it had gone. But no, it was still there. In fact, in the last few hours it did seem to have grown bigger and was now pressing against his ear like a turnip.

At the hospital a pleasant nurse received him, handed him a long white form and told him to fill it in. He did as she requested and then she took it back and looked through it carefully, making a mark with her pencil here and there.

"It's not a big operation, is it?" Jim asked, feeling foolish and embarrassed. The nurse smiled.

"Not at all. Sure you'll be in and out before you know it." She examined the completed form and then emerged from behind the counter. "Come with me," she said, and walked along the hall in front of him. She stopped outside a door marked *changing room.* "In here," she pointed, pushing open the door, "you can change in there. Take everything off and put this on," she handed him a long, loose garment. "You can leave your clothes on the bureau there, and when you've undressed just make yourself comfortable in the room beyond until I come for you." She began to leave, then noticing the strained expression on is face, she lingered by the door. "Don't worry you'll be fine. There's nothing to it. It'll be over before you know it," and she squeezed his hand.

In the waiting room were two other patients, one lad standing by the window looking out into the grounds. The other, and nearest to the door, looked up and said hello. The one by the window turned his head and looked sullenly around. His head and neck were swathed in bandages and Jim couldn't help noticing the horrid burn marks on his face and nose. He found it hard to pull his eyes away.

"Lye," the lad closest to the door mouthed, his own face a disfigurement of rent and torn flesh. He continued jabbering but it was impossible to tell what he was saying, his puffed up lips distorting every word. The bottom lip was split apart and the upper one so swollen it was hard to see his nose. A second bruise beneath one eye was so puffed up it had almost swallowed his eye. *The result of a recent brawl no doubt,* Jim thought, and looked away disgusted. At that moment the patient by the window spun around and quietly left the room. A few moments later he came back again, repeating the procedure, walking back and forth across the room like a man possessed.

Jim was glad when the nurse returned. She was pushing a small trolley bearing toiletries, a bowl of tepid water, a shaving brush and razor and a small glass containing cold water. A clean white towel hung over her arm. From her pocket she withdrew a puck-sized pill and held it out to him.

"Here take this, it will help to calm your nerves." Jim thanked her and gulped it down with the water she held out. She laid the towel across his shoulder.

"Right so. The first thing we have to do is shave off all this hair." She took her place behind him. After that his conscious mind deserted him, though he vaguely remembered walking beside her to the operating room. When he woke again, his own head was swathed in bandages, and he began to wonder about the lump. Was it still there, or had they cut it out? The nurse wouldn't tell him anything. After a week they discharged him with a notice to report to the clinic to have the bandages removed. It was then they told him the crushing news.

"Why didn't you come to see me earlier?" the doctor scolded. "How could you overlook a thing like that? You must have had some indication there was something wrong?" Jim had lied and said he hadn't for he couldn't see the sense of a confession now. Words weren't going to change anything. A disturbing feeling of lightness ran through his body. The doctor was right. For months he had known there was something wrong, had felt the affects and seen the signs. But he had chosen to ignore them, telling himself it was nothing that it would go away. But it had only gotten worse. By now the tumor had taken hold and there was nothing they could do. He had already begun to lose the sight in one eye and had lost hearing in his ear. Yet even now, even hearing the truth from the doctor's lips, he didn't want to believe it. Still told himself it wasn't serious.

"A tumor doesn't necessarily mean death, though, does it? A person can live with a tumor, surely."

"That depends on where and what type of tumor it is," the doctor told him sharply. "In your case, well....," he left the sentence dangling.

"So I'm going to die then, is that what you're telling me? Well, the least you can do is tell me when." The doctor sighed and shook his head, but Jim persevered, all the while trying to sound blasé. "Don't worry, I can handle it. It matters little in any case, as I have nothing left to live for." The doctor gave him a penetrating look, and then thought a moment before he said.

"I can't predict a thing like that. Something under a year I should imagine."

All that had happened in the spring. Time had passed and four months later on a sunny day in August, Jim was standing by the kitchen sink rinsing the dishes from the mid-day meal. It had been a scorching hot morning and he had left the front and back doors ajar, to catch the cool breeze from the river, when he heard the front one squeak open. Glancing up he almost dropped the teapot. Both eyes by now had begun to fail and for a moment he couldn't tell who he was looking at. He took a few steps closer.

"Paddy Pearce? It can't be! What! Where?" Unable to believe his eyes, he found a chair and sank down onto it.

Paddy laughed and hurriedly crossed the floor to embrace him. Thunderstruck, Jim had no words with which to greet him. They hadn't seen each other in over forty years, and Jim couldn't think of a thing to say. Numbly, he stared at the withered face. The face of a man who had suffered much, so scarred and creased with signs of trial and punishment.

"'Tis a pure pleasure to set eyes on you again," Paddy said. "For a while there I almost gave up looking." Jim finally found his tongue.

"Pleasure indeed. I ought to have you shot for what you did to me. All that time I had to do for you." He tried his best to sound irate, but it was no use. There was no resentment in his heart; too many years had passed for that. Besides, he was thoroughly glad to see him.

"Aye, I heard about that," Paddy said, "I wish it hadn't happened, but there was nothing I could do at the time. I was that desperate. I don't know what came over me." He pulled a chair out from the table and sat down. "The money wasn't for me you see, it was for our Rosie."

"Rosie!" Jim exclaimed, suddenly remembering. Rosie was Paddy's baby sister, a shy, timid little girl about twelve years old, but with the mind of a backward five year old. Paddy worshipped her and when she was a child, Jim remembered, he used to take her everywhere, making her laugh by doing silly things or telling her funny stories. Every Sunday at Mass he would offer up a prayer for her, always with the hope that one day a miracle might happen and the *healing light* find its way into the black hole inside her head. But the miracle never happened. Instead, at thirteen, some loathsome creature had violated her. Nobody knew how it had happened, or who might be responsible.

"All I can tell you is it happened," Paddy said, "and I was damned if I was going to let her suffer more. I had to get her away, don't you see, but to do that I needed money." Seemed the day after the robbery, he had sailed across the channel with Rosie by his side.

"So what happened then?"

"I took her to a clinic in London where they looked after her. Then I took her to my sister's house in Birmingham, where she stayed until she died."

"So she did die then?"

"Almost thirty years ago."

"I'm sorry to hear that." Paddy shrugged.

"Ah sure," he said, his eyes brimming with tears. "What can I say? We knew she couldn't live forever, not the way she was. But she had a decent life while she was here, I saw to that."

"So you went back in the ring I take it."

"How can you tell?" Paddy laughed, patting his flattened nose. "It was the only job I could depend on under the circumstances. At first I moved all over England doing odd jobs wherever I could find them, in construction mainly, building here and pulling down there." But that was never reliable. So, in the end he had returned to boxing. In a way, Jim envied him, for as a young lad he had often dreamed of traveling, and of being an engineer. He had even taken a course on it one summer.

"Oh, I'm not complaining. I did well enough by it and managed to save a few bob," Paddy said.

"I take it you never married then?"

"Couldn't take the risk. I knew the guards would be looking out for me and I had Rosie to think about then." His troubled face grew grave, and suddenly with a passion he declared. "There isn't anything I wouldn't do to try to make it up to you. Anything I can do I will." He began to talk faster, not wanting Jim to interrupt. Several times Jim tried, but each time Paddy talked him down. "I had to find you, Jim. I had to tell you I was sorry and should never have done what I did that day. But I was so distracted at the time, I wasn't thinking straight and I needed the courage of your company. To this day I've regretted it. I would have given myself up then and there if it hadn't been for Rosie. I knew if anything happened to me they would put her in an institution, and I couldn't live with that. If there is any way that I can make it up to you." Jim shook his head.

"It's in the past now Paddy. I say we leave it there. Seeing you again is all the making up I need." The truth was he was glad for Paddy. Glad he had survived and not spent his years in prison. They hadn't seen each other in over forty years, yet the bond of friendship from their childhood days was still strong.

"You're not mad at me then?" Jim shrugged.

"For a while I was, but I'm not now," he answered, unable in retrospect to describe the conflicting feelings he had back then.

"How did you find me anyway?"

"Well, it was the funniest thing. I'd been looking for you for the longest time, but nobody could tell me where you'd gone. Then just a week ago I was having a drink in a pub in Waterford, when who should walk in but this woman I used to know. As a girl, she went to the same school we did. She told me she was working here at the County Hospital and had seen your name in the surgeon's book. I couldn't believe my luck. It was just a matter of checking then."

"Well, I'm glad you found me anyway."

"Not as glad as I am," Paddy said, delving in his pocket for the bottle he had brought. "I know you're not one for drinking Jim, but we can have a drop together this once, can't we?"

"To be sure we can," Jim agreed, and went to fetch the glasses.

And so the afternoon turned into evening, and by the time the sun went down, each man had learned all there was to learn about the other. The bewilderment on Paddy's face when he heard about the cancer, reminded Jim of that fateful day in the jewelry shop. For a second he was tempted to bring the subject up again, to have it out with Paddy, and make him realize what a terrible thing he had done to him. Although he had long ago forgiven him, he had never quite come to terms with the consequences. He began picturing the life he might have had, if the incident hadn't happened, he an engineer, traveling around the world, building bridges and the like. But Paddy had robbed him of that chance. *But to every coin there are two sides,* he reminded himself, for had that dream become reality he might never have met Mary. He stifled the urge to interrupt, and instead listened quietly to everything being said.

Paddy was telling him about the bad times he had had in England, having to move around from place to place, especially that first year. He had to take work where he found it, he said, and at times was lucky to have a roof above his head. The second year he was there he came down with pneumonia and almost died. For days he had gone without food or help, afraid to go to a hospital. In the end he had dragged himself to an almshouse, where they looked after him.

Listening to him speak, Jim's heart began to soften. It was clear he had had his share of suffering and was not a happy man. A man, who by his own admission, was still chained to the past and not because he wanted to be. He had never married, and not because he never wanted to. How could he not feel sorry for the man? The light through the little window was getting low and

Jim got up to light the lamp. Then sat down again. The slightest movement of his head was painful.

Perhaps it was because of the time they spent talking, or the two drinks he had consumed, but whatever it was, by nightfall Jim's spirits had sunk to the lowest ebb and he felt a strong compulsion to get up and leave the room. He watched as Paddy poured himself another drink.

"We'll make up for all the lost years now Jim boy," he was saying, outlining the activities he had in mind for them. The things they had both loved doing while growing up, fishing, hunting and racing hounds. Jim found he couldn't answer, for though neither of them said as much, each one knew these things would never happen.

As the minutes passed a sort of listless quality entered the conversation and for no explicable reason, Jim found himself resenting Paddy's presence, and wishing inwardly he would go, while trying at the same time not to think that way. Paddy, for his part, seemed to sense what Jim was thinking and could see that he was failing; yet he didn't want to leave. But finally he knew he would have to go. He had promised to be in Waterford by a certain hour to help a young lad get through his first big fight.

"Will you be all right here by yourself?" he had asked, rising and Jim had answered sharply.

Of course he would, why wouldn't he? All he wanted now was to lie down in his bed. He was tired, more tired than he had ever been before, and the pain kept shooting through his head making conversation impossible. As he undressed and climbed beneath the sheets he felt a chill pass over him. He lay down as he had longed to do, the thoughts inside his head tormenting him. He began immediately to reproach himself. How could he have been so callous, as to wish his old friend gone. After all, the man was only trying to help and had gone to a lot of trouble to find him.

He was not by nature an emotional man, but the look on his old friend's face when he realized what Jim was thinking, was not a thing he wanted to remember. He realized he had spoken with more force than he intended, his voice sharp and wounding. He could make no sense of it, none at all. Yet thinking about it wasn't going to help, he would have to make it up to him next time he came. Ideas on how to do so began to crowd his mind.

He lay on his back in the darkness thinking, and watching the moon peep in at him. If he moved his head just a little bit, he could see it clearly through the tiny window. One moment it seemed to be sitting there not moving, and the next it seemed to drift away - a cloud passing over. Jim had always loved the moon and remembered how, as a boy it had confounded him, constantly outrunning him, and passing him at every corner. No matter how hard he tried to beat it, it would always get there first.

"Sure that's because it's made of lightening," Tommy Wall would explain.

"Don't be daft. The moon is made of cheddar cheese, everybody knows that," his friend little Mug would challenge. Until Paddy, after moments of silent giggling, would put in.

"You're both wrong. How many times do I have to tell you? The moon is made of glow wood, and I know that for a fact."

"How? How do you know? Who told you?"

"The man in the moon is a friend of mine and he told me, that's how."

"Aw! You're crazy, Paddy Pearce."

Jim chuckled to himself. He could see his old friend clearly now, the silly grin on his big broad face, and the memory of their foolishness helped him to relax. Yet he couldn't sleep, just kept falling off and waking up again. When he woke the final time it was the middle of the night and the room was in total darkness. For a moment he just lay there sensing something different. The pain in his head had left him, and he felt totally at peace.

Instinctively, he knew he was going to die and could almost feel the moment coming. *No use struggling against the inevitable,* he thought, wishing only that Paddy were still there. It wasn't that he was afraid of dying, only of dying alone. At least there was consolation in the knowledge that there would be somebody left to mourn him after all.

Slowly he closed his eyes again, allowing himself to drift. Someone touched him lightly on the shoulder – and then a voice from nowhere.

"Jim love. Jim. Open your eyes." Jim did as the voice commanded and saw Mary sitting beside him on the bed.

"Oh Mary! Thank God you're here," and he took the hand she held out to him

A LAST LAMENT

One fine Sunday afternoon as the sun was slowly sinking in the sky, I lingered on the bank of the river, in a spot directly opposite the derelict mill, hoping to catch sight of the Old Man. It was a place we often met from the time of our initial meeting almost eight years before. I hung around for the longest time, hoping to see his figure appear along the path but I couldn't see him anywhere. After some minutes passed, I decided he wasn't coming and had started back along the path, intending to cross the river at the narrow strait to the other side and home, when all at once I saw him. He was sitting low beside the river, his body completely hidden in the long green grass, his little pet goat lying by his side. If I hadn't been looking out for him I might never have seen him. Only someone passing close by could have ever noticed them.

The afternoon, or early evening as it was now, had turned quite cool. Yet I noticed he had laid aside his coat and scarf and was dabbling at the water like a little boy. I hurried over to join him, and when he saw me coming he raised his hand in his usual salute.

"Is it trying to get your death you are, going without your coat on a day like this?" I was parodying his frequent criticism of myself. "I thought you had more sense than that." He threw his head back and laughed.

"Ah! There ye are!" he said, coughing and taking a few moments to recover, before picking up the book that lay open on his lap. He dug his cane firmly in the bank, and supporting himself on the crook of it, rose to welcome me.

"Ye don't think I'd be sitting here doing this if I had any brains now do ye?"

He was still a big man, solid around the shoulders, though I couldn't help noticing how grey he had become, his once thick hair grown wispy and thin, and his friendly old face weatherworn and tired. He seemed happy enough to see me and I was pleased, for I had of late being neglecting him. He asked how I was keeping and I told him fine.

"Ye look thin," he said, looking me over with a careful eye. "'Tis so long since I saw ye, I thought you'd left the country." Ignoring the sarcasm in his voice I helped him on with his coat and scarf.

"Left the country? Now, what would make you think a thing like that?"

"'Tis what all the youngsters nowadays are doing, and I can't say as I blame them. Sure, there's nothing here for them. Given a chance and a few years youth, and I'd be off myself." There was nothing unusual about his words but I knew by the tone, he was out of sorts. I pretended not to notice the dark tenor of his voice, as I made a wide sweep with my arms around the valley.

"What! And leave all this. You can't be serious!"

The wrinkles on his face contracted and he gave a short laugh, but there was little joy in it. "Aye, and there won't be much of that left to care about at the rate they're going." He glared across the river to the scene beyond and the newly laid road slicing through the hills. Only weeks before that area had been green, virgin land with towering oaks and tall elm trees more than a century old. Now it was a barren wasteland.

"Why couldn't they have left it the way it was? We have no need of it," he moaned, analyzing its potential and its problems.

"The new road you mean?" I asked, intending to add that it was sadly needed.

But he had turned away from me, his eyes taking in the valley and settling scornfully on the piles of sand and corporation signs strewn out along the way. At one point in the road a cloud of smoke, from something the workmen left burning, meandered upward to the sky, and here and there the flat shape of a cottage recently demolished.

"Haven't they taken enough of the land already?" without fouling up the countryside with their motor cars and fuel-driven carriages."

I guessed he was referring to our affluent friends. People like the Blundens, the Belles, and the Smithwicks, whose estates spread out across the land. Contemptuously, he spat into the river, as though to demonstrate disgust for the egregious humiliations their kind had heaped on our kind through the ages. Then quite suddenly he said.

"Come then, we'll take a walk," and grasping his little goat by the rump he pushed her out in front of him and strode off along the trail, without bothering to check whether I was following. In all the time I had known him he had never done that. Not until we had reached the spot where the trail ended and opened out onto the bank did he stop and wait for me. I caught up with him and fell into step beside him, curious to know what else he had to say.

We continued out along the bank as we had many times before. The long green fields stretched away on either side, and in the distance one or two cars passed noisily along the gravel road. He shook his head dejectedly but said nothing. Clearly something was upsetting him, something other than the road, for I had never seen him in such a mood. I had known him always as a tolerant man, not given to ugly moods, and less inclined to criticize or moralize than most. I wondered whether he had drink in him? Earlier I had thought I detected a faint smell of liquor on his breath, but having no reason to support that thought I had dismissed it.

Picking up the threads of his earlier complaint, he began again. "When I was a lad there was none of that. People weren't afraid to walk. They'd walk for miles and think nowt of it. Nowadays they want everything made easy." I couldn't see the harm in it myself, and told him so without reservation. He leaped on my remark like an animal on fresh kill.

"Of course ye can't. How could ye? The outcome of these things is never clear at first, and can only be seen in the perspective of time."

"But surely that applies to everything?" I insisted, and he heaved a heavy sigh, neither agreeing nor disagreeing. I had opened my mouth to speak again when he interrupted.

"Hold your horses now and let me explain, and don't be trying to tell me what I know better." He stopped to take in breath. "What I'm trying to get across to you is this. Improvements are a good thing in and of themselves, and are always welcome when made for the right reason. But that's not always the case now is it?"

He described to me a number of cases in his own experience where, in the pretence of improvement, entire families were evicted from their homes and forced to live like animals in the fields. There was too much greed and selfishness in the world, he said, with minorities of powerful people constantly devising ways of imposing hardship on the poor. A shadow of pain seemed to cross his face as he mentioned this, and I looked at him without speaking, allowing the wisdom of his words to settle in my mind.

By the time we had reached the second field he seemed to have brightened. Yet scarcely had we set foot in it when he halted once again, one hand raised above his eyes, staring off in front of him. He took a few steps forward and then stopped, his sharp old eyes scanning the horizon.

"What is it?" I asked, following his gaze to a spot across the river where a rider had appeared cantering through the fields on a chestnut horse. We watched him circling the fields in an orderly routine, surveying the land and linkages, his back strong and rigid in the saddle. The intrusion clearly angered him. He rose on his toes like a fighting cock, his beard bristling, his knuckles grappling with his cane as though he had a mind to race across the field and strike the rider a blow with it.

"It's only Mr. Smithwick," I said, amused at his behavior for we had witnessed the scene many times before.

"So it is. So it is. But isn't that what I've been telling ye? For the likes of him that road is meant, and all he cares about is fences. What right has he to barricade the land?" I wasn't sure what my response should be to that because I knew full well there were few in our town ready to agree that Smithwick had no right to his inheritance, for not only did he own a great deal of the land, but the brewery too. Many families in the city depended on his brewery for a living, my own included. I tried to convey this fact to him, but his mind was set. People like them had no business here, land grabbers is what they were. They had ruined the country and left its people desolate.

He continued in this vein for a while, and even though I knew what he was saying to be true, and understood to some extent his bitterness regarding past events, I began to tire of listening. For no other reason but contrariness I told him I disagreed. That I thought he was being mean, and I asked what it was he had against Mr. Smithwick.

"At least he lives in Ireland and puts a little of what he makes back in the pockets of the poor. Surely that must count for something?"

It was a thing I felt needed to be said. Yet, it was not so much what I said, but the disrespectful way I said it. He took a moment to reply. His first reaction one of surprise, followed by exasperation. He canted his head to one side, and studied my face with his keen perceptive eyes. Then a grim smile spread across his face, and I knew right away I had offended him. I tried immediately to soften my remark, to erase the insult from his eyes, but it was too late. His hand went up to silence me.

"Very well child. Have it your way. What you say may be true, but ask yourself one question. Whose land is it that made him rich?" It was an age-old argument and though I was eager to defend my point, he had told me once that the quickest way to lose a friend was to beat him in an argument, so I simply apologized and kept quiet. He laid a gentle hand upon my shoulder. "No need to apologize alana. You're entitled to have your say and I expect you're right in any case."

We walked in silence after that, he muttering quietly to himself, and I thinking about the first time we met, almost eight years before. I was twelve years old, and had come upon him by accident, sitting watch at a glowing brazier beneath a starry sky. Curiosity had driven me to join the group of lads gathered around his feet, listening intently to his stories. As I have written an account of that meeting elsewhere, I won't go into it again.

Suffice it to say I had liked him from the start, and was drawn to his side as a moth is drawn to a flame. In him I had seen a man of candor and simplicity, an ethical man with an innate sense of what was going on in other people's minds, and who didn't hesitate to say what was going on his.

At first I thought he was using a sort of reverse psychology in order to have people respond positively to his position. But as time went on I realized that his purpose was not entirely selfish, but a way to invite participation with a view to opening up the *sealed doors* of people's minds. It was known that he distrusted the motives of the clergy and had little patience with the elevated notions people had about their priests.

To his way of thinking, priests were not in the same league as God and therefore not entitled to the same distinction. They were just ordinary men like the rest of us, simply a part of the rank and file, and with no more understanding of Divine Destiny. What the country needed was not more priests, but an end to the practice of bringing up children to be cut and polished into beads for the family rosary instead of jewels for the National Treasury. Myths, he used to say, are more brutal than reality and fables more fantasy than fact, and to try to convince a person otherwise, or expect them to devote their life to some arcane philosophy was shameful and wrong. Needless to say his opinions offended many, his blatant and often harsh remarks goading them to temper.

"That old codger, who does he think he's fooling, pretending not to be what the eye in him says he is, a cunning old fox." Cunning indeed, and old too, but never false or overbearing. It was my belief they were afraid of him. Afraid of the power of his independent thought, so dogmatically orientated was their own. Anybody suspected of proselytizing new ideas must have seemed like a threat to them. Yet, his words had opened up a whole new world to me. Weird is the only way I can describe how his thoughts kept mingling with my own that first night I listened to him speak. Half realized thoughts, and unasked questions that had been stewing in my mind but never quite spilled over into articulate form. I felt thoroughly and irrevocably drawn to him.

Many of the virtues I attributed to him back then probably had no genuine foundation, except as a product of my own imagination. But once in a while I think the world produces such a man, and whether he is accepted or rejected the result it usually the same, his influence diminishes with time, his grandeur fades, but the memory remains monumental. At times since, I have been drawn to certain people and listened to them speak, but never have I felt the same. That feeling of perfect harmony of mind, an association of ideas that made you want to listen.

As it turned out he had taken to me too, though I couldn't say why. Unless it was my willingness to listen, my naivety, or reticence to speak until spoken to. Who can say? Perhaps he simply saw in me a youthful reflection of himself. Whatever the reason we became fast friends, and I began to spend every possible moment in his presence. He had a way of making me feel good about myself, magnifying my virtues while minimizing my faults. Only when I reached my middle teens, was working for a living and had begun to notice boys, did I start neglecting him. All the time I had been thinking this, he had not spoken, but I could feel his eyes on me.

"Have you lost your tongue or what?" he asked finally, and I told him I had thought it best to hold it because everything I said, or tried to say, seemed only to upset him. He threw his head back and laughed, running his withered old hand lovingly across my head.

We paused along the path to let a young lad with a handcart rumble past. In it sat a younger, sadder boy clutching a small dog, and when asked why he was crying we were told he had stepped into a nettle patch, and scraped his ankle on a rock in his haste to get free. With a light touch to my arm, the Old Man steered me to one side and bent to inspect the injury. From his pocket he withdrew a handkerchief and wiped the tear-stained face.

"Janey Mac! Sure 'tis only a scratch," he assured the little boy, before shifting his interest to the dog, who had pricked up its ears at his approach but didn't bark or growl. "A Jack Russell eh! Great little ratter I'd say he is." He fondled the furry head and the young lad, ready to boast of the animal's accomplishments, quickly livened up. The Old Man listened patiently to everything he said.

"I don't suppose you'd be willing to part with him? I'd pay ye a good few bob," he teased, and made pretence of searching for his wallet. The little patient giggled.

"Thanks mister but he's not for sale," and he hugged the animal tighter to his chest. The Old Man laughed.

"You'd better go so before I'm tempted to run off with him." He straightened up then and with a gesture of his hand, stood back to let them pass. In the heat of his protestations earlier, he had lost the direction of his thought and I had made no attempt to revive it. Yet, no sooner had the two lads passed from sight than he returned immediately to the past.

"As I was saying before, when I was a lad my father brought me here to a house that used to stand right there," he pointed with his cane to a spot high on the slopes. "My mother's people lived in it. We used to stand on that hill and look out across the valley. My father loved the view and I loved it too. That's why I came back to it." Again he took in all the scenery and rubbed his forehead tiredly.

"There was a time, ye know, when all this land was purely Irish, and little Irish cottages adorned the hills. People spoke in the Gaelic tongue and were happy in their ignorance. Then that lot came and drove them out of it. Took all their land and left them nothing. That's what I have against them. It's not the man himself I mind, it's what he stands for."

It was important to him that I understand this, and to make sure that I was listening he gripped my shoulder tightly, leaning forward to peer into my face. Again I thought I detected a faint odor of alcohol coming from his breath. I was scrabbling for something intelligent to say, something that might impress but not offend him, when I noticed he had slowed his step and was searching in his waistcoat pocket.

Finding what he was looking for he pulled it out. It was a small bottle, a Baby Power of whiskey, which he held up to the light, remarking on its color and its purity. No amount of

Smithwick's ale could replace one drop of it, he proclaimed, as he pulled the cork out with a ploc and raised the bottle higher.

"More power said young Power when old Power was born," he called out in a defiant voice before bringing the bottle to his lips. One didn't need to be a connoisseur of beverages to know the taste best suited to his palate. When he had polished off about a third of it, he put the cork back in the bottle, pounding it in with the ball of his hand, then smacked his lips and returned the bottle to his pocket. All this was done with a great amount of gesturing and little side remarks, as though to demonstrate his disregard for anyone who might be watching. Luckily, nobody was.

We had reached the man-made bridge leading out to the Mulligan farm and were standing in the middle of the bridge looking down into the river, listening to the water sucking noisily at the rocks. The scene around was glorious, the green trees and swaying grass. The cattle grazing in the meadows, or standing knee deep in the shallows, their tails swishing across their rumps. The sun was slowly disappearing but still bright in the sky, and as we looked around the countryside our eyes fell on a field of corn. For an instant it gave the illusion of a field on fire, the last rays of the sun catching every blade in a blaze of gold. Close by, a flock of sheep bent nibbling happily on the lush vegetation. While across the field we could see the tall elm trees leading up to the Mulligan farm, and the small painted shed where Mickey kept his horse.

A small group of people had gathered in the lane, among them a man called Ryan, whose loud voice boomed out across the valley. The Old Man caught at the brim of his cap as a sudden breeze blew across the fields.

"D'ye know that man?" he asked sourly, and I said I did, for he was from our street and known to us as Mountainy.

"I wonder if he realizes how his voice carries?" That he wouldn't care even if he did, I told him truthfully, for Mountainy was known for his loud, regimental manner.

A ponderous man, with thighs as thick as an ass's belly and a moon-shaped face, he liked to stroll about the streets like a country squire in cavalry boots and leggings. You could pick him out in a crowd by the colour of his jacket, a bright rusty orange, and tan riding breeches which he never seemed to take off. No one questioned where he got the outfit for it was common in those days for people to wear the cast-off clothing given to them in kindness by others, regardless of style. We never knew exactly what he did for a living but suspected it had something to do with horses, for he had that smell about him and was never seen without his whip, which he would crack with mock ferocity whenever he saw us coming. A loud man, and poor, who liked nothing better than an argument, stopping people in the street when he had drink in him, but otherwise likable and pleasant.

"Ah he's all right," I said, defensively, "he means no harm." The Old Man straightened up and looked at me and I thought for sure he was going to start up again. But then his tone softened.

"No harm at all I dare say, but I'd hate to be a member of the constabulary and bump into him on a Saturday night." He began to chuckle then, enacting for me a scene I had seen many times myself, of Mountainy standing outside the barrack gate, his fists stuck out in front of him and he defying every officer inside to come out and go a round with him.

We laughed together over that and I told him about the time I had seen Mountainy accept a dare to ride a notorious stallion. No sooner was he seated on its back, when the stallion reared and took off across the field at a gallop, its rider bouncing up and down like a rubber ball on account of there being no saddle.

"He fell off eventually," I explained, describing how the stallion had come to sudden stop and thrown him over the fence.

"Is it the truth you're telling me, or lies?" he asked, doubling up with laughter. "Oh! He's a card all right. A great man for show is Mountainy. Sure day and night he wears that blinking uniform. Anyone would think it was glued to him."

"Might he ever have been in the cavalry?" I wanted honestly to know.

"The cavalry! Not a chance. 'Tis too bad he wasn't though. Maybe they could have made him a Brigadier General and be done with it." He struck the rail a ferocious blow, causing me to jump. "Ye know what it is I'm thinking? 'Twud serve him right if one day he were to meet a genuine commander and get a wallop in the eye for his masquerading." We went on laughing over that, but only a little while later when he was filling up his pipe and I was telling him another tale, a new sound came into his voice and I looked up suddenly and saw that he was crying. Big watery tears were swimming in his eyes and a loud sob broke out of him. He tried to hide the fact from me by coughing and covering his mouth with his handkerchief.

I turned away to save him the embarrassment and after a while he leaned his elbow on the rail and turned to me again, his grey eyes calm and steady. "What I was going to say about his voice carrying," he said, "there's a sick man in that house, so I wish he'd show a little more consideration." He told me then about Mickey's stroke of some days before, and how worried he was about his recovery. In his own particular vernacular he described how death, though it had struck with spiteful claws, had left its victim living. Mickey, it seemed, had rallied for a while, but was again failing.

"Better he had died right then," he said, describing Mickey's struggle to hold on to life, and his own fear of losing him. No sooner had he finished telling me when a loud peal of laughter came from the other side. He clicked his tongue in anger, his face tight, and to spare him further misery I suggested that we leave.

We retraced our steps across the bridge to the spot where he had left the goat. He called out to her and I saw her head rise above a bush as she came toward us along the path. She looked as though she had just come out of the river. All her hair was matted to her head and big blobs of water were dripping from her beard. She made a little yelping sound and dashed past us on the path. For the first time I noticed she was hobbling.

"What's wrong with her?" I asked, and he said he didn't know, but she had been limping that way for a while, and he had been meaning to take her to a vet, but the only one he knew was over in Dunmore, too far for him to travel.

We watched her now as she strolled ahead. Her limp, on second look, didn't seem so bad. Maybe it was nothing after all! He would hate for anything to happen to her, he said, because she was all he had in the whole wide world, the only one to care what might become of him. How could he have known that she would die before the year was out with cancer of the liver? For the present he was happy watching her, recalling the day he had found her. At The Puck Fair in Killorglin, he told me.

He had gone there one day to have a look around, and hoping to meet someone from home. A great dark storm had come up that day with rain the size of pellets and lightening the likes of which he had never known. Everyone had run for cover and somehow the goat had gotten left behind when the stalls had been taken down. She had crawled in under a pile of wood and one of the planks had fallen down on her. By the time he found her later that same day, she was all but dead.

"Only the size of a loaf of bread she was." He had wrapped her up inside his coat, taken her home and laid her on a blanket before the fire.

"The heat soon revived her because she stretched out her legs and looked at me. But when I tried to pick her up, she gave a groan. So I put some food beside her head and left her alone." Next morning he noticed that the food was gone. He stayed close by for a couple of days feeding her and tending to her injury. After that she wouldn't leave his side.

"Did you ever find out who she belonged to?" I asked, and he told me no because he did not try. He was afraid of losing her. The funny thing was, he said, that up until then he had never liked goats.

"You'd be lost without her now I suppose."

"I would faith. She's never out of my sight." He went on then to talk about his family, explaining to me why he was so alone. I was astonished to learn he had been married and had lost, not only his wife but his mother, father and brothers too. There was no one left to care what happened to him now, he said with a pitiful face, no one at all. We lapsed into silence after that. He, I supposed, reflecting on the things he had been telling me, and I not saying what I knew he wanted most to hear, that I cared about him, but thinking how much I wanted to.

The sky had clouded over and a light rain had begun to fall as the narrow footpath petered out and we came again to the old stone bridge from whence we had started, and must now cross on our way to our respective homes. He preceded me to the lamppost by the corner where, as was our custom we stood to say goodbye. His house was but a short distance from the river, the front door visible from where we stood. Meggie hurried up to it and waited for him to let her in. He delayed until I came up to him.

"'Tis hard to say if this rain will last," he said, peering at the sky, and asked if I wished to stand inside the door awhile and wait. I said no, that I had to be getting home. A look of disappointment spread across his face.

"Ah!" he nodded. "Well it was grand seeing ye at any rate. Will it be that long before I see ye again?"

He didn't wait to hear my answer, and I watched as he ambled off along the path, his back bent, his footsteps slow. Age had taken its toll of him, I thought, remembering how it had been in the early days, with him so strong and independent and I so eager and in awe of him. Yet something had changed between us, and though I couldn't quite say what, I sensed a strong emotion. Not a foreboding exactly, but an unsettling feeling as one might experience watching an ailing person, or maybe a dying one. The thought filled me with despair for we had come a long way together, and never once had it occurred to me that we were nearing our journey's end. He had shown me nothing but kindness and sincerity from the first day we met. Had taught me so many things and listened patiently to my worries and my constant tales of woe. Yet, never once had he let me down. Unquestionably, he had come into my life like a storybook knight, and at a time when I most needed him. I couldn't bear to think of him going out of it.

MOTHER

I never knew my mother, I lived in the same house with her for twenty-one years, but I never really knew her. An attractive copper-haired woman with a tiny frame and a slender, shapely body, she had a domineering manner, and would brook no challenge to her supremacy in the home. Yet, she was generous, industrious, and blessed with a hardy constitution. When I was a child I used to think that she was beautiful with her wavy auburn hair, unblemished skin and deep sapphire eyes. But then, I suppose, all children think that about their mothers. She didn't talk much, my mother, at least not with members of her family, but when she did speak, usually to comment on some current event or to explain how something should be done, you listened.

Having reared eleven children, she could at times display an acid temper, but I don't remember her ever hitting us; the odd swipe with the kitchen towel for some minor offence, but nothing more. Naturally, she had her faults, but cruelty was never one of them. Nor was it one of my father's, a mild, polite man, almost Victorian in his manner, he refused to lift a finger to his children.

"A man doesn't know his own strength," he used to say, and chastised his family with stern looks and warnings.

Except when drink released her temper, my mother had a jolly disposition and a kind, generous heart. Most people in the neighbourhood could attest to that, many taking advantage of her nature. Always calling at the house for money, or begging food and clothing. Mother tried to be kind to everyone, going so far as to take the clothes from her own children's backs to give to the more needy. The strange thing was, she seemed a totally different person outside the house, laughing and joking with the neighbors, for she had many friends. But as soon as she got indoors she would retreat into herself, her emotions bundled to one side like storm clouds in a sky. At times like that it seemed to me one couldn't do a thing to please her?

I remember once running home from school eager to show her the gold medal I had won. "A lot of good that'll do you," was all she said, not bothering to look at it. Today that may seem a cruel and uncaring attitude, and I must confess to a certain disappointment at the time. Yet, her response was not intended to disparage. It was simply a reaction to the inevitability of our situation, our lives a response to circumstance and environment, were not exactly geared to lofty expectations, and to my mother's way of thinking no good could come of allowing us to believe otherwise. Why should we expect to have what she never had? We must learn to be content in the station of life to which we had been lodged. Back then it didn't seem such a narrow philosophy, but looking back now I realize the damaging affect that kind of negativity can have on a person's self esteem.

In spite of the many drawbacks, I do believe that in the early stages of her married life my mother was content, for I have many clear memories of a vibrant, caring person dedicated to her beliefs and her family. Never one to explain her actions or express emotion, she invariably aroused my curiosity as I was growing up, and it used to worry me whenever she looked sad. Once in a moment of tactless curiosity I asked her why that was. Quick as a whip she lashed back at me.

"And what do you want to know that for?"

It was her usual reply to any impertinent question, and probably what I deserved. For I knew the rules and asking pointed questions, or prying into people's personal affairs was not only considered rude, but downright disrespectful. It was how it was with that generation. People had strict ideas about bringing up their children, and though we may at times have disagreed with their philosophies, parents were parents and we respected them.

Very little is known to me of my mother's past. Of her life before coming to Kilkenny, she seldom spoke. At one time I had the notion she had been a waif, and had visions of her running barefoot in a world of poverty and grime. From the little I did learn later I hadn't been far wrong. Though she escaped the burden of poverty and grime, her life at home had been anything but happy. Her mother, whom I envisioned as a figure dressed in black, a relic from another century, was apparently pious and church going, but a harridan nonetheless. A woman of mercurial nature and a firm advocate of the rigid approach, she rode her children mercilessly. Mother and she simply couldn't get along and quarreled frequently. To make things worse her father, whom she idolized, had died in her early teens and life without his love and support had soon become unbearable.

She had kept him alive in the locket on her neck, as she had the memory of Jimmy Cleare, the lad she was supposed to marry. Of him she tried not to think at all, though the years had compelled her to endure the pain. His parents, by all accounts, were a cut above her own, his father a politician, well known in the community. Jimmy was an only child and doted on by his mother; a fact responsible for people's belief that he would turn out no good. But he had grown up fine and shown good faith to Mother, especially after she had had to take that job at the Foundry, and the neighbors had started to look down on her.

Every evening he would wait for her outside the Foundry gate, so that people would know they were walking out and she had risen in their esteem again on account of it. Soon the whole village expected them to marry. There was no reason to believe his parents disapproved. Jimmy's mother, a quiet, genteel woman with a vacant face, who kept herself immaculate, made no objection, but kept her opinion to herself. Mother thought she was nice enough and often walked the distance to her house outside the village, and though Mrs. Cleare never asked her in, she always had a ready smile for her.

Then one day on their weekly stroll beside the river, Jimmy told her he was going away. He had no good reason to be going, and a quarrel had flared up between them. He would be back when he got things sorted out, he said, August or September, and it had given her hope. But August came, and September too with no sign of Jimmy. She had received one card renewing their pledge, but nothing more. In the end she had gone to see his mother, who had received her well enough, but would tell her nothing.

There was something odd about the way she looked at her. Something almost dishonest, her voice with an accent of forced concern, and only then had it occurred to Mother that she had probably had a hand in her son's departure. She didn't know what had transpired between them, but she was certain something had. Embarrassment had prevented her from asking more, and she had left without finding out the truth. Unwilling to face the public ridicule, she decided to run away.

It couldn't have been easy for a young girl like her to find acceptance in our town, for Kilkenny at that time was given body and soul to a form of nepotism apt to put any girl's social lights out in two shakes of a lamb's tail. All new arrivals in the town of later than a hundred years were resented, especially if associated with the economic weakness of the country. How then could my mother, a *blow-in* and mere *potwalloper*, hope to be accepted?

In reality, she didn't have to be, for one didn't need to be a noble in the house of Jack to enjoy the fruits of their own clean and honest labour. Aye! And there was the rub, for in our society nothing was so nearly a social absolute than cleanliness.

Even poverty, with all its evils and repugnance became respectable when scoured with Sunlight Soap and Carbolic. As it turned out, my mother's pot was amply polished because the one thing she had plenty of was cleanliness.

Besides, it was her belief that big fish swimming in shallow ponds deserved to be caught, and when my father, after months of serious courtship suggested they should marry, she readily accepted. Not that she considered him such a big fish, mind, but he had after all a steady job, a decent reputation and a held glimmer of hope for her prospective future. Consider, after all her position. She had arrived in our town like an angel in the night, with malice toward none and charity toward all, and might easily have found her way to another town had it not been for his persuasion. He it was who had directed her mind to the compensations of the matrimonial condition. So here she was and here she would stay, despite his mother's vehement opposition.

My grandparents, whom I never knew, lived in a modest house in Abbey Street and held a special place in the community. They were not wealthy by any means, but neither were they considered poor. Both were self employed, he a master tailor and she a tailoress. Years of British occupation in the city and a demand for fashion and fine tapestry had afforded them a decent living, plus admittance to a social circle they could not otherwise have managed.

"Beggars on horseback," my mother said, and maybe she was right, but they could see no harm in fraternizing with people of influential means, with an eye to furthering their own.

To grandmother's credit, there were no labourers in the family, two of her sons were respectably in business and both daughters were teachers. My father, at eighteen, was the youngest member of the family and already apprenticed to the largest retail marketer in the city. Grandmother's hopes for a favourable marriage within the boundaries of her twilight zone were properly dashed when she learned of his intention to marry my mother. Naturally she opposed the marriage with every fibre of her being.

It is difficult to understand the mentality of a small town if you have never lived in one, particularly back then. For one thing, everybody in it knew everybody else, which resulted in people dividing themselves into two main groups, those that had and those that had not. On top of that, there were clearly delineated rules of conduct and anybody found breaking those rules quickly became the subject of every street-corner gossip, and might even expect to find themselves outcast. What one's father did for a livelihood and how much money he earned was paramount. Yet strangely enough, the most important distinction was not necessarily the degree of one's wealth, but their educational background and level of respectability.

Unlike my mother, who was not slow to socialize, my father was an introvert and inclined to be reserved. When we were young we used to listen to his constant warnings about the perils of exposing one's private affairs to outsiders, and with no knowledge of our own to compare with his, we accepted his views without question.

"Familiarity breeds contempt," he was fond of telling us, and it was his habit to ward off certain people with the rigid handle of diplomacy. As for Mother, she didn't care what other people thought. Years of servitude and deprivation may have hardened her to the sensitivities of social decorum, but my father saw no reason to reject the habits of his upbringing. With the best will in the world it cannot be said that his determination contributed anything but misery to an already despondent partner.

Marriage, my mother had believed, would put an end to all her troubles, but she was wrong. For in addition to the vagaries of convention and the drudgery of everyday life, was the added burden of bearing children. Yet, in spite of the trials and tribulations, those years I believe to have been the happiest ones for her, the days when she could laugh and joke, finding pleasure in her children and in every little thing. Her chores she tackled with willingness and vim, first up in the morning and last down at night, perspiration sometimes in beads upon her forehead. Monday morning was her busiest time. It was then her back was bent for hours over an old tin tub scrubbing sheets, towels, and grime from the soles of her children's socks. The rest of the week she spent cleaning house, baking, ironing and darning. She had little time for gossip and felt that people who indulged in it were either lazy or had nothing better to do. *Never leave until tomorrow what you can do today.*

Shortly after the depression, about fifteen years into their married life, my father lost his job and it became necessary for Mother to try to find work to help support the family. This she did by applying as a domestic at the home of Mary Duggan, one of the wealthiest families in the city, and proprietors of the Monster House, the largest department store in the county. With her reputation for cleanliness preceding her, my mother met with little opposition. To Mrs. Duggan she owed the comfort of the following years, for it was through her generosity and honest affection for my mother, that our family was able to enjoy one of the nicest homes in the neighbourhood and the pleasure of clothing my parent's could otherwise not afford.

A whole year went by before my father found a steady job again, this time with an increased workload and lower wages. With his savings long depleted and growing mouths to feed a strict policy of thrift became imperative. Save more and spend less became his motto. Good advice in light of normal circumstances, but silent forces were at work as quiet and effective as those of Mother Nature.

It is said, and I believe, that loving eyes are often the most blind and that which is seen every day ceases to be different.

219

This must have been the case with my father, judging by his ignorance of the gravity of a situation that made any policy of thrift impossible to follow. For one thing, by now my mother was drinking steadily and spending every penny to support her habit. For another, her disappointment of some months earlier, when the Duggans left the city to set up business in another town, had not diminished. During the time she had been working in the Duggan home, she and Mary Duggan had become warm friends and my mother, not wanting to lose her patronage, had seized on the suggestion that she accompany them to the new location. From my mother's perspective it was a golden opportunity, the chance of a new life for all of us. From my father's, it was suicide. Maybe if he were a little younger or we children a little older, he argued, casting a complacent eye about the home he cherished. Yet, every time he spoke Mother knew he would never leave Kilkenny.

Filled with disappointment, she had accepted his decision, but in her heart she had despised him for making it. There are some questions, I suppose, on which women scarcely reason, they only feel intently, and this was one of those times. Disappointment dug itself deep into her heart and as time passed, resentment grew like lichen alongside of it. It just didn't seem possible that my mother's life, so happy and carefree in the early days, could become so miserable in the years to come.

It was only when I reached my teens that I began to realize there was something radically awry in our cozy home. That my mother was no longer the happy carefree person she used to be, and that the love she had once borne my father had long ago worn thin. They say that ripples spilled from an angry home spread far beyond its walls, sweeping innocent victims in its wake, and so it was with us as the arguments between my parents became more vicious and more frequent. One by one the family began to leave home.

I don't know when or why my mother began to drink, I only know she did. As a young girl growing up I never noticed it, or maybe I did but didn't register it. Yet, when I think about it now I realize, that while I may have had a distorted perspective about certain issues, I had a clear understanding of how things should be. Money problems and weekends fraught with ugly scenes were not exactly something even a child could overlook.

As time passed, it began to dawn on me that my mother had lost the capacity to be happy, and though I knew there had to be some serious reason, I couldn't figure out what.

"Some marriages were never meant to be," a neighbour said to me one day in retrospect analyses. At the time his observation angered me, but later I recognized the truth of his remark. My parents had not one single thing in common. My father so reserved and so attached to his books and music, and my mother, so gregarious, finding little pleasure in either. It became her habit to avoid the company of his friends, sensing I suppose that their sentiments were false. Only in the company of her own friends did she find contentment.

The problem was in her preference for the few whose manners offended my father's sensitivity; people he considered a direct affront to his efforts to exclude from our lives all that was coarse and common. The closer she adhered to their friendship, the wider the rift between them grew.

When I think about it now I realize I saw my mother mainly through the blurred lens of myopia, and had neither tolerance with, nor understanding of the psychological implications of her problem. Yet, any antagonism I may have fostered in no way diminished the love I felt for her. What saddens me most is the fact that as an adult I never found the courage to confront her, and maybe have helped her deal with the origin or nature of the pain that she secretly endured. Now that she is dead, I see her clearly, and am able to judge her fairly from a different point of view. Like many contributing mothers of her day, she no doubt longed for, but never received the acknowledgment to which she felt entitled. In the early years of marriage had she not, after all, been a dedicated wife, displaying genuine devotion to her family and its needs? Was it not she who had had to demean herself scrubbing, not only her own floors but other people's too, and all with the aim of keeping the family together at a time when her husband could not? So why hold him in such high esteem, while leaving her so tired and downtrodden?

Wounds of the spirit may not reveal themselves in torn flesh or blood, but they are nonetheless as painful, and perhaps it was that fact, more than any other that had eventually disheartened her, and driven her to seek consolation in *the bottle*. Dignity, they say, is a person's birthright. Strip them of that and you strip them of everything. Whatever the reason for my mother's fall from grace, it is impossible to judge her now by the standards of her day, and unfair to judge her by the standards of ours.

Theresa Lennon was born in Kilkenny,
Ireland in 1931. At twenty-one she left
for Brighton, England where she met
and married her husband Keith Blunt.
In 1957 she immigrated to Canada, where
she now resides. Tangled Webs is her
fourth book.